The Mrs. Degree

Sara Ney

Copyright

Love is a two-way street constantly under construction.

— Carroll Bryant

Chapter 1

Penelope

Today is over, thank god.

It started off with a bang. I was late getting my daughter to school, which is... honestly? My lateness is nothing new.

We're late most mornings. Usually, we're about to run out the door, and I'll look down to see that my daughter, Skipper, isn't wearing shoes after I told her to be ready. Or she won't have school clothes on and still be in pajamas.

Or she won't be wearing anything at all.

Today, Skipper decided to take the braids out of her hair as we walked through the front door because one of them felt too loose. She then insisted on having me redo them, crying until I relented on the front stoop while squirming and wiggling around like she had ants in her pants.

It made me late for work.

Then I couldn't find anyone to grab Skipper *after* work, so I spent my entire lunch break on the phone texting every mom I knew. At the same time, my boss stuck her nose over the top of my cubicle for a status update on an overdue report.

After word-vomiting an excuse, I snuck off to the bathroom a short while later and continued my mission there.

My boss? She isn't a parent—doesn't even own a pet—and has a lack of sympathy for working moms that rival any dictator's. It's not that I don't like her. Maxine Wallaby has her redeeming qualities, but compassion and patience are just not included.

In any case, none of this is my boss's fault.

None of it is Skipper's fault, either.

The little shit—who was picked up by my new hero, Raina, the mom of a little girl named Ivy, and let Skipper swim in their pool until I could pick her up—gives the back of my seat a kick with the toe of her shoe, causing the peppermint mocha I'd just splurged four dollars on to spill out of the cup and onto the front of my blouse.

Great.

Perfect.

Awesome.

With a loud sigh, I reach blindly for the package of baby wipes I keep wedged between the center console and the passenger seat, grappling for it with my fingertips. It seems they're wedged a bit too far down for an easy grab.

With a sigh, I settle for a dry napkin from the glove box and dab to no avail.

The blouse is ruined.

Skipper kicks me again, but I know it's not intentional. She's dancing to the music on the car radio, happily bebopping to the upbeat pop song, head tipping back and forth and side to side as she sings along.

Her cute little voice makes me smile despite the dark-brown sludge staining my powder-pink silk blouse.

"Mom, is Uncle Davis going to be there when we get home?"

Home.

My brother, Davis, lives next door. Technically, my house is *his* house because he owns it. Back in his glory days, he played professional football. I was a teenager when I got pregnant with Skipper, and Davis had gotten his first *big* paycheck. With it, he bought two houses side by side—one for him and one for me—and the day I brought Skipper home from the hospital, he moved me in.

He's looked after me for as long as I can remember. Our mom was single, too, and worked her ass off to keep a roof over our heads. Davis was tasked with babysitting when she was gone, and he still watches out for me.

Davis Halbrook is my brother, my neighbor, and one of my best friends.

I glance at my daughter through the rearview mirror. "I'm not sure, honey. I think he has a date tonight with Juliet."

Skipper bops her head to and fro. "Where are they going?"

"I don't know, sweetie. He didn't say." Now that my brother is seeing someone, he hasn't been around as much as he normally would. It's a nice change but a foreign one. I'm used to him being at the house and spending loads of time with us.

"Can we stop and get chicken nuggets?"

I glance back to see that she's munching on something already, probably something she fished from the cushions of her booster seat.

Hmm. "No, baby girl, I think I'm going to bake chicken tonight."

"Can we eat at Uncle Davis's?"

He has better apps on his television because he actually *has* a television with apps, and his refrigerator is stocked with more food. Plus, he buys Skipper snacks she likes, and his pantry is always bursting.

Unlike mine.

"Sure." I know I should ask my brother before I barge in on his evening now that he's dating someone, but I'm almost positive he won't be around. And if they come back to his place afterward, it won't take me but a few seconds to make myself scarce.

Besides, he won't care.

I don't have to run to the grocery store to bake chicken tonight. I have some things, and Davis will have the rest. I always know what he has stocked in his kitchen because I help make a list for his housekeeper when she does the shopping. And yeah, every so often, I steal a roll of toilet paper and a roll of paper towels, but that's what little sisters are for, aren't they?

At least that's what I tell myself when I'm being too cheap to go buy the shit myself.

When we get home, I change my entire outfit, swapping out the blouse for a hoodie, which I toss in the trash without bothering to get the chocolate stain out of the delicate fabric, and step into a pair of gray joggers.

Tossing my hair into a messy updo, I use about three small claw clips to hold it in place. Add a pair of fuzzy socks.

Voila! I'm ready to make some delicious baked chicken, settle onto the couch with a glass of wine, and spend some cozy evening time with my mini-me.

Skipper is hopping around near our front door when I walk into the foyer carrying a tote bag with some cooking supplies, the dress she wore to school long gone in lieu of a pair of rainbow leggings and a long-sleeved T-shirt with a rainbow heart on it.

My little friend is an energetic bundle who is always ready to roll.

We make quick work of the walk between our house and my brother's, the pair of homes united by a well-worn path between them that was forged through the many, many short journeys traveled.

Skipper scurries to the garage door, punches the code into the keypad, and disappears as it slowly rises into the dark garage as if she lives there rather than in the house next door.

I suppose now that my brother is dating someone (it's only been one date, but still—Davis hasn't dated anyone in a long time), my daughter and I should make ourselves more scarce. No sense in pissing off the Good Fairy because we're cockblock cramping his style.

With Skipper putting together a puzzle in my brother's living room, I have plenty of time to put together dinner. Popping the chicken in a pan, I add stuffing, then nuke some vegetables in the microwave and throw in a little butter for flavor. The entire meal is quick and simple and healthy, and one I know my daughter will eat. She's not exactly finicky, but she does have her favorites, and chicken is one of them. Chicken nuggets, chicken wings, baked chicken, chicken kebabs—if it's chicken, she will eat it.

Skipper yawns halfway through her dinner, which tells me she isn't going to last very long tonight, and I may have some free time to watch whatever show I want without an argument from a seven-year-old.

I'm not wrong. Shortly after she takes her last bite, she yawns again.

"Mommy, I don't think I want a bath. I'm tired."

Her eyes look heavy, and I wonder what they did at

school today that made her so exhausted so early in the evening.

"Of course you can go straight to bed." I smile. No way am I going to argue with her when this buys me some alone time. "Let's wash up, though, before we brush your teeth."

Instead of taking her home, I tuck her into the spare bedroom upstairs. Davis has it all tricked out for her anyway; lavender walls, a white double bed with frilly comforter, and enough stuffed animals to rival the FAO Schwarz toy department.

He spoils her rotten, but luckily, she's not rotten. We've been through this same routine dozens of times with Skipper and I coming to Davis's for the evening. She falls asleep in his guest room, and I hang out until he arrives home. They have breakfast in the morning, occasionally find an activity to go do (like the park or Target), then he brings her home.

Skipper yawns again as I blow her one last kiss before giving her one last backward glance and closing the door.

In the morning after she wakes up, she'll probably ambush her Uncle Davis and demand his world-famous fluffy pancakes with lots of butter and syrup and sometimes chocolate chips. My brother has none of that in his cabinets, so I should probably order some things for delivery tonight.

After cleaning up the kitchen, I flop down on the sofa and flip through the channels, unable to decide on a show to watch. I'm too tired from my hellish day and ready to slide into my own comfortable bed.

The laundry room door opens just as I lay my head back against the couch cushion, startling me. It's still relatively early. Too early for Davis and Juliet to arrive home.

They're laughing as they walk into the kitchen, his keys

hitting the counter at the same time as he notices me in his living room.

"I should have known you'd be here." He comes over to kiss me on the cheek and ruffle my hair. "Sorry I didn't text you back. We were eating, and then I was driving."

"I just put Skipper to bed. She tried to stay awake until you got home, but her little eyeballs couldn't fight it anymore."

"Really? It's so early."

My brother removes his coat and tosses it on the barstool in the kitchen. "She up in the guest bedroom?"

"She was at a friend's house today with an indoor pool. They swam and swam until their arms were noodles and their skin was all wrinkly. She's beat."

"Bet she'll be up at the ass crack of dawn, though."

"She'll for sure be up at the ass crack of dawn." I laugh. "I made chicken for dinner if you're hungry."

I shift so I'm cross-legged on the couch.

"We ate a few hours ago, but it smells delicious," Juliet says, taking an empty spot next to me on the couch. She dressed up for their date in black leather pants, killer high heels, and a floral blouse.

"Where'd you go tonight?"

"We went bowling."

Ha! "Who won?"

They both point at each other and laugh again. "We both suck at it."

You don't say. Is anyone ever good at bowling? I mean, it's not something a person does on a regular basis...

"We ate pizza while we were bowling," Davis tells me. "And appetizers. For some reason, I caught a second wind once I started kicking her ass and taking names."

Juliet rolls her eyes in my direction. "Okay, let's brag about it. We had the gutter guards up."

"Doesn't matter," Davis argues.

"Actually...it does."

"Are we always going to squabble like this?" My brother's voice is pensive as he walks over to join us girls on the couch, plopping down beside Juliet. He picks up her legs to rest them across his lap and immediately starts massaging her feet.

Like they've been a couple for years.

"Is that what this is? A squabble?"

I watch them both. "Aw, aren't the two of you just adorable?"

Gag.

My brother grins at me, all happy and shit. "I'd lean over and ruffle your hair, but you're too far." He wiggles his hand in my direction, out of reach.

"Good. I don't want my hair ruffled. I grew out of that in second grade."

"Liar. You used to love it when I would give you noogies."

"*Said no one ever.*"

Juliet laughs, kicking off her high heels and resting her head back on the sofa the same way I'd been doing before they came through the door.

"God, that feels like heaven!" She groans. "Those shoes were killing my feet. And after the week I've had..." She groans again, closing her eyes.

The doorbell sounds, and we all look at each other.

"Who could that be?"

Yeah, it is weird that someone is just popping by my brother's house this late at night without—

"Oh, shit!" I pop up from the couch like my ass has

suddenly caught on fire. "I forgot I ordered ingredients to make pancakes in the morning. We—and by *we*, I mean *you*—are all out of flour and vanilla."

Davis makes a show of beginning to rise from the couch, still holding his date's feet like a weirdo. "Sure you don't want me to get the door?"

They look way too comfortable for me to disturb.

I shoo him away, giving him a backward glance as I head toward his foyer.

"I've got it. Just be backup in case it's actually a murderer and not the delivery guy."

"Make sure you scream loud enough." He laughs.

Oh, I would scream loud enough, all right, but it's just the grocery delivery person, and typically, they've disappeared before I even make it to the door, sometimes leaving the bag at the garage.

Unlocking the deadbolt, I pull open the door, half expecting the bag to be on the stoop where it typically is. My eyes automatically cast downward at the ground, searching. Rather than a grocery bag, they land on an expensive pair of sneakers, then roam upward over dark denim jeans and a black hoodie.

The man standing outside on my brother's doorstep is most certainly not the DoorHub delivery guy.

He takes a step back, surprised.

"Holy shit. Penelope Halbrook. I wasn't expecting. I wasn't..." The man I haven't seen in many, many years—since college, to be exact—stuffs his hands inside his pockets almost bashfully as he stares wide-eyed at me. "I wasn't expecting you to open the door."

Of course he wasn't. This is not my house.

He was clearly expecting Davis.

But I'm the one who came to the door, and now I regret it.

This man...

He's a good man, but one I've been avoiding for far too long.

"It seems I'm not the only one who's shocked right now." I shift on my feet, my heart pounding inside my chest. I swear to god my blood pressure has to be through the roof because my heart is racing so hard.

Can't think.

Can't focus.

What is he doing here?

WHAT IS HE DOING HERE?

"Are you here to see my brother?" Obviously, this is Davis's house. What other reason could it be? They both play or played football at one point, though not at the same time and never as opponents.

With one hand on the doorjamb and another on the door handle, I have no idea what to do with myself.

"Please, um—come in."

He steps up into the foyer, hands still shoved deep into the pockets of his jeans, ball cap pulled down over his eyes. A bit older and bigger than the last time we were in the same room together but still very recognizable.

He looms, taking up all the space in the entryway. The air I'm desperately trying to breathe.

"Davis is in the living room," I babble, wanting out of the room and out of his presence.

Why is he here?

I lead him through the short hallway and into the living room. Immediately, my brother rises and extends his hand to the newcomer to greet him.

"Sorry to show up like this unexpectedly, but I'm in

town for a game and heard you still lived in the area." He removes his ball cap and runs a hand through his hair—it's thick and jet black and needs to be cut.

He looks down at me as he talks to Davis.

So much taller, which was one of the things I loved about him way back when, all those years ago...

He's staring back at me and has barely made eye contact with anyone else in the room, something I'm sure Davis hasn't failed to notice. My brother misses nothing.

"My agent, Elias, was able to get in touch with Silus Goodwyn," he's telling *me* as if we were the only two people in the room. "Your brother doesn't have social media, so I figured I'd pop in and see if he was willing to share your phone number. I wasn't expecting you to answer his door!"

I recall hearing the name Silus every so often, though it's been ages since Davis played football. Silus was—is?—the stadium manager and also happens to be a good friend of my brother's—not good enough apparently as he was willing to give my brother's address to a player outside of the ball club.

"Have you and I met?" Davis looks confused. "Do the two of you know each other?"

The color drains from my face.

"Are you here to see me?" my brother asks him slowly, still clearly perplexed. "Or are you here to see my sister?"

"Shit, I'm so sorry. I'm Jack Jennings." Jack extends his hand and re-introduces himself. "Penelope and I dated back in college. I'm not sure if she told you? Anyway, we lost touch way back, and I always wonder what she's been up to. I'm in town for a game." He's babbling nervously, shifting on the balls of his feet, plopping the ball cap back on his moppy hair. "I know this is weird, but I was hoping we could reconnect while I'm in town."

I paste on a smile, pretending I'm not about to toss my cookies all over the carpet at any moment from my stomach being in knots. "This sure is a surprise. How long has it been?"

"Gosh, I wouldn't even know, but—" Jack stops talking but looks as if he has the weight of the world on his shoulders. "Look. I'm going to leave you with this, and if you want to have coffee or something. Or drinks. Or...I don't know—maybe we could have dinner at The Tower Club while I'm here and catch up?"

Catch up?

He wants to *catch up*?

About what? What could he possibly want to talk about?

My heart beats out of my chest.

Davis snatches the envelope from his fingers once it's clear I'm too paralyzed to take it myself.

"Gotcha." Davis stuffs the rectangular card in the back pocket of his dress pants, ushering Jack back toward the front entry from whence he came, back toward the front door and the shiny black sports car parked in front of my brother's driveway. "Good meeting you, bro. If she wants to talk, she'll be in touch."

He's staring right through me when Davis abruptly closes the door in his face, no doubt leaving him standing surprised in the front yard.

On a normal day, I would say something like, "Why would you slam the door in his face?!" It was uncharacteristically rude and uncalled for when the guy was just stopping by to say hello to an old friend.

An ex-girlfriend who all but ghosted him.

But I don't.

Instead, I make a beeline back to the kitchen and brace

my hands against the cold countertop. My legs are weak, my arms shaking, and my breathing comes out fast and hard as if I've just run a marathon.

Dammit.

His showing up here was so random.

So jarring.

"Penn, what was he doing here at seven at night?" Aimlessly, my brother goes to the pan of rice and chicken resting on the stovetop and begins spooning a heap of rice onto a plate, keeping his idle hands busy. "You barely spoke to him."

My head jerks as I shake it. "No idea. Like he said, I guess he just wants to...um. Reconnect."

"You know who that was, though? *I* know who that was because he was drafted around the same time I hurt my leg. How do you know who that was?" He points the wooden spoon in my direction.

"That was..." I search for the words, not wanting to tell him the truth, leaning forward so my chin rests in my hands. "That was Skip Jennings."

Jack's nickname was always The Skip because anytime he would make a touchdown during a game, he would hop through the end zone as if he were being skipped across water—

Skipper.

"I know who Skip Jennings is, Penelope." He says it with an eye roll, unable to believe how stupid I'm behaving. *"What was he doing in my house?"*

"I told you!" I throw my hands up in exasperation. I just want to escape. "We used to know each other, and he wanted to catch up. How many more times do we have to say it?"

Eyes narrowed, I can see that he doesn't believe me.

13

"And he couldn't have contacted you like a *normal* person?" My brother is irritated, stuffing rice into his mouth, chewing, then adding butter. "Like say, oh, I don't know— texting you? How hard could it have been to get ahold of your phone number? Online, Facebook, Instagram, TikTok —literally any other way than showing up here in the middle of the night."

Probably not that difficult.

But it's hardly the middle of the night.

"It's seven fifteen."

Another sarcastic eye roll. "You know what I mean."

Years ago, I'd blocked Jack, so the messages wouldn't have been delivered even if he had tried to text me. The messages wouldn't have gone through, so he wouldn't have gotten a reply.

All my social media is private if I have an account at all.

I'm too busy trying to re-enroll in college and finally earn the degree I never received because I got pregnant, dropped out, and came crawling home to my brother.

"Penelope, you're shaking." My brother watches me intently, not having missed a single move or breath I've taken in the past forty seconds. "Are you afraid of Jack Jennings?"

I mean, in a way, you could say I'm afraid of him but not physically. He would never hurt me. No, I'm afraid of him for entirely different reasons.

Reasons I'm not ready to confess out loud to the man who has supported me emotionally and financially for the past seven years.

I rear back, horrified. "Afraid of Jack? No! What would make you say that?"

"Um, because you're *shaking*? Why would you be shaking if you weren't afraid of the guy? Did he do something to you?" Davis lowers his voice and gets closer. "Is he stalking you? Has he threatened you in any way?"

He has venom in his voice.

"What! No, no, nothing like that. *No*," I say again because I literally have no other words. I'm basically speechless. Stunned.

Spooked.

What a shock to open the door and have him be standing on the doorstep.

"He's not some creepy weirdo, is he? The last thing I need is some dude stalking you. I don't need the lack of peace of mind when I'm traveling, or I swear to god, I will bring you and Skipper with me."

He's gotten himself good and worked up, making threats and promises I know he would keep if Jack proved to be a danger.

Which he's not.

He's just a man with fond memories of a girl who broke his heart and left him right when he needed her most.

We were so in love.

But he was a rising star and on the verge of something great. He was training for football while also signing with an agent and entering the draft.

It was all so exciting...

And scary.

So very, very scary.

Leaving was the right thing to do, but the way I did it?

He will never forgive me once he finds out the truth.

"No, Jack Jennings is not some lunatic."

My brother hesitates and then moves from behind the counter, done with snacking, and snatches up the card Jack had given him earlier. The one I had failed to take from his fingertips because I'd been frozen.

"Well, in that case, here. Seems like he had some shit he wanted to say to you."

With hands that are still shaky, I take the envelope from his hand, grasping it like a lifeline.

"You sure you're alright?"

I nod, unconvinced.

I'm most certainly not all right.

"Skipper is fine to stay here tonight. I'll take her to breakfast in the morning so you can do what you need to do."

Translation: *I think you need to contact Jack Jennings and find out what the hell he was doing on my doorstep.*

"Thanks."

Robotically, I make my way across my brother's yard and through mine, cutting through the hedgerow separating the properties the same way I've done hundreds of times.

After removing my makeup, I take off my clothes and put on pajamas.

I don't touch the envelope again until I'm seated safely on the bed in my bedroom. After clicking on the lamp on my bedside table, I sit with my stomach in knots, hands trembling.

Hey Penelope,

I hope this letter finds you well. Hope you don't mind that I tracked down your brother's address to drop off this letter while I was in town, but it was a spur-of-the-moment thing not meant to intrude on your privacy, which is why I didn't contact you directly. I thought it would be best to leave this letter with your brother.

Remember how superstitious I used to be? Going through the same pre-game ritual from the minute I wake up to the moment I get in bed to sleep? Well, funny story—I've been dreaming about you lately, and it's been messing up that ritual, and I thought MAYBE if we connected, it might break the spell, and things could go back to normal. I've been shit at work. At the last game, I let two passes get intercepted, and the fans are beginning to turn on me, ha-ha. Thought seeing you would work, and I can explain more over coffee? Dinner? Either or both, I have a game Monday night, but Saturday or Sunday would be great.

I promise it won't be weird. Just two old friends catching up...

Here is my number in case you need it.

555-218-9950

Hope to hear from you,

Jack

I can't take my eyes off this letter, or that phone number, or his signature scrawled at the bottom in dark, bold strokes.

He's always been so sure of himself, and he's sure of himself now, confidence not eluding him the way it does with me. He walks tall, chin up, eye on the prize in a way that has intimidated me a bit in the past. I never had the confidence he did. I never walked into a room as if I *owned* it the way he does.

Commanding presence.

Self-assured.

Never any doubt he would accomplish what he set out to accomplish.

I'm not like that.

Staring down at the note, I worry at my bottom lip.

The ghost that has been haunting me for seven years has finally found me.

Chapter 2

Jack

D~~ear Penn,~~
       Dear? No, too personal.
       ~~Hey Penn!~~
Nope. Too casual.
~~Penn. I know it's been ages and first I want~~
~~Penn. I cannot stop dreaming about you. Can't sleep,~~
~~been tossing and turning. Call it superstition but I had to see~~
~~you to try to get rid of this curse you seem to have over me so~~
~~I can play.~~

Definitely don't tell her she's cursed, you idiot.

It had taken me a good hour to compose the note I'd stuck into an envelope and handed to her brother (along with my contact information), not knowing I would see Penelope in his home. When I pulled up that driveway, I assumed I'd be hopping out quickly and going to the door. I thought I'd do a quick intro—shake Davis's hand—give him the note I'd written, and be on my merry little way.

Bim, bam, boombalaka.

After all, I only had seventy-two hours in town. There was no time to dawdle.

18

She is not the person I thought would be opening Davis Halbrook's front door, and she certainly hadn't been glad to see me.

She had looked shell-shocked.

Pale, color draining from her face.

I mean, let's be honest, I'd known there was a chance Penelope wouldn't be excited to see me, but I was hoping for more than five minutes of her time once she answered her brother's door.

Ten minutes.

Twenty.

I'd held out hope that seeing me would spark a bit of something more. A memory? Our old friendship?

Shifting my car into gear, I back out of her brother's driveway with a pep talk the same as I'd pep talked myself on the ride over. I'd conned Halbrook's address out of Old Silus, made the trip over, and hoped for the best. I promised the old man I wouldn't abuse the address once I had it, telling him I couldn't get through to Halbrook's staff in order to send him a paper invitation to an anniversary party I was throwing for my folks.

My folks?

Both of them passed away in a car accident three years ago.

The lie felt as wrong as it had been, and I regret telling it as much as I regret ringing Davis Halbrook's doorbell when I should have just... I don't know.

Dug deeper for a phone number and called?

No regrets, Jennings.

Your life is not built on them.

Onward and upward, Jennings. *Forward looking.*

I shake it off—literally give my body a shake—as I rev the engine on this rental car. Punching in the hotel's address, I speed back toward the city as Halbrook's brick mini-mansion grows smaller and smaller in the rearview mirror.

I remember him well enough from his days playing ball because he was playing it long before I was. As my girl-friend's older brother, he traveled a lot when she and I were dating, but she had no interest in flying around the US to see his games. Not the same way I would have if I were his sibling.

Penn was content with the times he would show up unannounced on campus and take her to dinner somewhere fancy, then Costco and Target to stock her fridge and buy her whatever else she needed.

He paid her rent and tuition the way a parent would.

Back in his day, Davis Halbrook was something of a celebrity, short-lived as his career was. I've always been surprised he faded into obscurity and never became a broad-caster the way some retired ballers have.

Man, I looked up to that dude.

Never met him—but I admired him.

The shit he did for his kid sister?

Commendable as fuck.

I barely knew what to say to the guy when he'd stood. The speech I'd rehearsed on my way over flew right out the window the moment Penelope herself had pulled open the front door.

She'd barely spoken to me.

Hi—We've never been formally introduced, but I'm Jack Jennings. I am an old friend of Penelope's, and I've been having one hell of a time tracking her down. It's been years since I've seen her, and well, I'm in town for two nights for a game against the Mountaineers and thought it would be awesome if she and I could talk.

Then I was going to hand him a card with a note inside. Simple. Easy.

Ironically, I wouldn't have had to pass it along to him personally if she had taken it.

I'd known there was a chance she wouldn't be excited to see me, but I didn't think she would look so dumbfounded.

SHE IS THE ONE WHO DUMPED YOU.

She dumped me and wanted no contact, which I've given her for the past several years because that's what Penelope requested, and now she probably thinks I'm stalking her. Who just randomly shows up on a person's fucking doorstep like a love-sick fool who's been pining for her for all these years?

I'm an idiot.

I'm not a love-sick fool either.

It's just...these goddamn dreams won't let me live in peace.

They're so real. So vivid.

Keeping me awake at night and haunting me during the day.

I have to get them gone.

Still, I should have acquired her phone number and contacted her like a normal person.

Um, aren't you forgetting something? The last time you called that number, Penelope declined your call seven years ago, blocked you from calling again, then disappeared into oblivion.

Seven years ago, on the night of the NFL Draft, Penelope Halbrook had been my first call after the commissioner announced my name as friends and family flooded my inbox. She was the first person I called seven years ago as if she was my one last lifeline before entering a life sentence of hard work, dedication, and commitment.

Seven years ago, I called her and only her.

Not my mother, not my father—*Penelope*.

She did not take my call.

She never called me back.

I've been through Chicago a few times since my career began for games but never had the urge to contact her quite like this.

It's been seven years, and I've gotten Penelope Halbrook out of my system for the most part. I've dated other women and even fell in love with someone else for a little while.

But recently, I've been having these dreams...

Wild dreams about *her*.

Us.

Dreams so wild they felt real.

Just *maybe* if I tracked her down to get in touch, the dreams would stop, eh? They're every night, and it's becoming a distraction. I wake up thinking about Penn and think about her before closing my eyes. This is not normal.

She isn't in my life anymore, so why would the universe play with my head like this? I haven't seen her or heard her voice in years. Haven't even tried to creep on her online.

I gave that up years ago. I'm not the same love-sick fool I'd been when she last saw me. I am a grown man who made his dreams come true with hard work and determination. When it became clear she wanted nothing to do with the life I wanted to build, I had to let that part of my life go.

The same way she let me go.

As if I meant nothing.

But lately? Damn, if I'm not having nightmares. Dreams where I wake up soaked in sweat, seeing her but not being able to touch her. Sinking into the water and watching her face disappear above as she watches me drown. Me reaching out my hand to her and watching her fall. The last time I touched her skin, kissed her lips, and felt her hand in mine.

The dreams will not stop.

In fact, the bastards have gotten worse. More intense.

"Dude, God is trying to tell you something," my agent and best friend, Duke, told me after I confessed to having these dreams.

"What could he possibly be trying to say by having me toss and turn every single night?"

"Didn't she ghost you?"

"Yes. Thanks for bringing it up."

He laughed. *"Do you think it's possible that you need closure for the dreams to stop?"*

Closure.

Duke may be right, but I wasn't about to make an ass of myself with Penelope, who wanted to stay hidden.

Except...

I've been having the damnedest time focusing while on the playing field. I haven't been able to concentrate during practice, either. Games? Eh—I've been able to tune the thoughts of Penelope out long enough to get through them, but *damn*, if I catch sight of a young woman in the stands who even remotely resembles how I picture Penelope Halbrook in my mind?

I spiral.

Call me superstitious, but don't call me a fool. I know in my heart these dreams have affected my playing, and there's only one thing I can do about it.

Go see her.

Get the closure I need to move on and play the kind of football I'm famous for.

Staring up at the ceiling of the hotel once I've rinsed off

in the shower, checked in with the coaching staff, and stripped down to my skivvies for bed, I climb under the covers wide awake.

Blink up at the ceiling.

Close my eyes only to see Penelope's face behind my lids.

She's beautiful with long dark hair and blue eyes.

She came to the door wearing sweatpants and a sweatshirt, but damn, she wore it well. I didn't want to look her up and down, but when she'd led me to the living room to her brother, I couldn't resist giving myself a glimpse.

Penelope is a pixie.

Petite but curvy, at least from what I can remember, I'd tripped on a pink scooter in the foyer on my way through to the living room only to discover more toys there. I'm assuming Davis Halbrook has had a few kids of his own by now. The other woman in the room must be his wife?

I wouldn't know because Penelope didn't introduce me.

She seemed more shocked than horrified to see me, so I guess I'll take that as a good sign.

Checking my phone, I make sure it's not on silent.

Checking it again, I make sure I haven't missed a message.

She isn't going to contact you, Jennings.

She isn't going to dinner with you.

Why are you being a Debbie Downer, Jack? You don't get anywhere by giving up, and you certainly don't give up on the first try. But I'm not giving up. The ball is not in my court any longer. I've passed it off to her, and only she can dictate how the story goes. All I need is to see her, tell her about my dreams, and ask her why she disappeared in the middle of the night and never returned any of my calls.

Easy, right?

Who am I trying to kid? Penelope Halbrook is a flight risk. She proved that in college when she left me high and dry, just a naïve kid with a goal and a dream who thought he had his life mapped out for himself. I was a kid with a college girlfriend who found out the hard way she wasn't in it for the long haul.

I thought we were going to get married.

I thought we were going to help each other realize our dreams. She wanted to be in advertising. I've often wondered if she was or still is.

I thought we were going to start a family. We had talked about having kids once we both had careers and enough money that we wouldn't have to worry about bills or where the next meal was coming from. She hated relying on her brother for tuition and grocery money, but the jobs on and off-campus didn't pay nearly enough.

Just a boy and his dreams.

Ha!

A boy who stands at six foot three, is built like a tank, and runs faster than most mortals is now a man who can't get a woman to use his phone number.

Some things never change.

Chapter 3

Penelope

Jack has not changed his phone number since we were kids.

When I programmed it into my cell, I was surprised to see it was already there—blocked contact, sure, but still...

It was there.

My fingers hover over the two words UNBLOCK CONTACT. My thumb hesitates while my eyes are stuck on that name his friends used to call him.

Skip.

I hated that name back then, but I hear it every single day now.

"Penn, this is our friend Jack—everyone calls him Skip because it looks like he's skipping across water in the end zone." My friend Natalia, whom I met in a mass comm class, shoves a guy at me unlike anyone I have ever seen.

I wasn't planning on drinking or flirting at the house party and wasn't even dressed up. It was finals week and the beginning of football season, so everyone was out and in high spirits. The rookies on the team—along with the veteran players—promised to take our team to the championships.

I wasn't a huge football fan myself, but the games had an energy that I loved. Electric. Fun. Loud and obnoxiously chaotic.

Since my brother played football professionally, I was used to it. I'd also gone to his games with our mom when he was in school before he'd been drafted.

"Penn?" Someone nudges my arm, and I glance up.

"Your name is Pen?" the guy, Skip, says. "Like pen and pencil?"

"No, like Penelope." I was blushing, but I was also hot in this sweater, in this house, under his gaze.

"Nice to meet you, Penelope," Jack says, extending his hand for me to shake. Rather than take it, I give it a long, hard look, unable to slide my hand into his.

"Nice to meet you, Jack." I refuse to call him by his nickname the same way everyone else is. Not only because it sets me apart but because it feels easier.

There's a tepid cup of beer in my hand, and I raise it to my lips, needing my hands to be busy. Not wanting anyone to see me shiver when Jack smiles down at me. His warm and friendly smile has butterflies in my stomach spreading their wings and fluttering.

Heart skipping a few beats...

Skip.

He was always more mature than everyone else. His goals always felt loftier. He knew he wanted to play in the pros, and nothing was getting in his way. Laser-focused, he kept himself on a strict diet and worked out religiously.

He didn't miss curfew, didn't break the rules, and did what had to be done to stay on the right path.

He was funny, and he loved me.

The first time we slept together, I'd been a virgin. Scared but excited, he had more experience but was nervous just the same, probably because the connection we had was so strong.

"Are you sure about this, Penn? We can wait." There was no rush, but I loved him. I loved him the moment I laid eyes on him and felt respected by him, too. I hadn't felt rushed to sleep with him at all. The urgency was on my end.

He was happy making out like teenagers and going down on me and getting blow jobs. I was the one who craved more.

"Yes, I'm sure. Are you going to make me beg?" I was teasing but also serious. It felt like he was holding back. I knew it was because I was a virgin, and he didn't want me to have regrets. "Oh my god, stick it in already."

"Gee, when you say it like that, it doesn't make my dick want to shrivel up at all." He laughed into the nape of my neck, his warm breath sending shivers down my spine. I could feel his erection pressing against me and squirmed, wiggling my hips back and forth to urge him forward.

"I'm not fragile, Skip. I won't break."

Skip. I only used his nickname when he irritated me, and he knew it.

"I know you won't break, but you're so small."

I felt feminine and womanly beneath him, and I wanted him inside...

"You feel so good, Jack."

He groaned.

I couldn't understand why he was hesitating. I wasn't the first girl he'd been with. Far from it. I knew he'd gone through that same phase so many athletes went through, with girls chasing after him. The cleat chasers propositioned him.

The young women on campus were lining up to lock down Jack Jennings, and I was not his first sexual partner.

"I love you so much, Penelope."

It hurt when he took my virginity, but we more than made up for that first night. The many, many nights that followed were full of sex in every position, on tables, in the shower, living room, bedroom, and even airplane bathrooms those times I flew to his away games.

No, his number hadn't changed.

He had, though.

He was all man now, no naïvety of youth shining back at me in his astonished eyes.

Dark, dark eyes.

The same eyes I see every day.

Suddenly, I wish Skipper was home, sleeping in her own bed so I could go into her room and check on her. I'm feeling very... uncertain right now. And sick to my stomach.

I do not feel like a good person, or a good mother, or even a good human being. There's only one thing I can do, and that is to text Jack Jennings. I have no other choice.

The first thing I do, though, before firing off my message is to change his contact information from Skip to Jack. It's late, so I doubt he'll be up to answer, but I send it anyway.

Me: *Hey Jack, it's Penelope. I just read your letter, so I wanted to...well. I guess I'm open to having drinks or something. I owe it to you.*

He has no idea how much I owe him.

None at all.

Dread pools in the pit of my stomach when the phone dings with a notification only a few seconds later. Shit, he's awake.

Jack: *Great. I was beginning to give up hope.*

Me: *Ha, no. I just had to think about it first.*

Jack: *I wouldn't have blamed you for needing a few days to think it over first. It's been a long time. I can certainly catch you on a different weekend or fly back to town if this weekend does not work.*

Jack: *There is no pressure.*

There he goes, being sweet and understanding.

Ugh, it would be so easy if he was an asshole. So much easier if he was a piece of shit scumbag. I literally have no excuse for my actions other than being young and stupid and scared.

Now it's time to be an adult and own my mistakes.

Me: *No, this weekend is fine. There's no need for you to make a special trip back from, um. Where is it you're living now?*

Jack: *Denver.*

Duh. He plays for a team in Colorado.

They're champions, as a matter of fact, and if I wasn't such an idiot, I could lay claim to knowing him as a friend.

Me: *Sorry, I'm tired.*

Jack: *I honestly wasn't expecting you to respond to me at all, let alone tonight. You should be in bed!*

Me: *LOL—you're the one who should be sleeping. Don't you have like, training and stuff this weekend?*

Jack: *Yeah, I'll see my trainer and probably work out, but no practice or anything. Game on Monday, obviously.*

I can't help but wonder if he purposely came to town these few days early to see me. There is technically no reason for him to be in town already. He could have flown in on Sunday night.

Jack: *So you're up for drinks? I have to shake these*

weird dreams, so I appreciate you meeting up. You can sage me or something, ha-ha.

He'll want more than sage on him after I tell him my secret, and he hates me forever.

Me: *Sage?! It can't be THAT bad.*

Jack: *Trust me, it was worth humiliating myself in front of your brother to show up at his door. He looked confused and annoyed at the same time.*

Me: *I'm sure. Davis isn't used to men showing up on his doorstep unannounced specifically to see me.*

Jack: *Ah, so does that mean you're not dating anyone?*

No, Jack—I don't have the time. Not really. Or haven't made the time, considering I have a daughter to raise, want to finish my college degree so I'm not living off my brother's charity, and work full time...

Me: *It means Davis only has his buddies over so unless you're there with a pizza or beer, he's going to look surprised to see you. LOL*

There's a long pause before Jack's next message.

Jack: *How is he doing now that he's retired?*

Me: *Good. He doesn't talk much about the old days. He's pretty focused on his career. Really glad he got that degree in finance. Many of his clients are former teammates.*

Jack: *It's good to know there's life after football, ha-ha.*

Me: *Indeed.*

I stare, not sure what else to add. Or what to say.

This whole conversation was a huge leap for me. My tummy churns in a way that makes me want to vomit or use the toilet, whichever comes first.

Jack: *So tomorrow night works for you?*

I'll have to see if Davis or someone can watch Skipper, but it's now or never for the news I have to share.

Me: *Yes, tomorrow works just fine. I just need an address.*

Not twenty seconds later, an address comes through along with the map app.

Jack: *Or I can send you a car?*

Oh god, there is no way I'm letting him send a car. This is not a date, and he doesn't have to be so polite. His chivalry is only making me feel worse. Like a horrible human.

Me: *Thank you, Jack, but that's not necessary. I'm not far from the city, so it shouldn't be an issue.*

Jack: *It's not an imposition. I can even come grab you myself.*

Me: *And be trapped in the car with me on the way home? What if the evening is a trainwreck?*

Jack: *Somehow, I doubt that.*

Me: *Still, it's probably best if I just drive on my own, although I do appreciate the offer!!*

Jack: *So...7:00 then?*

Me: *Yes, 7:00.*

Jack: *Great. I'll see you tomorrow night then.*

Me: *Yup, tomorrow night.*

Jack: *Hey, Penelope?*

Me: *Hmm?*

Jack: *I'm looking forward to it.*

I stare at that sentence for a good long while before responding, knowing full well that soon enough, I'll be knocking whatever smile he has off that handsome face.

Me: *Me too.*

But not really.

I google the address he sent me to look up the place where we're meeting. As one of the fanciest restaurants downtown, it was voted the city's most romantic three years in a row. Situated high in the sky, the Italian restaurant is eighty stories up, so it overlooks the entire cityscape. Dimly lit with candlelight at each table and fantastic food.

A quiet place to talk.

Shit.

There is nothing casual about this spot.

There is nothing casual about this meeting.

Either Jack is trying to impress me or he's genuinely clueless about the spot. Or maybe he does not care that it's romantic and better suited for a first date or Valentine's Day or an engagement proposal than to tell a woman about your bad dreams.

Sick to my stomach, I lie in the dark unable to sleep, counting down the hours.

"Who are you going out with?" my brother asks, seeing me in my dress. He looks me up and down as if seeing me for the first time. First time dressing up for a date, that is.

I hadn't told him who I was going out with tonight when he agreed to watch Skipper, but he also hadn't asked.

It's true that I manage to go out and get dressed up plenty with my girlfriends, but rarely with a man. So the dress and the hair and the makeup must be throwing him off.

"Jack Jennings."

Jack's name hangs in the air between us while Skipper is already getting her dolls out of the leather trunk my brother uses as a coffee table. Everything she loves is inside: Dolls, puzzles, books, stuffed animals.

My brother steps closer. "Penn. What aren't you telling me?"

He's studying me with a shrewd look in his eye, brows furrowed as if he already knows what I'm going to say.

"What do you mean? I'm going for a drink with Jack. He has a few things he wanted to get off his chest. Something about superstitions so he can play?" I'm shrugging into my jacket, and I can't even look at Davis.

He knows me too well.

"So that's what this is about?" He pauses. "He's having a hard time playing or something because of these dreams?"

"Yeah, I guess." I pull on my gloves. "Remember, we dated in college?"

"Yeah, I remember you dated in college." Another pause. "Seven years ago, to be exact."

Both our eyes stray to Skipper as she sets her ponies on the carpet, laying them out on the floor one by one.

My brother's eyes bore into mine, and without saying it, we both know what he's thinking, except I'm not ready to say the words out loud.

I barely have the courage to put one foot in front of the other and go through the front door to meet Jack, who waits blissfully unawares downtown at some fancy, bougie restaurant.

"That's it. That's the only reason you're seeing him." He makes it a statement, not a question, and it makes me feel defensive.

"Yes, Davis. That's the only reason I'm seeing him tonight." My chin goes up a notch, but I'm anything but confident, my gusto inflating like a balloon that's been pinpricked.

"I hope you know what you're doing, sis."

I don't.

That's the whole thing of it.

I haven't the faintest clue what I'm doing, but I'm going to fake my way through the best I can.

"I hope so, too."

Chapter 4

Jack

Damn, she looks gorgeous.

Stunning.

Prettier than anyone I've been on a date with since the day she walked out on me.

I try not to stare as the maitre d' pulls out her chair so she can be seated and puts the napkin across her lap. I try not to stare when she tips her head up to thank him.

It's impossible to say whether or not Penelope put in a maximum amount of effort into dressing up tonight, but I appreciate the long wavy hair and the emerald-green dress that clings to her body—both of them silky. So silky I want to reach out and touch her, run my hand over her thigh, over the fabric that looks as if it were made for her, and *that is not the reason we are here.*

Shit. What if seeing her tonight makes my dreams worse? What if instead of exorcising the demons of her running through my mind, I have even more dreams about her?

The thought hadn't occurred to me until now. This dinner was supposed to cleanse my body of her. Cleanse my mind so I can sleep and eat and concentrate. The past couple of weeks have been an exercise in refocusing my thoughts away from Penelope.

We are no longer kids. No longer college students who lived in a bubble of naïvety.

I grew up the day she walked out on me without a word or explanation. I'm a man now with real responsibility, who makes a fuck ton of money in a fast-paced world where people fight for my time...sitting with a woman who wants nothing to do with me.

Keep telling yourself that, Jack. You have to keep reminding yourself that Penelope doesn't want you in her life —you're only here to sage her from your mind.

We don't speak until after the server has come to take our drink order. I order a cocktail on the rocks while she orders a glass of wine. It's strange to see her drinking. She never did while we were in college. She claimed she never had a taste for it.

This is not a date, this is not a date, this is not a date.

I look up from my menu to find her watching me—dark hair, dark eyebrows, blue eyes—and it takes me a solid few seconds to remember that I have to speak actual words from my mouth and not just sit here gawking at her. I'm more affected than I ever thought I would be. Why did I legitimately think I could meet her and act like a normal person?

Because I'm a cool guy. The entire world wants to get to know me, and here I am, nervous to be on a date with my ex-girlfriend.

We've had sex.

I've seen her naked.

I've seen her cry.

"This isn't awkward at all," she jokes, picking up the glass of wine when it's set in front of her and sipping from it, eyes watching me from over the brim, berry red lips leaving a stain on the edge of the glass.

"Is this awkward? I hadn't noticed."

Good, we're bantering.

This is good. This is good.

It was better than I'd hoped for because I hadn't known what kind of woman Penelope had grown into, so it's nice to see that she has a sense of humor. A rude, snotty bitchy one? A label whore? The uptight, conservative type?

She had not looked glad to see me on her brother's doorstep in any which way.

Penelope is staring at me in a way that people usually don't look at me. As if she's staring at my face to memorize every line and detail. Is it because she hasn't seen me in so long? Is it because she's trying to reconcile the differences between the boy I used to be and the man I've become?

In any case, I feel like I'm under a microscope, though not in a negative way.

I feel like she appreciates what she's seeing and wants to drink in every detail of me.

"So. You looked surprised to see me yesterday."

"That's an understatement."

"Really? How so?"

"I mean, who opens the door to someone else's house and expects to see their college boyfriend there?"

College boyfriend. First boyfriend.

The guy she lost her virginity to.

"I really didn't mean to freak you out. I know I could have slid into your messenger or something, but you know how that is. I didn't know if you'd see it if you had social media or whatever."

"And you thought showing up at my house was the easiest way to go about it?" She chuckles, taking a sip of wine. "My brother's house, I mean. Gosh, and you were so close, too."

"So close? What do you mean?"

"I live next door. In the house next door."

"To your brother?"

"Yes." She takes another sip of wine, and if she doesn't slow down, she'll need another glass and a ride home. "The house directly next door. Sometimes it sucks, but most days, it's awesome."

"Wow. You must be doing well."

She gives her head a little shake. "Not really. He bought it when he was in the pros and thought it would be cozy to keep us close by. Me close by." Penelope sets her wineglass down, pushes it away from her body, and straightens her spine. "One house over and you wouldn't have had to leave your letter with my bro."

Her bro. "Dude looked so confused."

I sit up straighter too, righting the napkin on my lap and picking up the menu to peruse over the starters, giving the landscape below us a cursory glance.

The sight is breathtaking.

It's a shame this isn't a romantic date because the view is stunning, the lighting dim, the atmosphere quite...magical, if I'm being honest. Not to sound poetic or anything.

"I've never been here," Penn tells me, chin in her hand and staring down into the dark cityscape dreamily. "It's gorgeous."

She is gorgeous, but I don't say so. I don't want to be weird.

Showing up unannounced was weird enough and crossing boundaries. I don't want to make her feel any more awkward than this already is.

Clearing my throat, I go back to looking at the appetizers, giving the bread basket a brief glance as it gets set in the center of the table.

My stomach growls.

"Do you want any appetizers? I really love calamari or even a crab cake, but I'll leave it up to you."

This isn't a date, but I want her to have what she wants. I mean, we're all dressed up, so we might as well enjoy ourselves. It wasn't originally my intention to bring her somewhere so fancy, but the second I saw her—the moment I laid eyes on her beautiful face yesterday, the one I used to love with all my heart—I made reservations here.

All previous plans for something a bit more casual flew out the window.

"Sure, I always love a good appetizer."

I remember that about her. She still always orders calamari and crab cakes. Even though we didn't have a lot of money in college, we would make it a point to taste test the calamari and crab cakes anywhere we went. Her favorite thing to dip them in was always a marinara and ranch, but this doesn't seem like the type of place that will bring us cups of salad dressing to dip our appetizers in.

She sets down the menu.

If her look was saying anything, it's saying you remembered. Even though she's not moving her lips, her eyes are speaking volumes, and they're wide right now as they regard me from across the table, her hands tucked away on her lap where I can't see them.

Penelope hides her face by lowering her head and focusing her gaze back on the menu the same way I've been doing.

"So," she says, lifting her head at last. "You've been having dreams about me? Do tell."

"Ha-ha, get your mind out of the gutter. It's not those

kinds of dreams. They're the kind that has me waking up sweating. The kind where I'm drowning, and you're reaching for me, but you can't touch the surface or reach for my hand."

"That's so Jack Dawson of you." She smiles, referencing the scene in the movie *Titanic*, where the girl lets go of her one true love, only to watch him sink to the bottom of the ocean when she could have shared her spot with him on the floating door.

The smile does not reach her eyes, so I know she's taking this seriously despite the teasing words.

"Well, it's becoming a problem because I'm having a hard time focusing at work with all this lack of sleep."

"And you seriously thought seeing me was going to help? That's very optimistic of you."

"I'm not the kind of athlete who has to wear the same socks to every game or who never changes his underwear like some people. So when something affects my game, I have to get rid of it. Or at least make it make sense, if that makes sense?"

"Of course that makes sense." She nods. "Are you forgetting who my brother is? I remember him doing the same exact thing every game day when I was living in his apartment before I left for college. Every game day, he would wake up and eat the same breakfast—a bagel, five eggs over easy, half a pound of bacon, hash browns, and orange juice. Then he would leave for the stadium, but he would always tap the doorjamb three times before walking through it, then kiss his index finger and his middle finger. I never saw his entire ritual set once he left the house, but I can only imagine it was bizarre." She shakes her head as if she finds this all very funny. "Your dream problem hardly seems even remotely as superstitious."

"I like to think of it as less of a problem and more of a nuisance I'm trying to get rid of. Like, oh, I don't know...a demon or an evil spirit."

"Whoa, that seems extreme. Really? Dreams of me are like an evil spirit?" She laughs, tipping her head back, causing her chest to rise and fall in the sexiest way. She tosses her hair in a casual, natural way that sends it spilling down her left shoulder.

I clear my throat. "You know what I mean."

"You know you could've told me all this in a coffee shop. It would've saved you a ton of time and a lot of money." She laughs.

"Who says I'm the one paying the bill?" I wink at her, hoping she realizes it's a joke.

I have every intention of paying the bill.

Penelope blushes furiously. I can see it from across the table even though there isn't a lot of light in this restaurant. I know she's blushing because I know Penelope, and that is the sort of thing she does when she's embarrassed.

"I didn't m-mean..." she stutters uncomfortably. "We can do Dutch. We'll go Dutch."

Oh shit, I made her feel bad. "No, I invited you out, so I am paying the bill. I shouldn't have made the joke. It was tacky. I want nothing more than to catch up with an old...friend."

Friend, my ass.

We were more than friends.

I wanted to marry Penelope Halbrook more than I wanted a career in the NFL, or at least the same amount, except I never had the chance to tell her.

I thought she knew.

Or maybe she did know I cared and loved her that much, and she didn't give a rat's ass?

42

In any case, I raise my glass to her for a toast. "Here's to old friends and this exorcism, and may I sleep through the night so I can play somewhat decent tomorrow."

She rolls her eyes at the same time she toasts me from across the table. After drinking from the wineglass daintily, she wipes at the corner of her mouth. "Drooled a little bit." She giggles. "And you know you're going to play decent tomorrow. Is there any actual doubt?"

"Yeah, I have doubts. That's why we're here. I can't keep lying awake every night staring at the ceiling. I'm like a zombie now."

She nods slowly. "There's no reason to have nightmares about me. I wonder what brought it on."

"Me too. Here I was, minding my own business when all of a sudden—boom—I'm having dreams about an ex-girl-friend who hates my guts."

"That's harsh. I do not hate your guts."

"Really? Then why did you leave?"

There, I said it.

The question I've been waiting to ask her for years.

Why did you leave?

"It's...complicated." Her sentence drawls out slowly.

"Everything is complicated. This isn't Facebook. You don't get to tick a blanket statement box to explain it away."

I realize I sound pissed—because I am—so I take a few deep, steadying breaths to cool my nerves. I'm flustered and frustrated, and she's not explaining herself at all.

Lucky for her, she's saved from answering by the server delivering the starters to our meal, easing directly into taking our dinner orders.

Penelope serves herself some appetizers, taking some calamari out of the bowl and placing it on her plate, then cutting off a fraction of the crab cake and doing the same.

There's only one sauce available, and she spoons a small heap of that, too. Once she's completed the task, she looks up at me.

"I have made a lot of mistakes, Jack. Mistakes I am not proud of making with you. And I know it sounds like I'm making excuses, but it was a very difficult time for me, and I didn't want to bur—"

"Mr. Jennings? Sorry to interrupt your meal." A man stands next to the table, interrupting Penelope, holding out a cocktail napkin. His wife hovers behind him with her phone, looking embarrassed. "My son is a huge fan, and well, we were wondering if you would autograph this napkin for him?"

Typical fan behavior? Absolutely.

Am I used to it? One-hundred percent.

Convenient? *Not at all.*

I take the napkin with a smile and scrawl my name on it with the pen he's also handed me, then my eyes go to the phone in the woman's hand. "Did you want to take a picture?"

Might as well get it out of the way so they'll go back to their table or leave, and Penelope can be left in peace.

"Would you?" the wife enthuses loudly. "Oh my gosh, we're so sorry to interrupt, but we figured we would never get this chance again. How often do you bump into celebrities? And we know this happens to you all the time—" She gestures with her arms toward Penelope in an "I'm so sorry" manner. "Miss, I am so, so sorry," she gushes. "Our son loves him so, so much."

So, so sorry.

So, so much.

Still, Penelope nods with a pleasant smile glued to her face as if these people weren't imposing on us and our appetizers weren't getting cold. "The things we won't do for our kids."

I pose for pictures with the husband while the wife snaps the photograph—a dozen of them, judging by the way she's snapping this way and that and moving the phone around to different angles. Penelope sits patiently as she waits for them to finish.

The couple leaves us with a chorus of thank-yous and handshakes, disbelieving their good fortune for having bumped into me. They walk out with their heads bent together, no doubt poring over their photo gallery.

"Where were we?" I try to loop around to the conversation we were having before we were interrupted by my fans. But Penelope just smiles again. It's the beautiful, lovely smile that made me weak in the knees as a kid. I remember the first time she smiled at me at that college party and how it made me feel like I was the only guy in the room.

I've never been the type of guy who thought he could have any woman. So many of my buddies are conceited assholes who think their shit doesn't stink. They think they can have any woman they want.

That is not me. It never was.

When Penelope first set eyes on me in college—when she returned my feelings, and we started dating—I felt like the luckiest bastard in the whole wide world.

Like I could *take on* the world.

She's giving me that same look now, but this time, it's one only a person from your past could give you. One of friendship and camaraderie.

I'm curious about her personal life and wonder how I can dig without being nosy or sounding jealous. It's hard not to when we have a history. Obviously, I'm going to want to know a bit about what her life is like now, yeah?

We might have only spent a few years together, but like I said, I wanted to spend the rest of my life with this person.

"What have you been up to lately?" I ask as I run the crab cake through the hollandaise sauce it was served with.

She considers this question, tilting her head and staring off into the distance before replying. She swallows the bite she's just taken and wipes her fingers on the napkin. "Well, I work a lot. Does that count?"

"Tell me about your job. What's it like?"

"Um. I'm pretty sure my boss can't stand me. I think I irritate her, which sucks because I'd like to be in her position one day, but I don't think she's going to promote me anytime soon. It's safe to say I don't love my job, but I really want to love my job?"

"She can't stand you? How would that even be possible? You're adorable." Or were. Was. Is?

I keep reminding myself that I don't actually know this person anymore. We are seven years from knowing one another. I know I sure as hell am not the same guy I was in college. So much has changed.

"She's very businessy, if that makes sense. All work and no play. Doesn't joke around, doesn't join us in the break room, and never cracks a smile. If we don't work late—like seven or eight o'clock at night—we're not working hard enough." Penelope sighs. "I know I'll have to quit eventually, but there aren't many jobs in the marketing field right now that would hire me without a degree."

That's right. She never graduated.

"So what are you planning to do?"

She sits up straight again. "I haven't told anyone this yet, but I contacted State, and I can finish online in less than a year. I'm close, so I'm going to try to get my degree. Business and Mass Comm. It will be a juggling act, but if I don't, my options are limited."

"You can just start back up where you left off?"

She shrugs. "Pretty much. I mean, they have all my transcripts, and I was getting great grades..."

Which is why it made zero sense when she bailed.

No fucking sense at all.

There must be something she isn't telling me.

Another guy?

Something with her family?

I have no idea who else would have been in the picture back then, but what the hell do I know? Apparently, not much.

"What's held you back before from getting your degree?"

Her shoulders rise in another shrug, and she pulls the hair from her left shoulder, tossing it over her right. "Time, mostly. Money, of course. Motivation, time." Penelope laughs.

"So...time?"

"Pretty much. I forgot about it for a while, but recently, with how freaking much I dislike working for my boss—I want to be the boss. I don't think I can do that unless I get my bachelor's."

We look up when the servers approach, carrying our meals. The plates are set before us, and ground pepper is added to my steak, and they take our empty drink glasses before leaving us alone.

"But enough about me." Penelope sets to cutting the scallops she'd ordered. "Tell me how your life is, barring the nightmares about yours truly."

"You know, the usual. Practice, work out, practice, sleep, game day. It's all the same now."

47

She glances up before putting a fork of risotto in her mouth. "No time for dating?"

"No." No time for dating and very little interest. "I've tried, but—no."

I seal my lips shut, not wanting to discuss my personal life but being insatiably curious about hers. There are a hundred things I want to ask but won't. God fucking forbid I look desperate or digging or like I still care.

Penelope broke my heart.

She was my best friend.

I still love her, but it took one helluva long time to move past the betrayal of her leaving and realize it wasn't about me at all. She must have had demons that didn't include me and reconciling that fact took me years.

We eat for a bit in silence, stealing glances at one another between occupying our time with eating, drinking, and responding when the servers come back and forth to check on us.

"Do you feel like seeing me will help you sleep?" Penelope asks as she dips her fork into a piece of cheesecake, licking the frosting from the fork after the bite is in her mouth.

"We'll see tonight."

"How will you let me know?"

Reaching into the pocket of my sport coat, I pull out an envelope. "I'll tell you tomorrow in person how I slept."

Her eyes flicker from me to the envelope and back again. "What are these?"

"Tickets."

"Tickets for what?"

I roll my eyes. "The football game tomorrow. Do you have plans tomorrow? There are two tickets in there. One for you and one for a friend."

"A friend."

"Sure. Bring anyone you like." Including a dude. "Your brother maybe? A girlfriend?" I throw out suggestions like "no big deal." "Go ahead, take them. If you can make it, awesome. If not..." I shrug to let her know I'd be unaffected if she let the prime seats go to waste.

The seats are in the WAG section, where the players' families sit, but she doesn't need to know that.

"Thank you, I'll think about it."

I nod. "That's all I ask."

"I want you on top so I can look at you." I run my hands through her thick hair and roll, pulling her along with me. She straddles me, a furious blush crossing her cheeks.

Penelope has always been a bit shy about being naked, but that's one of our differences I love. While I don't mind walking around my apartment as naked as the day I was born, she's more comfortable covering up her body with a tee shirt or actual pajamas.

I love looking up at her on top of me with her tits in my face and hair falling in long, dark waves.

She adjusts herself, sinking onto my dick with a groan.

There's nothing shy about her now. She places her hands on the headboard as her hips begin to move, leaving her completely in control.

"Do you like that?" she asks.

"Yes..."

She stops. "Do you like that?*"*

"No."

Penelope laughs, leaning in to kiss me on the mouth and brushing her breasts against my chest. "I just wanted to tell you I forgot to pick up the refill on my birth control yesterday, so I didn't start my pills until this morning." Another kiss is placed on the tip of my nose as I begin thrusting into her.

She feels so fucking good.

So right.

I brush the hair out of her face to look at her. Really look at her. Flushed and beautiful, she's young and full of life.

"Jack, did you hear me?"

I thrust. "Yeah, I heard you. I trust you."

My hands go to her hips as we move together, the broken thermostat in this dumpy off-campus apartment I'm renting making the room so warm that sweat beads on my forehead.

A baby cries in the background, louder and louder until I shove her off me, and she lands on the bed beside me.

I kick off the remaining covers because I'm hot.

So hot.

"She's fine," Penelope says. "Let her cry."

"Let who cry?"

There is no baby. We don't have a baby.

Someone pounds on the wall of the apartment. "Shut that kid up!"

I wander through the apartment, naked, opening one door after another, a labyrinth of mazes I can't find my way out of.

"Jack, come back!" Penelope calls my name.

The baby cries.

The neighbor bangs.

"Where is the fucking door to this place?" I shout, sweat dripping from my forehead and between my pec muscles. "WHERE IS THE FUCKING DOOR TO THIS PLACE?"

I shoot to a seated position in bed, gasping.

Breathe in, breathe out.

I remember that I'm in a hotel room in Illinois and not in my condo in Colorado.

Shit.

That dream felt so real. Well, most of it anyway.

It has me lying here a long while, doing the same damn thing I've been doing the past few weeks—staring wide-eyed at the ceiling with the game day looming only a few hours away.

Chapter 5

Penelope

I couldn't sleep last night.

Obviously.

What woman in their right mind would be able to sleep knowing they just had dinner with the father of their child and didn't tell him her secret? I didn't tell Jack that he has a seven-year-old daughter who was sound asleep upstairs in the same house he was inside of just the day before. Jack Jennings is going to hate me when he finally hears the news.

I put a hoodie on Skipper before we exit the vehicle. The valet parking at the stadium was a convenience I hadn't expected when I finally decided to use the tickets and bring her to the game.

Beside me, Skipper hops up and down with excitement as we approach the gate. It's a VIP entrance I used when I went to my brother's football games, and a pang of nostalgia hits me.

In the envelope with the tickets Jack had given me was a hand-written note instructing me to come to this gate. *Go to the gate at the back of the stadium, not the main entrance.*

It's chain link and slides, and there is a guard booth there. That is the private entrance if you want to use it. Someone will show you to your seats.

Well la-di-dah, Mr. Fancy Pants.

Skipper takes my hand as we follow a man wearing a security jacket and carrying a walkie-talkie down a sleek tunnel-like hallway.

What am I doing here?

The better question is, *what am I doing here with my daughter?*

The nerves don't quit. They worsen during the announcements, Jack's face, number, and stats on the Jumbotron as players are broadcasted and cheers echo.

Skipper covers her ears but wears a huge grin.

"Mom, this is so fun!"

It doesn't take long before she's eating a giant pretzel and dipping it in cheese, content to snack as her short little legs dangle over the edge of her stadium seat. Obviously, she has little interest in the actual game, but she is obsessed with the food, people watching, and everyone high-fiving her when the home team gets the ball, scores a touchdown, or makes an interception.

It is all so exciting for her, and our seats are fantastic.

We're in the center of all the action, right where my daughter can see, hear, and practically taste the action. The players are right here in front of us like large giants on the sidelines. The presence of the media and staff just add to the thrill of her exciting day.

My eyes are glued to Jack Jennings as if it were my job to watch him.

I hadn't intended on staying for the entire game. My plan was to leave early in the fourth quarter to beat the rush and traffic leaving the stadium, but the game went so fast, and the time got away from me. Before I know it, a man taps on my shoulder. It's another official with a security jacket on and a walkie in his hand.

"Are you..." He glances at the paper in his hand. "Penelope Halbrook?"

Since he's wearing the outfit of an employee, I'm not suspicious and nod my head.

"I am. Is everything all right?"

"Everything's fine, ma'am. If you're ready to head out and you'd like to follow me, I can lead you back downstairs."

"Oh, outstanding!" This will save me from having to navigate back down to the VIP tunnel. I have no badge to give me the credentials to go wherever I want, and my car is parked in a place where not many people can go.

After grabbing my things and Skipper's hoodie, we rise to follow the man back up the stairs, past all the concession stands, to an elevator at the end of the corridor.

He needs a special card to access the lower levels.

Back through the sleek hallway, he leads my daughter until we end up in front of a large, green, windowless door. It's open, and when I peek inside, I see it's a room full of fancy-looking people.

Men, women, and children.

"I'm confused?"

"This is the reception area, ma'am. You can get some more food here or swag. There's a vendor table in the corner, and you can take what you'd like."

I put my hands on Skipper's shoulders as we slowly wade into the room, my eyes skimming over women and children—presumably the wives of players? They can't be anyone else. There are barely any men in this room. I mean, there are—but they're older, so most likely fathers?

Not to mention these women? They look expensive.

The kind of expensive that only comes with millions of dollars in contracts per year, fillers, Botox, and diamonds the size of my thumbnail.

Before I can back out of the room and get the hell out of there, Skipper breaks away and makes a beeline for the snack table. I don't blame her. It's loaded with fruit platters, meat and cheese trays, hot dogs, hamburgers, and candy— all the things we had to pay for back in the stadium seats and all things my seven-year-old daughter loves.

Not only that but there are also gifts.

T-shirts and hoodies, along with bumper stickers and toy footballs. Cups, pilsner glasses, sports-themed Monopoly, and tote bags.

Skipper is in heaven, already loading down a plate with food even though she ate while we were watching the game. It's still being streamed now on the television sets in every corner of the room, leather furniture laid out so anyone in the room can sit and comfortably watch the game.

That doesn't seem to be what anyone in here is doing. They're all chatting amongst themselves, and it's obvious they're all well acquainted.

I'm the odd man out.

Feeling like a fish in a fishbowl, I casually stroll to grab my daughter, who continues piling on snacks as if she were at a birthday party with eyeballs bigger than her tiny stomach.

"Sweetie, take it easy," I tell her quietly. "We're not staying, honey. We have to get out of here before the traffic gets bad. The game is almost over."

Six minutes in the last quarter can take an eternity, but I'm not taking any chances. I want to leave, and I want to leave now.

But Skipper doesn't cooperate.

She wiggles out of my grip, ducks to dodge me, and slithers to the opposite side of the room to a small group of little girls her age. She plops herself down and begins chattering away.

Shit.

How am I going to get her up and out of here without causing a scene?

How are there only four minutes left in the game?

Colorado is winning by a landslide, so everyone in the room is in high spirits. As no one is worried about Chicago gaining a lead, only a fraction of the room continues to watch the game.

I hardly know what to do with myself. The last thing I'm going to do is stroll over to the wives and introduce myself. Like—what the hell would I even say? *"Hi, I'm the mother of Jack Jennings' child, the one he doesn't know exists, who's in the corner playing with your child right now? I haven't seen him since I got knocked up, but he showed up on my doorstep, and here we are."*

Yeah, no.

Forty-nine seconds left in the game.

Thirty.

Fifteen.

The room erupts into cheers with merriment all around. Skipper leaps up from her spot to jump up and down with the other kids. They hug and dance, shaking their little booties while eating their snacks.

Skipper has a hot dog dangling out of her mouth.

Dear lord, it looks like she's been raised with no manners.

"Hi, I'm Lana Macenroy." A blonde appears out of nowhere, sashaying up with a smile on her face and a

Southern accent to boot. When she extends her hand, I take it, though hesitantly. "You look lost."

"I feel lost?" I decide to be honest because I'll probably never see this woman again. "One moment I was sitting there, thinking I should leave to beat traffic, and another minute, I was being ushered into this room."

"Oh, you're from here?"

"I am."

She tilts her head and studies me. "They don't indiscriminately let people in here."

Indiscriminately? Dang, Lana sounds smart.

"I'm..." Let's see, how do I put this? "An old friend of Jack Jennings."

"Oh!" She bobs her head with recognition. "That makes more sense."

"My brother used to play for the Sprinters." I have no idea why I share that random piece of information other than: I do not want her thinking I'm a fraud who doesn't belong here even though I don't belong here.

"The Sprinters?" She wrinkles her nose with a laugh. "We killed them last year."

"I said *used* to." I laugh too, mostly because I'm nervous and have no idea how to behave right now. I feel as if Lana has been sent over to retrieve information on me and isn't here chatting me up for a new best friend.

"Well, my husband is Robb Macenroy—number twelve."

Everyone with a pulse knows who Bobby Macenroy is. Quarterback and MVP, he is no longer a rookie, makes a zillion dollars a year, and is beloved by the entire US of A.

"You must be so proud."

"I am." Her eyes shift to the corner of the room, to

Skipper and the other children. "My two are the blond kiddos."

They look just like her. "Speaking of kiddos, I should be grabbing mine to leave. The traffic is horrible on a regular day, so I can't imagine what it will be like trying to get out of here." Ugh. I loathe the thought of Skipper being trapped in the back seat because she'll be impatient for the long ride home.

Lana nods. "Well, it was nice meeting you. Maybe I'll see you around someday."

Probably not. "So nice meeting you." I add, "Thank you for introducing yourself to me."

This makes Lana smile. "I wasn't sure if you were dating a player or whatever, and it's never fun being the new girl in the room, so I wanted to make sure you didn't stand here alone the whole time."

Very thoughtful.

I like her.

Eventually, Lana and I part ways, and I'm over trying to wrangle my rambunctious child away from the fun, which would be a momentous task. Once Skipper is set on something, she's determined to see it through—playing, taking all her time in the shower, playdates. And if she sees an animal, all bets are off.

Prying her away from a cute dog?

Impossible.

I pick up my daughter's jacket and shoes that she's removed and discarded on the floor, then take her plate to the trash. While I'm doing that, I lose her again to the small group of children and have to do it all over again. At this rate, I'm never getting out of here.

The door opens, and a man walks in with wet hair and a smile. Several of the kids fly toward him and squeal.

Another man walks in, then another, until at least a half a dozen football players are in the room with the rest of us. One looks like a giant, more than one? A team of giants.

My heartbeat quickens.

Please do not let Jack come into the room, please do not let Jack come into the room, please do not let Jack—

He appears in the doorway, his wide frame massive, eyes scanning the room until they land on me. He smiles, then moves forward, albeit a bit hesitantly and unsure. His hands go into the pockets of his athletic pants.

"Hey, you made it."

"Yep, didn't have anything else going on today, so..."

He looks over at the food table. "Get enough to eat?"

"Yup, got enough to eat." This conversation is killing me softly. It's so awkward and stilted I'm actually embarrassed. There have to be people listening to this exchange right now wondering what the hell is going on between the two of us.

My eyes meet Lana's, and her brows are raised. My face flushes.

"Hi, who are you?" My daughter's face pops up from out of nowhere as she inserts herself into my conversation— it's something she is known for. Skipper has no couth and the manners you'd expect an excited seven-year-old to have.

"I'm Jack, but my friends call me Skip." Jack gives her his famous name with a grin. "Who are you?"

"My name is Skipper too! I've never met anyone with the same name ever in my life," she declares, dancing a little jig and pulling her face into a goofy little grin. She's being a ham, and Jack laughs.

Me, on the other hand? I'm dying inside.

"Is that really your name, you silly goose?" Jack asks Skipper, a quizzical look on his face.

Skipper nudges my elbow. "Mom, what's my real name?"

Oh, god. I die inside when I look at his face as he looks down at Skipper. His daughter.

I pull her in front of me like a shield, hands on her shoulders. "Sorry, no one ever calls her by her actual name." I ruffle her hair, which has come out of the sleek braids she started with. "It's Harper."

Harper, the adult, has been one of my best friends since childhood and is my daughter's godmother. She was there in the delivery room with my mother, and I couldn't have done it without her.

She's the sister I always wanted, and it was an honor to name my daughter after her.

"Oh, that's right!" Skipper giggles, skipping in place on one foot. "I always forget I'm named after Aunt Harper!"

She's practically shouting, which makes my face flush hotter as people turn their heads in our direction.

Jack stares at her long and hard before he looks back up at me with a wink. "She's cute. Where'd you find her?"

My teasing shrug holds no enthusiasm. "Oh you know, by the churro stand upstairs."

"By the churro stand!" Skipper giggles loudly. "Mom, you found me at the hospital!"

Jack looks at me.

Looks down at Skipper.

Back at me, down at Skipper.

She resembles me but not nearly the same way she resembles *him*—dark hair, dark eyes, dimple in her cheek. *You'd have to be blindfolded not to see it.*

"We should go," I weakly say, for lack of anything more intelligent, pulling my—our—daughter's arms into her sleeves as she squirms like she's gotten a bucket full of ants dumped down her pants.

Jack only nods, his dark eyes looking back and forth between Skipper and me.

It's impossible to tell what he's thinking right now. His expression is unreadable, his face a wall of stone.

Jaw clenching.

If he's doing the mental math, he seems to be on the right track.

Chapter 6

Jack

"I don't want you to think I'm dating you for the wrong reasons."

"Why would I think that?"

"Because, Jack, the girls at this school are horrible. Everyone wants to date the athletes, marry them, and become wives of professional athletes. You have no idea how many girls are just here for their M-R-S Degree."

"M-R-S Degree? What the hell is that?"

"You know, attending school at a Big Ten just to meet a man to marry?"

"Oh, now I get it. Missus Degree, ha-ha." I give her a quick kiss on the lips. She's so stinking cute when she's worried.

My little over-thinker. "That's not you, Penn. I don't think you're a gold digger." I pause. "And besides, there's no guarantee that I'm going to get drafted. We may end up broke, living paycheck to paycheck because I can't find a job after graduation."

"Please. You're amazing."

She's not wrong. I'm one of the best this school has ever

seen, and it's not me saying that. It's the media and the press and schools still trying to get me to transfer.

There's talk about the Heisman trophy.

Agents have already been contacting me, and I'm a sophomore.

Too bad my parents would kill me if I left school my second year to play professionally. What if I end up like Tim Tebow, who everyone thought would be the golden child of the NFL but wound up retiring after three seasons.

"If I go at all." I pick at my hoodie. "I'm not sure it's what I want. What if I don't have what it takes?"

Penelope makes herself busy by folding the few blankets on the couch. "Are you saying you'd rather work a regular job and have a few kids instead?"

"Kids? God no." I snort. "I mean, no offense to anyone because I do want kids, but not for a few years."

I remember sounding so adamant then, more passionate than I probably was, but honestly, I wasn't thinking about kids in those moments. I was thinking about my career. Not school or classes or grades or how I wanted to spend the off-season.

Football was my job and my future.

Penelope was the love of my young life.

I needed nothing else to complicate things. I had too many balls juggling in the air at the same time as it was.

"Mr. Jennings?"

I crack an eyelid to look at the flight attendant staring down at me.

"Can you please stow your tray table? We're preparing to land."

Sure. Fine. Whatever.

After putting the tray table up, I rest my head back

again and close my eyes. I try to fall asleep for the next twenty minutes, but I only see Penelope behind my eyes.

I haven't contacted her since yesterday, but she's not the only one haunting me.

That little girl.

Her daughter.

Penelope's daughter—the one she found at the churro stand.

The thought brings a smile to my face as I sit here, tired, thinking of everything I have to do when I land—grab the dog from my buddy's house, order groceries for delivery, send my agent a note to thank him for getting me in touch with Penn. It hadn't helped to see her. If anything, the dream last night was worse, and there's no doubt in my mind that I'll dream of her again tonight.

"That's my name too!" The squeaky little voice echoes in my mind.

Skipper...is that what she called her?

Weird.

They called me Skip even in college, and the media took a shine to it when I was drafted, giving me the nickname The Skip anytime I make it to the end zone. *Why would she name her daughter Skipper?*

After an ex-boyfriend? Makes zero sense.

I shift uncomfortably in my seat.

Dark braids.

Dark eyes.

"Dude, the kid looked just like you," Robb Macenroy had said when he passed by me on the tarmac as we made our way to the plane. *"Like put a wig on you, man."*

I can't nap.

My brain won't shut off as my head flops on the seat uncomfortably.

Get out of your own head, man—you're imagining things. Shut the brain off, Jack. Shut the brain off.

My eyes squeeze shut, but all I see is that kid, Harper. I remember Penelope's best friend. They were childhood friends who lived in the dorms together and never fought or argued. Inseparable except for when I came around, and even then, Penelope often included Harper. They joined a sorority together, did intramurals together, and took care of one another like sisters.

Skipper.

What a cute kid.

Looked about...shit, I don't know how old she looked. I know nothing about children.

The only kids I come in contact with are my teammates' kids—and the one time I dated the single mother with five-year-old twins, but Harper looked a bit older than that?

Hair in braids, she had giant eyes and teeth a little too big for her mouth, and cotton candy stains in the corner of her mouth from the candy in the green room. Amusing kid.

She seemed smart.

Super outgoing and chatty, she definitely was in no mood to leave the action.

Penelope had Skipper out the door shortly after I'd arrived to say hello, but I certainly wasn't expecting her to have a child along. I assumed she'd bring a friend. Even a man. And the only reason I'd popped into the room was to see her. I normally have no reason to go into the family room, but I'd had a member of security go fetch her after confirming she'd used the tickets.

When the flight lands at the airport, I head to my vehicle the same way I do after every game and toss all my crap into the back of my SUV. I grab Kevin, my Springer Spaniel, and head home for a long night of resting with my feet up on the coffee table and binge-watching trash dating shows. I can't believe these people actually date while they're in a pod, then get engaged after ten days—insanity!

I could never do it, although it's probably a good way to make sure someone is dating you for the right reason and not simply because you're a professional athlete. My face is on billboards and on television, so it's pretty damn difficult to meet the right woman these days.

I'm not going to say I was hoping to have a romantic connection with Penelope after not having seen her for seven years, but *in a way, I was hoping to have a romantic connection with Penelope.* I told her that I'd wanted to stop dreaming about her so I could play, which was true! But the fact is, I'm sure a part of my subconscious was wishing we still had a spark.

I scratch Kevin behind the ears, and he lets out a loud, content sigh.

"Dude, the kid looked just like you."

Did she? So what.

She looked like her mom. She and I have the same dark-brown hair, so it would stand to reason that her daughter would, too.

But that dimple in her cheek...

"Dude, the kid looked just like you."

Kevin nudges me with his nose when I stop scratching, and I stare blankly at the television set, not registering what's on the screen.

"...the kid looked just like you."

It cannot be.

Penelope would not have kept something like that from me. She is honest and good and loyal.

Loyal? Bro, she left you.

But why? Did she ever actually say?

No.

She didn't because we got interrupted by fans before she could explain, and then we never broached the subject again after they left. I thought I knew all the answers: she fell out of love with me. She met someone new and didn't have the guts to tell me. She flunked out of school and was embarrassed. Her family needed her.

The list went on and on, and I never could quite settle on the actual truth.

On the night of the draft, I'd wondered if she was watching. It was televised, and though we hadn't been together for a year, she had to have known I had entered and was favored to go early—to be chosen by Colorado as their first pick. It hadn't been my dream team, but it ended up being the most lucrative contract that year. The most publicized and scrutinized.

I couldn't take a shit without the paparazzi wanting to film it.

The night of the draft, I'd been in the expensive, fancy suit my agent had bought me, sweating bullets as the studio's lights where they filmed it shined down on everyone in the room—the college players, their agents, and families.

My parents hadn't made it. New York had been too far to travel for my father, who'd recently been hospitalized from complications from the flu. When Don Bacchus, the NFL Commissioner, announced my name as the first pick for Colorado, no one was more surprised than me.

I knew they were picking me, but at the same time, I wasn't. It was a pipe dream. I was about to become one of the big men on TV that little kids fantasized about. That was going to be my life.

I did not call my parents.

I did not call my best friend.

I called Penelope.

I called her after twelve long, silent months. I wanted her to know I'd made it—we had made it. That I'd accomplished what she and I had planned for me to do. That the best team in the league wanted me. After the photographs and the smiling and Mr. Bacchus moved on to the next pick of the draft, I'd stolen away and called Penelope from a small room I'd found.

She hadn't answered.

Hadn't returned my texts.

Why?

Why.

Rising from the couch, I'm frustrated and suddenly a ball of energy.

Kevin follows me, and I feel guilty for waking him from his cozy snuggles, the burden of following his human on one of my daily quests. He sits when I go into the kitchen.

He follows me into the bathroom.

He follows me back into the kitchen, wanting to nap but living with the ever-present *fear of missing out.*

I pat him on the head as I stand next to the counter, mindlessly looking through the large, panoramic windows with a view of the city outside.

"...the kid looked just like you."

"...the kid looked just like you."

It couldn't have been...

Penelope wouldn't have paraded her around if she was.

That was not my kid.

That was not.

My.

Kid.

Is it a coincidence that Harper's nickname is Skipper? I wander back to the sofa but don't sit down, confusing Kevin, who is half up, half down on the cushions. '*Are we staying or going?*' his big puppy dog eyes ask.

The Skip.

Skipper.

Way too coincidental.

If Penelope wanted nothing to do with me, then why would she give her kid a name that's the *same* as the person you want out of your life?

Skipper.

Skip.

"*...the kid looked just like you.*"

Fuck.

She did look just like me. She did. Even I could see that, and I know nothing about children.

Why did she bring her to the game?

She didn't know she was going to see you, idiot. She was trying to do something nice for her daughter.

My hand rubs at the back of my neck, the tension there growing by the second. Instead of getting answers from Penelope, I have nothing but more questions.

Shit.

Fuck.

I'm tempted to call her, or text, or video chat, but a knot is forming in my stomach.

You have a bye week, Jack—no game on the horizon—you could fly back and find out. It's true. I do. Plenty of time to land back on her soil and sort this out.

"I'm sorry, bud. It looks like I'm going to have to leave again." Kevin whines as if he understands the words coming out of my mouth. "I'd love for you to come with?" His ears perk up. "But this is official business."

His ears go down.

He can fly— of course, he can. I've taken him on planes

before and he's a rockstar traveler, especially if I'm not flying commercial.

"Next time. I promise. " I walk toward the bedroom, the dog trailing me, and this time, he gives up and jumps onto the bed, curling up. Then he just watches me as I go through my nightly routine of washing my face, brushing my teeth, and throwing on pajamas.

A few minutes later, I climb in under the covers, tuck my arms behind my head, and lace my fingers together.

In the morning, I'll get this sorted.

I just hope Penelope isn't horrified by another visit, but I have to know. I have got to get rid of this nagging feeling in my stomach and the tightness forming in my chest.

"She's cute. Where'd you find her?"

Penelope shrugs nonchalantly. "Oh you know, by the churro stand upstairs."

"By the churro stand!" Skipper giggles loudly. "Mom, you found me at the hospital!"

She's cute, and she looks just like me.

Chapter 7

Penelope

"Who is Jack Jennings to you, Penn?"

I'm in my own kitchen, minding my own business, when my brother butts in. Making himself at home, he pulls out a stool at the counter and plops down.

"You know who Jack is, Davis. He's an ex-boyfriend."

He's quiet for a few minutes while I put dinner together. "I've always given you your privacy where Skipper is concerned. I figured you would eventually tell me who her father was, and I figured you had your reasons for...withholding the information."

He's right. I did have my reasons, although suddenly, those reasons seem petty and childish.

But I've dug a hole—a deep one—and it seems there is no getting out of it.

I had my chance, and I blew it.

Twice.

I continue whipping the mashed potatoes as my brother watches me.

"I know I was busy when you were in college, and I

knew you were dating a football player. But until he showed up on my doorstep, I didn't put two and two together." My brother hesitates. "Why was he here?"

"Superstition."

"What does that mean?"

"It means he hasn't been able to sleep because he's been dreaming about me, and he wanted to see me to make it stop."

Davis nods as if that makes total sense. "So what you're telling me is a man flew all the way here and showed up on my doorstep—looking for you—because he had a few bad dreams?"

"No, I'm telling you he flew here to play in a football game and was multitasking by showing up here."

He nods slowly, skeptical. "Right." Then he looks me up and down. "That's the only reason? What aren't you telling me?"

Everything.

All of it.

I'm not telling him anything.

"Who is Jack Jennings to you, Penn?" He pauses. "Better yet, who is Jack Jennings to Skipper?"

Shit.

Shit, shit, shit. He's got me there, and there is no getting around this. Jack has already laid eyes on her himself. If he's a smart man, it won't take him long to put two and two together, and he'll be beating down my door for the truth.

"Her father."

Davis drops the protein bar he had been about to take a bite out of.

It falls to the counter. "Are you fucking serious?"

His voice holds a host of emotions. Surprise. Shock. Outrage.

"Does he know?"

I shake my head.

"Are you fucking serious right now?" My brother stands straight, his face turning red. "You never told him? You never told the man he was a father?"

My mouth hangs open. Davis has never spoken to me in this way. "I was young. I didn't know any better."

Excuses, excuses.

He laughs bitterly. "Well, you're an adult now, and the man was in my house. Did you tell him when you went on your little date last weekend?"

Another shake of my head. "No. But it's not as easy as you would thi—"

"You are fucking *un*believable."

My brother heads for the door, leaving me staring after him in shock.

"Where are you going?"

"I can't be around you right now. I'm so disappointed."

"You're my brother. You're supposed to—"

He whips around to face me. "Don't stand there and tell me I'm supposed to blindly sit by and watch you fuck things up worse than you already have." Davis inhales a deep breath to deliver his next diatribe. "Not only have you denied Skipper of her father for seven years but you've also denied him the baby years, the toddler years. All those milestones. For *what*? Because you were embarrassed you got pregnant when you were in college? You hid from your friends, you hid it from me until you started showing, and now I find out you hid it from him when all these years, I thought Skipper's father was some piece of shit burnout who skipped out on you and didn't deserve either of you."

I mean—yeah. That's exactly what I'd done.

But hearing him say it in that tone makes me feel gross and ashamed, as only one's sibling can make a person feel.

He's the closest thing I have to a parent. Our dad walked out on us when we were kids, and Mom died a few years back, so it's just him and me. A few aunts and uncles stay in touch, but not the large, boisterous family we'd always wanted as kids.

Davis keeps going to walk out the front door but stops himself every time, unable to resist lecturing me.

My bottom lip trembles. "I'm going to tell him."

"Skipper is *seven*, Penelope—seven! You've had seven years to grow a pair of balls. It's not like the man is hard to find, and he found you without even trying."

"I know that! Stop yelling at me!"

Davis narrows his eyes. "I don't feel sorry for you."

"I'm not trying to gain your sympathy. I just don't want you to raise your voice."

"No, you're deflecting." He rests his palm on the doorjamb, standing in the doorway. "So what is your plan?"

I don't have a plan.

Shrugging, I evade the question. "I mean…he's not in town anymore. I can't tell the man over the phone."

"So you get on a plane, and you go tell him in person. I'll pay for the plane ticket."

"I don't have any more personal days at work. If I take off, my boss will fire me."

"You hate your job."

"That's easy for you to say. You have your degree. I don't."

"You know what it sounds like to me, Penelope? You don't want to tell Jack Jennings he has a daughter because it's hard. Because it's embarrassing because you waited so

74

long. And *sure*, he will *probably* take you to court." He says it so matter-of-factly that it takes me off guard.

Court?

I hadn't thought of that.

Like. At all.

"Wait. *What?*"

Davis rolls his eyes and crosses his arms. "You honestly haven't thought about that? Once he finds out he has a child that you've been keeping from him, he'll probably take you to court for some kind of visitation. Unless he's a total bag of crap, which I highly doubt. A man who doesn't care would never show up at an ex-girlfriend's home out of the blue unless he gave a shit about her, and from the looks of it, Jack Jennings still has feelings for you. This is going to gut him."

"Gee, thanks."

"You want me to be honest? Or should I lie to you?"

The way I've been lying to myself? Yes, I'll take some of that, please. It makes it easier to sleep at night.

"This is a mess, Penelope."

A giant mess. "Yes, I know."

I'm trying not to pout. I am a mother, for heaven's sake. Best leave the pouting to the child.

But it's hard.

Facing this issue of my own doing is difficult. Taking accountability is something I have faced, but only to myself. Over the years, my brother has stopped asking about who Harper's father is, making assumptions and scenarios I've been all too happy to let him run with.

The truth came knocking, and Davis didn't like what he saw. Only...he discovered I was the problem.

He discovered what a coward I am.

The lies.

Skipper's dad isn't a loser. A creep.

A dead-beat.

He is a successful, nice, funny, and famous athlete who still thinks highly enough of me that he sought me out for dinner and drinks.

I didn't want him in my life, not the other way around.

Shame on me.

Shame.

On.

Me.

"Seems like you have a lot of thinking to do. I'll take Skipper tonight so you can have some time alone. And I don't want to give you any ultimatums, Penn, but if I were him...and I found out...I would be devastated. I'm a family man and want kids, and maybe he did too."

I shake my head. "But he didn't."

"Penelope, seven years ago, he was a boy, so of course he didn't want kids. He was in college, for Christ's sake."

That's another thing I had reconciled myself to over the years as I grew up. *Perhaps he'd spoken in the moment, and I'd taken him literally.* I realized this only after becoming a mother, which turned me into an adult overnight.

At that point, it was too late.

The damage was done.

Skipper had been born, and the only thing I could do to honor him was give her his nickname because I wouldn't give her his last. In a perfect world, she would be Harper Rose Jennings, not Harper Rose Halbrook, though I always thought both had a beautiful ring to them.

Once I have my daughter settled at Davis's—he has toys and snacks at his place already, forever the world's best uncle—I return home, only to wander the house, restless and sad.

Guilt-ridden.

It eats away at me as nighttime falls, and the darkness only has me pacing more.

I cry in the kitchen.

I cry in the shower.

I cry while putting on my pajamas and while I'm shoveling ice cream into my mouth, alone on the couch.

What have I done?

If I could go back and do it all over again, I would have told Jack about my pregnancy. But at the time, I didn't know how. I thought it would break his heart and ruin his career.

I thought he would think I did it on purpose to trap him.

Gold digger.

Cleat chaser.

Wanted out of school by way of the Mrs. Degree.

It was such a hard secret to keep, one of the only true burdens I've ever felt in my life.

Guilt plagued me then, and it plagues me still, much more so now than had Jack never shown up to find me.

He did, and there is no going back.

This was a sign from the universe.

Now what do I do about it? I have a few options:

1. Show up on his doorstep and tell him in person.
2. Text him.
3. Video Chat.

That's it. Those are my options, and the second two feel cheap and like a cop-out, except...I can't exactly afford to hop on a plane to Colorado, get a hotel, and pay for food just to tell a man he's a father.

Then again. *It would be a small price to pay for my sins.*

All three options leave me feeling nauseous.

Head in my hands, I bury my face, tears flowing once

more. With my heavy heart, I'm loudly sobbing. I've never been a cute crier, even if it's simply at the movies or tears of joy. My nose always turns red, my eyes always get puffy, and the snot always runs.

So gross.

I'm miserable.

I'm glad I am alone to wallow—it serves me right.

The next day, I'm still unsure of what to do or how to proceed. I spend most of Sunday clicking away on the keyboard, researching airfare to Colorado. Checking and double-checking my savings account and credit card balances for the extra cash, so I don't have to burden my brother. Skipper has come and gone between our houses several times, and now that I've laid eyes on her father, I cannot stop seeing him in her eyes. Every feature she possesses belongs to Jack Jennings.

The goofy smile, the tilt of her nose—even her laughter sounds like his.

She's gone back to my brother's house, having picked up a craft project she wants to do at his place (bead necklaces), slamming the door behind her as she always does.

Small but mighty.

I'm startled twenty minutes later when there's a knock on the front door...followed by the ringing of the doorbell, which is strange because Skipper usually just barges in, considering she knows the codes to half the homes on the block or where the keys are.

I swear, that stealthy little shit will be a cat burglar one day.

The grin I have when I pull open the door is wiped

straight off my face, another round of "shock and awe" as I'm greeted by the likes of Jack Jennings. Only this time, he isn't just as shocked to see me standing here as I am of him.

He knew where to find me.

Davis...

Thanks for the heads-up, bro.

Taking a deep breath, I open the door wide so he can step inside.

Jack declines, stuffing his hands into his jacket pockets with the shake of his head. "I don't think it's best I come in just yet."

I nod, one half relieved, the other half confused.

"What are you doing here?" *It's déjà vu all over again.*

"I had a bye week. No game."

That's not what I meant, and he knows it. "What's the other reason?"

"I think you know why I'm here." His eyes seem to scan the area behind me, over my head, searching for something.

Or someone.

Skipper.

Panic fills my belly, and I fill the doorway. Though my daughter—*our* daughter—isn't home, I feel the need to protect my space.

Regardless, he doesn't seem interested in an invitation to come inside.

"Can we go somewhere and talk? Like a coffee shop or something?"

I hesitate. "Um. Sure. Let me just..."

I need to get my coat and text my brother.

Let me just calm the fuck down. Chill. Stop my racing heart. Check my pulse because I swear I'm having a heart attack.

Jack tilts his head toward the car in my driveway, a

black sedan that's surely a rental. "I'll wait in the car. You can follow me if you want."

I want.

Being in a car with him would feel as if I were being kidnapped. Stifling. Like I was trapped with no way out...

"I'll follow you."

A small mom-and-pop coffee shop is on the corner not far from here, not even a mile away. I'm assuming that's where we're headed, and to be honest, it's kind of perfect. Quiet, private, and slow without much foot traffic—not with the giant coffee retailers down the block a little farther sucking up all the customers.

I text my brother to let him know I would be leaving. My hands shake as I hit SEND.

Davis: *Don't chicken out this time. You owe him the honest truth no matter how much you don't want to tell him.*

I know.

Me: *I won't. I promise.*

Davis: *Skip and I are getting lunch with Juliet and taking her to the movies. Don't worry about hurrying back.*

Me: *Did she see him when he came to the door looking for me?*

Davis: *No, I put her to work unloading the dishwasher and she was busy with her beading.*

I smile sadly.

Skipper and her messy beading...

I don't bother checking my reflection in the mirror on my way out. Jack isn't here to date me, romance me, or judge me by how I look. He's here because he knows, and he wants me to say it to his face.

The man has more balls than I do, that's for sure. It seems he has bigger balls than most. He always knew what he wanted in life and never gave up. Now, answers from me are the next item on his agenda.

The man flew across the country to see me, which is more than I can say for myself.

Opening the garage door, I give him a small wave as I climb inside my car. I watch him back out through the rearview mirror, then back my own car out of the driveway and follow him down the street to the cute and quaint little coffee shop I will probably never want to set foot inside again. The memories I'll create within the next few minutes will be life changing.

Life changing not just for me but also for my daughter and for Jack.

My knuckles are white as I grip the steering wheel, pull into the little parking lot, find a spot, and put my car in park.

I need a few deep breaths and a few seconds to myself before I'm able to step out of the vehicle. I'm wearing black leggings and an oversized sweatshirt, along with neon pink sneakers. My hair is thrown up into a messy topknot—literally the messiest topknot you've ever seen in your life—but at least I'm comfortable.

Jack, on the other hand, looks like a million bucks: dark denim jeans, a black leather jacket with a hoodie underneath that adds an "expensive but I don't give a fuck" vibe, and sunglasses. He looks one part *Mission Impossible*, one part Dad I'd Like to Fuck.

I trail him reluctantly, insides tangled, not sure I can stomach anything to drink or eat.

But we're on neutral ground, which is what he wanted.

He's smart.

Insightful.

My phone vibrates, and I remove it from my pocket to see another message from my brother.

Davis: *You know him, Penelope. There is no reason to be scared. He might be big and tough-looking, but he's about to be the most vulnerable human on earth. Give him a chance to be mad at you, but remember, this will all work out in the end. This is the universe's plan for you.*

The universe's plan for me? Since when is my brother so altruistic?

This is what having a girlfriend is doing to him, turning him into an even bigger romantic.

Jack orders a coffee, turning to ask if I want one, too.

I don't, but I find myself nodding anyway. My hands will need to be occupied, and I can't sit at the table jingling my keys nervously. "Yes, please." I pause. "Thank you."

Compared to our night out, this feels sterile and formal. Stiff and forced.

I'm extremely uncomfortable already.

Guess it would have helped if I had prepared a speech on my ride over rather than wiping sweat from my armpits.

Jack carries the cups over after adding a sweetener for himself, dropping a few onto the tabletop for me as he takes a seat. He leans back only to silently watch me from across the table for a few seconds.

Is he waiting for me to say something first?

Stop being a baby, Penelope. You owe the man.

You owe him a lot.

I feel as if I've committed a crime. One against humanity or at least parenthood, my sin one without a fitting punishment. My level of discomfort can be no match for Jack's inner turmoil.

I inhale a deep breath and wrap my palms around the warm coffee cup, cradling it.

"When we first met, it was love at first sight for me." I begin telling Jack a story I'd never told him before, from the beginning. "I remember everything about that night—what you were wearing, what I was wearing. The time at night when my girlfriends and I arrived at the party where you were." I pause to recollect the memories and give him time to do the same. "I think at that point I was still scared. I had never dated anyone before, and here you come along, already larger than life."

Jack shifts in his chair, the tension he had in his shoulders when he arrived beginning to fade.

His body relaxes but only a fraction.

I continue. "I didn't come from a small town, but I came from a small school, and Davis and my mom sheltered me. My brother had chased off any guys I'd ever been interested in. First, it was through intimidation—because he thought that's what big brothers were for—and then through the simple fact that no guy wanted to mess with Davis Halbrook's—of the Lions—sister. No one wanted to find out if he would actually appear to kick their ass. They cared more about him, his reputation, his rising star than they ever cared about me."

That truth still stings me to this day.

"So when I met you, I could already see that you were different. You were mature and worldly—or so I assumed—and so very confident. It intimidated me at the same time as it drew me in. All I wanted after that first night was to be around you." *I loved him so much.* "At the same time, I didn't want to hold you back."

Jack narrows his eyes as he listens. "You never held me back."

"I'm just explaining that at the time—when I was twenty years old—that's how I felt. I'm not saying you did," I say, hands leaving the rim of the coffee cup to hold my palms up. "I knew you had goals much bigger than mine, and I felt…" I search for the words. "I felt…that mine weren't as important. I was never going to be a big deal. I was going to work in a corporate office, work for someone else—some entry-level, shitty job, probably with an asshole of a boss. Long days and long nights." I'm basically describing the job I have now, only rather than earn a business degree to go along with it, I'd dropped out. "You, on the other hand—were going to play professional football."

Jack hardly moves a muscle, but his jaw clenches.

"You never made me feel anything but wonderful. I felt like the luckiest girl in the world. I was dating The Skip—the most loyal young man on campus who had the world at his fingertips." He was charismatic and funny. He made the dean's list every semester. He volunteered in the community when he had the time. He made time for me and never made me feel as if he was giving me his scraps.

His dark eyes seem darker.

"Then I don't understand why you ghosted me."

"I don't know if you remember this, but one night—we'd been dating over two years at that point—we had a conversation about our futures. You were a junior, and you were talking to agents, and we both knew you were going to enter the draft. We both knew you were going to have teams looking at you. Every single thing you did. Every move you made. Your family, your friends." I take a deep breath. "Me."

He nods slowly.

"Anyway. During that conversation about our future, kids came up. You were having serious doubts about playing football professionally. It was the first time I'd ever seen you doubt yourself. I asked you, *'Are you saying you'd rather work a regular job and have a few kids instead?'* and you said—"

Jack interrupts me. "I snorted and said *no offense to anyone because I do want kids, but not for a few years.*"

"Right."

"I wasn't being literal. I was twenty-one years old. Does anyone want kids when they're twenty-one? No."

"I know now that you weren't being literal, but try telling that to twenty-year-old me. I was a *baby*. I was dating The Skip. I was dating Jack Jennings, the guy everyone wanted to be around. I was insecure, and in my mind, you were the most important person in the relationship because that's what people were telling me. *Showing* me. You were the one signing autographs and speaking on television in post-game interviews."

It was a lot for me back then, a young girl from the Midwest, thrust into some quasi-celebrity because of her boyfriend when all she wanted to do was live a quiet life, have a family, and do some traveling. "I hadn't realized my self-worth. I was putting it all on you."

That's the thing about becoming a parent. It forces you to grow up. And when your child is a daughter? A girl? You instinctually become tougher—more fierce. A big believer in girl power and empowering women and self-worth because that's how you want your daughter to feel—like the most important person in her world.

You want your daughter to feel as if she can do anything.

Be anything.

"So you'd said, '*I don't want kids for a few years,*' and all I heard was, '*I don't want kids.*' Period." At this point, I decide it's wise to take a drink of my coffee, so I stop talking and gather my thoughts. I've said a lot of words, and he has said almost none.

Wonderful listener.

Great communicator.

"That I don't want kids hit me a few weeks later in the gut. I hadn't gotten my period, and although I was on the pill, I had missed a day when I'd forgotten my prescription at the pharmacy."

He nods, remembering.

"And the day I took a test, I was..." Paralyzed. Panicked. Scared. Horrified. Embarrassed. "Ashamed. I wasn't coming from a place of, 'this is happening to us.' I approached it from a place of 'this is happening to me.' You had said you hadn't wanted kids, and I freaked out. I couldn't study, couldn't eat, couldn't focus on anything. I pushed you away because I thought I was doing you a huge favor."

"What did you think I was going to do?"

"I don't know. My immature brain thought you would drop out of school or something and get a shitty job just to pay the rent and buy formula. I thought having a baby would crush all your dreams."

Jack screws up his face. "You didn't think my talent was going to carry me forward? Like the NFL was suddenly going to decide I was shit because my girlfriend was pregnant?"

"Okay, when you say it like that, it sounds totally idiotic."

"Well, sorry, but it is. That's not how that shit works. We're not living in the 1950s. This is the modern millennium."

"I'm aware of that."

Jack is silent then, stirring his coffee aimlessly with a silver spoon.

"I was home when I took the test. My brother had a bye week and was home, and I didn't want to be alone." I hear how horrible those words must sound to Jack and wince. I wouldn't have been alone if I'd gone to *him*. But I hadn't. I had fled home, to my brother, afraid to put my trust in my boyfriend. "So I hid away. From you and from him. Like I thought I might be pregnant but to see that positive test was..." Jarring. Emotional. "Surreal."

I resist the urge to tear open a sugar packet and dump it into my cup for the sake of having something to do with my hands. I'm nervous, obviously, but now that the floodgates are open—and he's not screaming at me or flipping tables—it's hardly as difficult as I've made it out to be in my head.

Then again, he still does not have all the facts.

"I...went back to school, but my head wasn't cooperating with my body. It was pointless. Staying would have been a waste of my brother's tuition money, and I knew if I told you, you would try to talk me out of moving home. I told my academic advisor, and I told my brother, but I couldn't tell you. Not when you had so much going on."

Jack shifts in his chair. "I remember being confused with your about-face. One day you were fine, and when you came back to school from being gone the weekend, you were...acting strange. I didn't think you'd actually disappear." He lays his spoon on the cup's saucer. "I was worried about you. The only reason I knew you weren't dead or kidnapped was your roommate. She's the one who told me you went home."

Why didn't he chase me?

Why didn't he show up at my house the way he'd shown up at my brother's?

We were both so young and foolish, but I was the one shouldering the burden of being pregnant at twenty and left to raise a child. Of my own doing, of course. It was all my own doing.

A life without parole I'd sentenced myself to.

"I want you to look me in the eye right now and say to me what you should have told me before you ran away in college." Jack's voice is low and steady—a challenge for me to tell him the truth.

"My intention was never to...lie. Or hide." What a foolish thing to say. I try again. "I did what I thought was best."

"Those aren't the words I want you to say." His mouth is set in a straight line.

He wants me to tell him he has a child. A daughter.

He wants me to say, "Skipper is your daughter."

I hold my breath, my bottom lip trembling.

Jack nods once.

"Exactly how old is she?"

I have a lump in my throat. "She just turned seven last month."

Uncle Davis threw a huge party for her in his backyard. He rented a bounce house and had a giant, three-tiered cake made, and she had gotten to invite all her friends from first grade. Davis even hired princesses and someone to paint faces.

It was a huge spectacle, and Skipper loved every minute of it.

"Let me see a picture."

I dig my phone out of the pocket of my sweatshirt, scroll through the photo gallery, then slide the phone across the table toward Jack.

He doesn't touch it, only stares down at his daughter. A picture of her laughing, a gap in her front teeth, and glitter in her hair because we had gone to *Princesses on Ice*. She'd worn a blue Cinderella dress with her white faux fur coat and little shearling winter boots.

Jack stares holes into that photograph.

Then he looks up at me with a blank expression.

"I wish I knew what you were thinking," I blurt out, uncomfortable. This moment is horribly disarming. I've never felt so exposed.

"Trust me, you don't want to know."

He stands, pulling on his ball cap.

"Where are you going?" I ask as he walks toward the door, conscious of the fact that the baristas are now watching us with hushed whispers.

Jack barely turns around. "I have to think."

Helplessly, I have no choice but to watch him go. Watch him through the windows as he strides purposely to his car and slides behind the wheel.

Watch as he sits perfectly still, staring off into nothing as if he were numb, hands clutching the wheel. Watch as he eventually puts the car in reverse and backs out. He pulls into the traffic and takes a right at the light.

I watch Jack Jennings until I can no longer see his car driving off into the distance, wondering where he's going and what thoughts are going through his head.

Chapter 8

Jack

"*I love you.*"

She glances up at me from the couch, the pencil in her hand halting above the notebook she'd been writing in—whatever essay she had due was neatly scrawled in longhand. Penelope loved pens, notebooks, and journals, and the one she was using I'd given her last week.

I found it in the bookstore when I was there buying a novel for one of my English lit classes.

"*What did you say?*"

"*I said...I...*" *I stumble on my words, loathe to repeat them.*

I feel like a moron.

Had she really not heard me? Or was she so appalled I'd said them that I had to clarify? I wasn't confident one-hundred percent of the time. I had an ego and pride this girl could easily crush.

God, why is this so hard to say? "*I love you.*"

I'll admit, it comes out as more of a whisper. At this point, my tail is between my legs, afraid of how she'll react.

"*You love me?*"

I can do nothing but nod. "Yeah." I do.

A lot.

For the first time in my life, I was in love, and I couldn't keep it inside. Not saying anything was driving me nuts.

Penelope sets down her notebook and pen, clicking it closed before rising from the couch and crossing the room to meet me in the middle, wrapping her arms around my waist and squeezing. Her soft lips kiss my neck.

"I love you, too, Jack."

I love you, too, Jack.

The love of my life had always been the game of football. All my time and energy were spent on only that. Girls were never a part of the equation. They were not my focus, and they hardly mattered.

Until the day I met Penelope Halbrook.

Penelope was the first girl I loved.

When I'd said those three little words to her, it had been the first time I'd told a girl I loved her, and I'd meant every word of it.

I loved Penelope Halbrook!

Loved her smile and her kind heart. I loved how sweet she was. How she never had an unkind word to say about anyone. How she worried about her grades and her mother and her brother.

She wanted to take care of everyone, including me.

A ball of nervous energy, I drop to the floor of the hotel room and do twenty push-ups, then jog in place a few minutes when what I should do is go downstairs and use the gym.

I have a daughter.

I have a seven-year-old daughter that my college girlfriend gave birth to without telling me. She even named her after me but never told me the child existed. I'm not even sure how to feel right now. A million feelings run through my head, and the last thing I want to do is fly home tomorrow.

I thought maybe it would be a quick trip here and back home. Penelope would tell me I was overreacting, that Skipper was not my daughter, and then I would fly to Colorado as the same person I was before and resume my normal life—my best life, never looking back.

Never look back. *The way she did.*

What kind of woman in a great relationship has a baby and doesn't say anything? What kind of woman just vanishes without a trace and leaves a man wondering?

We were good together.

She loved me the same way I loved her.

I'm angry again, frustration consuming me. I don't know what to do with it. It's hardly productive to get angry without having anywhere to direct it. I could go jog or run this energy off, but I don't have tennis shoes with me.

I wore these ridiculous loafers.

I have a daughter. A little one who likes princesses and has missing teeth.

I should call my lawyer, obviously, but that feels premature. I don't have all the facts. I mean, I have the main fact: there is a seven-year-old on this planet with my eyes, my nose, and my smile. She has my same coloring, too.

Dark hair.

Dark eyes.

A dimple in her tiny face.

Jesus Christ, *she looks exactly like me.*

I knew it the second I laid eyes on her in that green room at the football game. It just took me this long to make sense of it in my brain.

Logically, I know I need lawyers. Logically, I know I'm

going to be taking Penelope to court. Logically, she owes me... but what? How does a person make retribution for a child they kept from you? It's not as if I can take custody of the kid without traumatizing her. Penelope isn't an unfit mother because she was too afraid to tell me I got her pregnant when we were in college.

I don't think my publicist, manager, agent, or a lawyer are going to see it that way, but a part of me wants to keep this between Penelope and me. Why get any of my people involved?

Is that stupid? Does that make me an even bigger fool?

God sent me to Illinois for a reason, I'm sure of it.

I take a knee next to the window, hands folded, face toward the sky.

"Mom and Dad," I pray. "If you're watching me now, tell me what to do." I pray to my parents—my guardian angels and spirit guides—the same way I do almost every night, asking them for guidance and telling them my inner thoughts. This fear is a big one and could possibly be my greatest challenge.

You loved her once.

It's as if my mother is speaking directly to me inside this hotel room even though she's not here. I can hear her words. They're the same words she would've said to me if she were alive today.

Always supportive. Always rational.

Always sensical.

"She lied to me, Mom," I reason. "Penelope lied."

You love her still, son. You still love her.

I bow my head, wishing it weren't true. It would be easier to hate Penelope for keeping secrets from me. Not just any secret.

A child.

93

I want to be angry. I want to be.

"What should I do?" *What the actual fuck do I do?*

I rise to a stand, staring out into the dark night at the city's lights below, hands behind my head, the sound of my mother's voice echoing through my head. *You loved her once.* So? That isn't going to get her out of this mess. The fact that I felt something the second I saw Penelope in her brother's doorway means nothing right now.

We can't turn back the hands of time. You can only look forward.

Still, I have people I'll have to explain all this to. Managers and PR people because the media will find out, and no doubt they'll spin this into something embarrassing. A love child, they'll call Skipper. They'll make it seem like Penelope is only out for my money. They'll make it seem like I knew about the child and ignored her on purpose. They'll...

The media will try to blow up any bridge between us we try to build in the upcoming days.

No.

It's best I say nothing—not even to Elias—though he is one of my best friends.

I pull my cell out of my pocket and check to see if anyone has texted. Correction: check to see if Penelope has texted.

I'm disappointed to see that she hasn't.

Disappointed to see that I've only gotten messages from a teammate, my agent about an endorsement deal, and my cousin Robbie, who's getting married and giving me details about his bachelor party.

Unable to stand it any longer, I fire off a message to Penn.

I'm hungry for more information. More details. More pictures of Skipper.

My daughter.

Holy shit, my daughter.

Dark hair.

Dark eyes.

A dimple in her tiny face.

My heart squeezes, and I take myself to the couch, sitting down. Resting my face in my hands, I feel myself begin to cry.

I have a daughter.

My mother would have been a grandmother. Dad would have been a grandpa.

My shoulders shudder when the tears come, thinking about all those wasted years.

Gone.

Would Skipper have come to find me once she got older? Would Penelope eventually have told her? Kids ask these things, right? At some point in her life, Skipper would have begun to wonder why there was no other parent, yeah? Don't kids do that sometimes when they get old enough to compare?

Will she blame me for not being around?

Will she like me? What if I scare her?

You don't scare her. She's met you already. She walked right up to you and sized you up, brave little shit.

I want to know everything about her, and I want to know it yesterday.

Suddenly, I'm restless.

I cannot sit in this hotel room. I cannot sit here idly waiting for tomorrow, not when there are things I want to know.

"How long are you here?" Penelope is walking alongside me down the street. A walk to nowhere. No plan, no destination, no agenda.

I just knew I couldn't stay cooped up in that hotel room, and I also wasn't interested in having a conversation over the phone. Or text. Or video chat.

We were together hours ago, but I had to see her again.

I shoot her a sidelong glance. "As long as it takes."

She nods, shuffling along in her warm jacket, hat, and mittens. It's not freezing out, but I'd told her I needed to walk.

Walk and talk and think.

She's as cute as a button, and I hate myself for letting my brain go there. This person who betrayed me.

Betrayed Skipper, too, in a sense.

"Does she ever ask about me?" I pause. "I mean, not me specifically, but..."

"I understand what you mean, and...yes, she does sometimes ask. She is well aware at this age that she doesn't have a second parent. Uncle Davis does his best to fill that gap, but yeah, she's beginning to ask every now and again. Sometimes after she has a playdate at a friend's house, if the dad is home, she'll ask where hers is." Penelope hesitates. "And her friend Madison has two moms, so she asks where her other mom is, too."

We walk on in the quiet night, the streetlights flickering, seemingly lighting up one by one as we pass a large park on our right.

I gesture to enter it, and we head in, both meandering toward a bench at the far side.

"Are you going to take me to court?"

"I don't know," I tell her honestly. "I think we should start with...a playdate or something. I want to meet her again. Get to know her." Start there. Realistically, I wouldn't be around much. Not with my schedule, not with all the games and the travel. Being on a championship team takes time and dedication, so it isn't as if I would be fighting for full custody. Who would watch her, a nanny while I worked? But I am her dad, and I will need a DNA test to confirm it, and I want the time with Harper that I am entitled to.

"A playdate?"

"Yeah, like we could go do something together so she can get to know me. What about..." I rack my brain for ideas. "The zoo or something."

Penelope pulls a face. "Um, *sure*."

"What's that look for?"

"I hate the zoo." She laughs. "Don't ask me why. I've just never liked it." She begins babbling. "It feels too much like a chore and isn't a ton of fun. But we can do the zoo if that's what you want."

"Oh. With *that* ringing endorsement? No thanks, I'll take your word for it."

She seems to be giving this some thought. "There's a trampoline park in Oak Park."

"Where is Oak Park?"

"It's a suburb. It takes about twenty minutes to get there from here, but it's a small town. We've only been to the trampoline park once, and Skipper was so excited she almost lost her mind."

"Can grown-ups jump?"

"Totally."

"Aw, sweet. Did I ever tell you I took gymnastics when I was younger?" Not many people know that.

97

"I think I remember you saying something about that." *But we were together a long time ago, so I've forgotten many things about you,* are the unspoken words that follow.

"Does...Skipper do any activities?" Do any activities? Ugh, that sounded lame. "Is she in any?"

Penelope nods. "She loves baseball and soccer. In the summer, I have her in swim lessons. But nothing like ballet or gymnastics. They have teams at this age, but it's a hefty commitment that I don't have time for."

Right. She mentioned she works a lot at a job she loves but also hates.

It's strange to be discussing any of this stuff with her. Strange that I'm asking questions about a daughter I didn't know I had. Strange that I'm not angrier.

It's as if I have no idea how to be mad at Penelope.

I want to be.

Honestly, I do.

I tried. Listed all the reasons I should be good and pissed off. All the reasons I should chew her ass out and give her a piece of my mind:

1. She lied to me.
2. She lied to my daughter.
3. She deprived me of many years of knowing Skipper.
4. This whole situation has me feeling clueless and useless as if I never mattered.
5. This whole situation has me confused, frustrated, and emotional.

I don't know how to act. How to behave.

What to say or do next.

The one thing I do know is that anger won't help. It

won't get me any answers, and it won't allow me to know my daughter.

Shit, I can't believe it. I can say that same sentence over and over a thousand times, and I can still barely believe the words.

My daughter.

Our daughter.

I don't just have a child. I have a kid. An elementary school-aged girl. One who likes soccer and baseball.

"We can do the trampoline park. That sounds good." I shoot her a sidelong glance. "Does tomorrow work?"

Penelope hesitates, then nods. "Sure."

She's in no position to argue. I'm not looking for a debate or to fuck up her day even though she's just done a number on my entire life.

It will never be the same.

No one knows I'm in Illinois. My friend and agent, Elias, thinks I'm home during this bye week, working out at the gym and taking it easy.

Little does he know I'm a plane flight away and about to meet the girl I'm going to spend the rest of my life with.

"What else is she like?"

"Well. She talks a lot. Loves the sound of her own voice." That makes me smile. Where Penelope was rather quiet, I talk a lot too, for the most part. "And she loves cheese."

"Cheese? That seems random."

"Kid can't get enough of it." Penelope laughs. "She hasn't had a Barbie phase yet, but she likes reading and is already into some shorter chapter books. Definitely likes to spend time crafting and making things, beads, pictures. Pictures with beads."

"So basically, she likes making messes?"

"Basically." Beside me, Penelope shrugs. "If I'm baking something or making dinner, she always wants to help, and she enjoys watching that *Kids Baking Championship* show on TV even though there aren't many seasons so we have to watch them over and over."

Sounds painful.

"Sounds like you don't enjoy the kids baking show."

Penelope makes a groaning sound. "What I enjoy is heckling the participants even though they can't hear me. I'll shout at the TV—say, a little boy baked a cake, and he forgot to add flour so it didn't rise, and he starts bawling. I'll yell for the judge to get him off the show, and Skipper will shout at me for being mean to little kids."

"Okay, that's something I can get behind. I also love shouting at the television, but usually, it's a professional football game or something like that." Whatever floats Skipper's boat.

"I don't think there's anything that kid doesn't like," Penelope tells me. "There isn't much she won't eat. I didn't prepare special foods just for her when she was younger. She had what I had for dinner. It's made life so much easier now that she's older, and I know Davis appreciates it when he watches her."

The casual mention of her brother causes me to turn my body toward her and get serious.

"Does he watch her a lot?"

A pit forms in my stomach that feels something oddly like jealousy or resentment, although I can't quite pinpoint it because it's so new. Another strike against her, perhaps? The fact that she had another man help her raise my daughter when I wasn't good enough to do it?

This isn't me being petty—these are facts.

"He wasn't around as much when Skip was a baby. My

mom was still around, and she had been living with him at the time. When Skipper was born, Mom moved into my place with me and helped out. Then Davis got injured and had to retire, and everything revolved around the baby. In some ways, she saved our family."

Penelope chances a look at me. She'd been staring off into the distance as she spoke, almost hesitantly saying the words. She instantly regrets them by the looks of her.

I must have a look on my face.

"But if you're asking if he raised her? No, he didn't. He helped out when he could, but he most certainly didn't raise her, and no, she doesn't think of him as her dad." She pauses. "Sure, he is her only male influence, but...it's not the same."

I shift on the bench, not sure what to say.

"I'm sure it was a blessing to have their help. You were so young."

"Yes." She nods. "Young, no degree. No job. A new baby. It was...a struggle. Obviously, my mother freaked out. She was hysterical when I told her. I'd assumed she would be supportive from day one, but it took her months to come around. Once she did..." Penelope fiddles with her hands. "She was great. I'm glad she was able to spend that much time with Harper before she died."

Wouldn't it have been great for my mother and father to spend time with their granddaughter before they died? It's on the tip of my tongue to sarcastically ask.

I don't because I have zero desire to sound bitter when we're in the middle of being civil.

Instead, I clear my throat. "I'm sure it's nice being so close to your brother, just in case."

"It is. Plus, he owns the house, so I don't have rent or a mortgage, which is helpful."

More information that makes my ass cheeks clench, though it's information I already knew. It doesn't make me happy—not when I'm the one who wanted to own a house with her, not when I'm the one who could be supporting her while she worked toward her degree.

That's what she wants, yeah? To finish school so she can get a promotion and one day become her own boss?

But no.

She relies on her brother, and that's just how it is.

Relax, dude—this has nothing to do with you.

Wrong. It has everything to do with me.

*Every*thing.

I'll be honest, this conversation is starting to make me uncomfortable. Making me feel inept and resentful of both her and her brother. I can't stop the feelings, and I won't apologize for having them.

"I want to say something, and I hope you believe me." Penelope turns toward me, shifting her body to face me, one leg crossed on the bench, the other still on the ground. "I knew what I did was wrong, Jack. I knew it then, and I know it now. Not a day has gone by when I haven't hated myself or punished myself in some way. It was wrong." Her head gives a little shake of sadness. "I wasn't old enough to be a mother when I got pregnant. Clearly, my decisions have exhibited that lack of maturity. But I can't take any of those decisions back. I can't rewrite all the wrong I've done."

Nope. She sure can't.

"I'm so sorry," she whispers. "I'm so, so sorry, Jack." Her head bows as if she were crying, and when her shoulders give a small shudder, I know that she is.

I rest my hand on her shoulder, pressing gently,

comforting the woman who did me wrong. "Don't cry, Penn."

That only serves to make the tears fall even more. "I don't know what to do."

"We'll figure it out."

"I loved you so much." She whispers again as if she were only speaking to herself and not to me. "I loved you so much, and I didn't know what to do."

A tear escapes from my eye, too, my head bending toward hers as we sit on the bench in a park under the glow of the lamplights.

"I loved you too, Penn." That's why I was so crushed when you left. When you wouldn't see me. When I started my career and didn't have you beside me.

I'm not sure what I would have done if I'd found out she was pregnant. I have no idea how I would have reacted because I didn't have the chance. But I am a grown man now, and things are different. I have a somewhat stable job and a fantastic income, with limitless potential post player.

"I'm sorry, Jack." Penelope lifts her tear-soaked face.

"We'll figure it out," I repeat after moments of silence.

We'll figure it out.

Chapter 9

Penelope

He's at the entrance of the trampoline park when we arrive, leaning against the tall, glass door, one leg bent behind him, looking all kinds like a male model. Buff arms, ball cap pulled low, and well-worn jeans —the look of his face isn't the only thing making my heart ache.

It's the look on Jack's face when he spies us and sees Skipper climbing down out of the car.

He stands up a bit straighter and pulls at the hem of his shirt, straightening it as if this were a date and he had someone to impress.

He wants to impress his daughter, a small voice tells me. *He wants her to like him.*

I'll be the first to admit that impressing a seven-year-old isn't always easy. In fact, most days, it's exhausting. It's as if I'm raising a twenty-six-year-old influencer who has an opinion, wants what she wants, and considers everything and anything a negotiation.

Jack pushes himself off the building and shoves his hands in his pockets nervously.

Skipper bounds forward with zero chill. "Hi! I know you!"

We prepped in the car on the ride over about how she was meeting a friend of Mom's who was a boy, and how he was special and a member of the family. I haven't sat her down yet to discuss Jack being her father, but that will come soon enough, and we'll do it together, he and I.

Now isn't the time.

For now, she just needs to...get *used* to him.

"Hi, Skipper," Jack greets her as she hops on one foot to demonstrate that she is indeed a skipper.

"Look." *Hop, hop.*

"Whoa." He laughs.

Our eyes meet over the top of her little self as she runs onto the sidewalk and jumps onto a decorative boulder near the park's entrance.

"She is not short on energy today."

"She never is."

Up at six, even on Sunday. Chatters from sunup to sundown.

Jack pulls the door open, and Skipper bounds forward. It's surreal watching them walk through the door together, side by side, two nearly identical figures.

She is his mini-me. A tiny replica. Spitting image—you get the picture.

I knew she resembled him but never knew how much.

It's...

Wow.

My body physically reacts to the sight of them, legs getting a bit weak, my stomach in knots. Jesus, how did I get myself into this mess?

Once inside, Jack pays so the three of us can jump—not

that I want to. I left the house without a sports bra, so this isn't going to be pleasant. Yeesh.

I somewhat expect him to hang back and not be as interactive with Skipper as I would be, helping her take off her shoes, put them in the lockers provided, and making sure everything is good to go before we head toward the giant, blow-up trampoline set up throughout the park.

But I'm wrong.

Jack is extremely participatory, taking her little jacket off and hanging it on a hook, then making sure her shoes are properly put away—all without prompting or interference from me.

I'm surprised, though I shouldn't be. He was always a no-nonsense, self-starting individual. He wouldn't be where he is today if you weren't. If he were the type of guy who stood around waiting for things to happen.

Suddenly, I feel like the third wheel, trailing them as they take off toward one trampoline after the other, jumping and hopping and screaming, delighted by the thrill. Skipper can't jump high enough. She can't show off enough to her newfound friend, this man she's only just met. One whom she is the spitting image of.

She hasn't noticed. Of course she hasn't.

She is a kid. Do they notice those things?

Because Jack is a celebrity, many dads have taken notice, and some younger boys are taking the opportunity to bounce with him and laugh as if he were a regular dad there with his kid.

No one takes any photographs, at least...not that I've noticed.

Skipper bounces, shouting, "Skip, LOOK AT ME!" over and over again, doing tricks that aren't actually tricks and leaping this way and that. What she lacks in skill, she makes up for in enthusiasm, and her father is right alongside her, doing much of the same: showing off. Kicking his legs out.

"You're going to sprain something if you're not careful," I tell him. "We're not getting any younger."

"With my luck, I'll sprain my groin, and you'd have to nurse me back to health."

That gives us both pause, Jack realizing too late what he's just said out loud in front of mischievous ears.

"What's groin?" Skipper innocently asks.

Jack looks at me for answers.

I shake my head. "No way, pal. You're the one who said it, so you can be the one who explains it."

He's got to learn to watch what he says. The little stinker sees and hears everything!

Jack stops jumping and points at his inner thigh. "It's this."

"Your *wiener*?!" Skipper shouts, hopping and giggling and hopping.

"No, not my wiener." He sounds like he's in pain, wanting this conversation to end. "Here! By my leg. My leg!"

"Wiener, wiener," Skipper hops and shouts.

Jack looks at me for help.

I laugh, jumping in the opposite direction so he can't see the smile on my face with the playful echo of "wiener, wiener" lingering behind me.

Kids and their potty talk.

We bounce, jump, and hop from trampoline to trampoline for the next hour, tossing balls at one another and playing games. They have basketball hoops throughout the gym, and every so often, a beach ball makes its way into our hands, and we play with that, too.

Jack lobs the beach ball at Skipper, and it bonks her in the head, causing another round of giggle fits.

This was the perfect way for them to spend their first few hours together.

"I'm hungry!" Skipper announces, bounding her way toward me, and I check my watch to see that it's well past her lunchtime.

She never misses a meal. Not if she can help it.

Lucky for us, the trampoline park has a nice food court with plenty of options. Skipper is not a picky eater, so it's easy, but she has to be in the mood for junk food. Collectively, we hobble down off the trampolines to put on our sneakers so we can walk on the tile floors and not get our feet gross.

We have to scan one of those little cube code thingies taped to the table to see what's on the menu. After waiting ten long and painful minutes, a less-than-enthusiastic teenager walks over with a tray of lunch. A slice of pizza and two hot dogs.

French fries.

Vanilla milkshake. Two bottles of water.

And a fruit cup.

For a few moments, all is quiet. Well, it's loud in here, but the table is quiet. No one is talking while they eat—until Skipper decides she has something to say.

"What should we do next time?" She wants to know, little teeth biting down into her massive hot dog. It's the kind of hot dog they serve at ballparks and at Costco—the really thick kind that fills you up fast.

"What do you mean?" I ask.

"What should we *do* next time?" She repeats herself with a heavy shrug. "Next time we have a day of fun! Isn't this fun?" She's chomping down hungrily, a little bit of ketchup squishing out the opposite end of her bun.

Jack's brows go up. "You're having fun, huh?"

"Oh yes, this is so fun." Our daughter has actual perspiration on her forehead, and her mini face is red from exerting herself. "Where are we going next time?"

Oh, that's what she meant.

Jack ruffles her hair. "I don't know. Do you have any ideas?"

Skipper chews her food and swallows before responding, thank god. "We could see a movie? Or go to Build-A-Bear!"

"You have enough Build-A-Bears," I tell her with chagrin, although it is a fun place to visit—expensive but fun. Definitely something Jack could do with her when they're ready to have independent playdates without me.

The idea makes my stomach sink.

You have to share her now.

It has occurred to me—of course it has!—but it wasn't a reality until now. Until *he* was sitting on the same side of a table with us, sharing lunch and laughs and fun. Skipper has been mine for seven entire years. Actually, since before that. Since the day I found out I was pregnant.

I didn't actually think the test was going to be positive. My period had been late before, and I was under a lot of stress. Classes were great, but I was killing myself studying because none of it came easy. I wasn't exactly making the dean's list, but I wasn't average either. But the pressure to get good grades was taking its toll.

School was stressing me out.

I was searching for a job so I could at least pitch in with my rent. I still didn't think it was fair that my brother was paying for all of my expenses. He was not my parents. He wasn't my father, and he wasn't responsible for me. I was an adult, too. Why did he feel the need to pay for everything?

Plenty of people had student loans.

I could have them, too!

Anyway, things with Jack were good, but I was still rather insecure about our relationship. Everyone knew we were dating, and people began to look at me differently. I noticed girls judging me when we went out to the bars.

I knew they wondered what he saw in me. I wasn't flashy, and I wasn't popular. I didn't have big boobs or blond hair or a spray tan. That seemed to be the look a lot of the athletes on campus were attracted to and dating. There certainly seemed to be a type among that crowd.

This month, my period was late.

Two days late, but still.

To be on the safe side, I'd ordered a test online. I didn't dare go to the local pharmacist or Walgreens or even Target. God forbid I bumped into someone who knew who I was, knew who Jack was, and caught me holding one.

The rumors that would spread...

Like wildfire.

And so I shut myself into the bathroom once I got home from my evening mass communication class. Jack had a team meeting and wouldn't be by until later—if he came over at all. I followed the instructions on the box, hands trembling, and stuck the white stick between my legs as I sat on the toilet. I tried to hold it steady under the flow of urine as I peed, not sure how long I actually had to pee on the stick for it to work. I didn't have a cup or anything to put it in once I was done, so I sat there holding it, watching as that little blank box filled with two blue lines.

I hadn't even needed to wait the full three minutes.

My hands shook.

Do I throw the test out or save it?

I didn't want to keep looking at it. The results were the cold bucket of reality I hadn't wanted or needed today.

What was I going to do?

What was I going to say to Jack? Worse, what was I going to say to my brother?

Oh god, he was going to be so disappointed in me.

Here he was, working his ass off to send his kid sister to school only to find out she got pregnant by the first long-term boyfriend she's ever had?

And one who's a player?

Jack can't know. This will devastate him.

Devastate *him?* How?

He has goals. Plans. Dreams much bigger than yours!

Think, Penelope, think. What are you going to do?

I take a deep breath and raise my eyes toward the mirror, gazing back at the terrified face there. Wide eyes that look as if they've seen a ghost.

Bright red cheeks.

Raising a hand to my forehead, I press my palm to my face. It's hot, temperature high. I'm blushing furiously from fear and shame, no longer worried about the scores for the test I'd just taken and probably bombed.

No longer worried about rent or gas money or what I was going to wear on my date with Jack tomorrow night on his one weekend off.

Don't be stupid. You're not going on that date.

If you sit across from him at that table, he will know

something is wrong. He's going to think you're being weird and ask a million questions you're not prepared to answer.

Fumbling for my phone, I do the only thing I can think of to do. I cancel on him.

That was the beginning of the end for us.

I would take another test over the weekend when I was home, just to be sure.

And now we're here, watching that little girl I was pregnant with when I was practically a girl myself.

I shake my head, lost in thought.

"Mom, want a french fry?" Skipper is wobbling a limp fry back and forth in front of my face, wearing a cheeky grin on her chubby face. "They're *soo* good."

I take a bite of it while she's still pinching it between her fingers, chomping like a shark. "Yum! Thanks, baby girl."

My daughter rolls her eyes. "Mom, I'm not a baby."

I smooch her face, emotional despite myself. "You'll always be my baby, baby girl."

"Gross." She gives Jack a bite of the french fry. "Jack, isn't that gross?"

He nods along with her, commiserating, but the sentiment doesn't quite reach his eyes. In fact, he's looking a bit emotional himself, face as flushed as mine feels while he's lost in thought.

"I don't know if I'd call kisses from your mom gross," he finally allows, shoving some pizza into his mouth while avoiding my gaze. "I would call them slimy."

"Slimy!" Skipper and I both shout at the same time.

I pick up a fry and toss it at him, close range, with a laugh. "You brat."

"Ew!" Skipper kicks her legs, her mouth puckered as if she'd swallowed a lemon whole. "You kissed my mom?!"

The idea of it repulses her.

"Are you my mom's boyfriend?" Skipper pulls another sour expression but smiles at the same time, blushing, her cute little freckles popping out in the sweet way I love so much.

She gets those from me.

"No, I'm not your mom's boyfriend."

Our daughter absentmindedly nibbles at the end of her bun. "Then why were you kissing her?"

So innocent.

"Because I was her boyfriend."

"Oooh." Skipper pauses. "When?"

"When we were much younger."

"Last year?"

"No, longer than that."

She tilts her head, and I watch the interaction. Jack is handling it beautifully, so there is no need for me to jump in and save him.

"When?"

"When we were in school."

Skipper's eyes widen. "First grade?"

Jack and I laugh. "No, college."

"Oh, college." She nods in a way that would make you believe she understood, though she has no actual concept of what college is or how old a person is when they attend it. "That makes more sense."

She hands Jack a few more french fries, and he eats them, watching him intently the entire time, happy for this new friend of ours.

Skipper chews on her hot dog, contentedly munching away. "Hey!" Her little hand presses itself to Jack's hand. "Look. Your thumb looks the same like my thumb!"

Jack examines his hand before examining her tiny one.

"Oh yeah, they do look the same. Two different sizes, would you look at that. Why do you suppose that is?"

Skipper tilts her head so she can properly think. "Hmm." She thinks and chews. "I don't know. Maybe 'cause we're family."

Jack's head snaps up at me, brows shooting up into his hairline.

"In the car on the way here, I told her you were a good friend and that we were family," I hasten to tell him. "I didn't know how else to..."

Explain.

My daughter—correction: our daughter—gets up good and close to Jack's face, ketchup on the side of her mouth, still chewing her lunch. So close it's like she wants to share something or tell him a secret.

Total invasion of his personal space.

She squints into his eyes. "And don't you think it's funny we have the *same* name?" She giggles, most likely blowing hot dog breath into the poor man's face.

Once again, Jack raises his eyebrows in my direction. "I *do* think it's funny. Why do you think that is?"

"Well." Her little butt lowers back into its seat. "Mom said we're family, but do family people share nicknames?"

"That's a good question." He's nodding. "My dad's name was Jackson, and my name is Jackson, but I go by Jack."

"I have a friend named Shelly, and her mom is Mrs. Stacy." Skipper fiddles with her braid before scrunching up her cute little face. "That's not the same."

"They start with the same letter, though," Jack praises her. "What grade are you in again?"

"First."

"How are you liking first grade?"

Skipper shrugs. "It's fine. We don't have enough recess, and the boys stink."

"Harper Halbrook!" I chastise. "The boys do not stink."

"Yes, they do, Mom. On Monday, Bryce Hanson peed his pants, and he had to change into lost and found pants, and Roman stinks like peppermint."

I share a glance with Jack, who can't keep the grin off his face. "In that case, I would say Bryce was probably scared to tell the teacher he had to take a pis—he had to use the bathroom."

"Were you going to say piss?" Skipper asks matter-of-factly. "My uncle says piss all the time."

Oh jeez.

Jack is literally going to think I'm an unfit mother, teaching our child horrible manners, bad words, bad habits, bad—

"Yeah, I was about to say piss. Stopped myself just in time."

Skipper bobs her head, empathizing. "Mom swears sometimes." *Chomp, chomp.* "Especially when she's driving."

What the heck?

Why is she ratting me out like this, the little shit?

"Oh, does she?" Jack leans in, interested. "We call that road rage."

Skipper nods. "She flipped off a grandma yesterday. A grandma in a minivan."

I'm sorry, but that woman was going fifteen under the speed limit and probably shouldn't have a driver's license!

"Okay, you two, that's enough."

Okay, you two, that's enough—words that a mom says. Words that I've dreamed about saying as a playful warning to a partner, words I dreamed about saying if I ever had more kids when they got up to mischief. *"Okay, you guys..."*

"What else does Mom do?" Jack asks Skipper to tease me, and it works.

I shoot him a "don't you dare encourage her" look, but sadly, the child needs no further encouragement. She would sing like a canary and sell me out any ol' day of the week!

"Mom eats brownies from the pan, but she yells at me if I do it."

"What?" My mouth falls open. "I do not!"

I do.

"Yes, you do!" Skipper accuses me, pointing her little finger at me. "And you always make me put things on plates. You also tell me to recycle, but you threw a water bottle into the regular garbage yesterday."

Monster!

Jack just laughs. "I love brownies from the pan, don't you?"

Skipper nods enthusiastically. "Yes, if she lets me."

"Fine." I huff. "How about next time we make brownies, I'll let you eat some fresh from the pan." It's only fair, I guess, since I do it when I think she's not watching. The trouble is, the little turd always seems to be watching!

She nods. "Deal."

"Do you have any pets?" Jack asks his daughter.

"No. Mom says we don't have time for one."

He nods. "Makes sense. They're a lot of work. I have a dog, but right now, he's probably sad because we're not home. He is with a babysitter."

"Oooo," Skipper sympathizes, making a sad little noise. "Poor dog. What kind is he?" She scoots closer to Jack as he gets the phone out of his back pocket and scrolls through it for photos of the dog.

"This is Kevin."

"Kevin? That's your dog's name?" Skipper bursts into hysterics as if that's the funniest thing she's ever heard, holding her little tummy as she laughs and baring her teeth while her chin disappears. "That's so funny!"

She's adorable. I want to squish her cute cheeks and give her a giant kiss on her sweet face. I just love her so much.

Jack catches my eye over the top of her head, his expression one of the saddest expressions I have ever seen in a moment so filled with joy.

What is he thinking right now?

What could he possibly be thinking?

It looks as if he swallowed a bug. Or has a lump forming in his throat.

Oh, no.

No.

Is he going to...

Cry?

Too late, Skipper notices once she's done whooping it up over the goofy dog with the funny name, lifting her hand to wipe the tear on Jack's face.

"Don't cry, Skip." Wrapping her little arms around his waist, she squeezes, which only seems to make it worse. "Shh, it's okay. Kevin is fine. He's not sad."

Tears well up in *my* eyes, and *my* lip is trembling, and this can't be good...

Suddenly, I'm crying, too.

"Don't hate me." I mouth the words over our daughter's head once he raises his tear-soaked eyes at me.

"I want to, Penn," Jacks says earnestly, throat hoarse. "But I can't. I can't because I love you too much."

Skipper hears it. She hears his gravelly words—the ones he'd barely spoken out loud.

"You love my mom?" She's still consoling me, patting me on the back with her tiny hand as if to say, *"There, there, Mom."*

Jack only nods, not repeating the sentiment, nor confirming it as his daughter flops back down on her rear, seated between us, two grown adults with a lot of growing to do.

Chapter 10

Jack

"*You love my mom?*" That little voice echoes in my brain all through the night, and suddenly, I'm dreaming about kids and dogs and babies and not Penelope Halbrook.

The dreams where she was letting me drown beneath the water, reaching a hand out but letting me go?

Those were gone.

"You love my mom?"

Did she sound hopeful when she'd said it? Sure sounded like it, but then again, what the hell do I know about seven-year-old kids?

I settle into the bed in my hotel room, literally googling "what do seven-year-old kids like" and hit SEARCH. Instead of the buttload of information I'm expecting to pop up, a gift guide populates instead. And rather than searching for something new, I tap on the THIRTY BEST GIFTS FOR GIRLS and scroll through the toys.

Legos. Barbies.

Books. Bath bombs, lab kits.

All this shit is so lame. Who's buying this crap? So

119

okay, maybe Legos aren't lame, but what kid wants to sit and stare at a rock tumbler for hours at a time? Better yet, what parent wants to listen to that shit? I had one as a kid, and I remember my mom putting it in the garage so we didn't have to hear the damn thing rolling rocks for days on end.

None of these toys are cheap.

I scroll on, googling one article after the next, reading psychological studies about girls raised with only one parent, the effects, how to tell your child you're splitting up. How to talk to your child about their biological parent.

My head hurts as much as my heart aches reading this stuff, and before I know it, it's well past midnight, and I'm still wide awake with thoughts of Penelope and Skipper consuming me.

I thought I had my life figured out. I thought I was at a place in my life where I was...good again. After my parents died, I realized that there are no coincidences in life, merely events put in our path as lessons.

People, too.

It took me years to learn from Penelope leaving me. She taught me that I was capable of loving—and loving hard. She taught me I could be faithful and loyal to the right person, even with the obstacles that being an athlete throws at me. Women, money, fame. None of that is as important as love.

Then the lesson was impressed upon me again the night of my parents' accident, shattering my world.

Changing my life forever.

My goals.

My priorities.

Gone was the man who dated casually but never got serious. Gone was the man who wasn't ready to settle down.

Gone was the man who assumed he'd have kids... someday, maybe.

The night Mom and Dad died, my life flashed before my eyes, too, in that way fate and karma and destiny have a way of presenting itself.

Suddenly, the man who wasn't ready to settle down longed for a family. Began dreaming about the one time in his life he was truly, madly happy and in love.

I haven't known a love since Penelope. I've never actually allowed a woman to get close because yes, I was still in love with her after all those years.

Everything happens for a reason...

Even the everythings that feel shitty and take aim at the gut and go for the jugular.

I have to believe that, or I'll go crazy. Why else would the universe put all these obstacles and signs in my path?

All these things happen to show us how much people mean to us and how we have so much to be grateful for. Moments, times, and places.

I turned around, and she was gone.

The county fair was packed. It was opening day and wrist bands for the evening were half off, so it feels as if everyone in the state was there. Besides that, a band from my parents' generation was playing that could still draw a massive crowd, and the crowd tonight was enormous.

The sea of people was as wide as the actual ocean and just as dense.

My heart was in my throat. Not that Penelope was a child and I thought she would be snatched, but the idea we were separated made panic rise with every second the space between us filled with people.

Had she walked off, or had someone dragged her off?

Was she in the bathroom?

Had something happened to her?

We'd been holding hands, headed toward the one largest thrill ride the fair had, one she'd begged me to go on just once. "Just this once, and I'll never ask again..."

I hated rides.

Any ride, even the tame ones.

I think I was traumatized as a kid on the Tilt-A-Whirl, barfing on my cousin as soon as the ride began twirling in circles, round and around, dizzy and nauseous and wishing I hadn't eaten a chili dog for lunch.

He'd wished I hadn't eaten a chili dog, too, when it landed in his lap and on his shirt and in his shoes.

I hated that ride, and I hated the fair, but Penelope thought it would be a fun date night. The evening was cool, and she was able to bundle up in a cute sweater and leggings, snuggling up to me as we walked arm in arm through the massive crush.

Until we hadn't been.

Glancing around, I frantically shout her name, eyes scanning the area where the rides ended and the games began, unable to catch sight of her dark hair in its flirty pony-tail, tied with a pretty white ribbon.

It matches her sweater.

I go up on my toes to scan above whatever heads aren't taller than me. Several people recognize me and smack me on the back to say hello.

I have to find my girlfriend.

Three seconds from shouting her name at the top of my lungs, she materializes through the crowd, holding a pink puff of cotton candy in one hand and a blue snow cone in the other.

Licking it, she offers me a taste. "Where'd you go?" she asks, big doe eyes staring up at me.

My heart pounds in my chest, da-dum, da-dum, da-dum.

"Where did I go? Nowhere, I was looking for you." I can barely formulate a sentence, wanting to take her by the shoulders and say, *"I was worried! I thought you were lost, or stolen, or...or..."*

Penelope hands me the snow cone, pressing a cold hand to my cheek and giving it a pat. *"Aw, you poor thing. You were worried? I told you I was going to grab treats."*

She did? *"There are too many people here, babe. Maybe we should leave."*

It was stifling.

More so than any stadium, and I'd been in plenty.

"Leave?" Her eyes go wide. *"I wanted to play a game! Or at least walk around and look at the booths. Can we do that?"*

Play games? Everyone knows those are rigged. *"Which game?"*

She plucks off cotton candy and sets it on her tongue, shrugging her way through the crowd. I have no choice but to follow if I don't want to lose her again.

"I don't know. Don't you want to win me a prize?"

I suppose that wouldn't be too hard.

I follow her closely, reaching for her hand, letting her pull me along toward the Strong Man—or, High Striker, as the large red sign proclaims.

It rises high in the air, and the silver bell sits at the top, taunting me. The yellow ruler is labeled with weights all the way to the top, and the black plate at the bottom waits to be struck by the hammer.

"Step right up, test your strength!" the carnival worker calls out, despite the fact that we're already standing in front of him. Penelope waits patiently for me to pick up the mallet and take aim.

"*Three swings for ten dollars,*" the man tells me with a toothy grin. "*Or five for fifteen.*"

Prizes hang on the fence behind the worker—stuffed animals large and small, and some little things, too.

I fish a ten-dollar bill out of my wallet and begrudgingly hand it to the man, who makes a show of giving me instructions. He tells me how to hold the mallet while encouraging the surrounding onlookers to heckle me.

I pull back the hammer, holding it behind me, and aim for the middle of the rubber plate.

The metal ball shoots up halfway to the bell, then falls back down unceremoniously.

Hmm. I know I can do better than this.

"*Try to get it right in the center, babe,*" Penelope encourages me from behind, picking at her sweet treat as if she hadn't a care in the world.

"*Three small prizes make a medium,*" the man tells me with a smirk.

Three small prizes, my ass.

I rear the hammer back and smash the plate again. This time, I send the ball up three-quarters of the way, but I'm still unable to ring the bell.

There must be a trick to this I'm not aware of.

"*Right in the center, babe.*" I hear.

I nod. "Right in the center. Gotcha."

Swiftly, I watch the center of the plate where I have to strike carefully—same as I would watch a baseball being pitched to me, the way I'd watch the bat strike the ball, keeping my eye on it the entire time.

Lo and behold, on the third try, the ball fires like a shot, striking the bell and ringing it loudly, much to the glee of my girlfriend, who bounces up and down like a child to celebrate my victory.

"I knew you could do it!"

The man isn't as excited about my triumph, but he walks toward the wall of prizes, showing us what we've won—two mediums, one big, three smalls, or this, that, and the other thing.

"It's not for me to decide," I tell him. "She's in charge."

Penelope smiles, eyeballing the animals and the blow-up guitars. The blow-up hammer. The horrible blow-up aliens. She stares into bins of mini slinkys, yo-yos, and sticky hands, and plucks a small shiny object from obscurity, sliding it on her finger.

It's a plastic emerald ring, and its green stone is surrounded by gaudy plastic diamonds.

"That's it?" the guy asks. "You don't want that big Daffy Duck?"

Penn shakes her head with a laugh. "No thanks. This is perfect."

She holds her hand out, letting the fake rock shimmer in the carnival lights. "We can go now."

"Oh, we can go now?"

"Yeah. I'm happy. We've had dinner and our fair snacks. Let's go back to your place and get in our jammies and watch a movie."

Penelope goes up on her toes so she can kiss me on the lips.

"Whatever you want, babe."

I hadn't wanted to come here anyway. I certainly hadn't wanted to go on any rides, and I sure as shit don't want to waste more money playing any more games.

"Let's go."

I wonder if she still has that ring.

She was so happy keeping things simple. She never wanted or expected me to buy her gifts—so on the rare occasion I'd buy her flowers (from the grocery store, usually) and surprise her with them, she would be over the moon as if I'd spent hundreds of dollars on them.

Everything happens for a reason.

I knew that now.

She is back in my life not just because the universe was pointing me in this direction with the dreams and the memories and the thoughts—but God had thrown a huge wrench in the reveal by presenting me with my daughter. Unexpected and shocking, to say the least.

Why now?

Why did fate choose now? These moments?

No one from above responds to me as I lie here alone, searching for the answers. Waiting.

Waiting for my mother's voice.

Or God, whoever comes first.

It's late, but I'm full of energy, so I pick up my phone and shoot Penelope a text. Perhaps she'll be awake and in the mood to chat.

Maybe she's got a lot on her mind, too. Maybe she can't sleep.

Me: *You awake?*

Penelope: *I am. Unfortunately.*

Me: *Today was heavy, wasn't it?*

Penelope: *It was. I'm not sure I was mentally prepared for it, but I'm glad we went.*

Me: *It was time.*

Penelope: *It was...*

There is a long pause before Penelope texts me again.

Penelope: *I have a lot of regret, Jack. More than you know, and if I could go back in time and do it all over again, I'm sure I would do so many things differently.*

Me: *I didn't text you to make you feel guilty. I texted you because I'm here, wide awake, doing a lot of thinking.*

Penelope: *I imagine you have. That's all I've been doing, too.*

Penelope: *I am just glad you're speaking to me. You would have been well within your right to shut me out.*

Me: *That's true—but that's never been my style. That's never been me. I face things head-on, even when they suck.*

Penelope: *True. I've had to grow a lot because my first instinct is always to...run from my problems. I'm not sure why since no one in my family ever ran out on me.*

Me: *That's not true. Your dad did.*

She's silent for a few moments, the three little dots on my phone's screen appearing and disappearing as she decides what to say and how to respond.

Penelope: *It took me a very long time to realize I had some abandonment issues. And my mom, too—though she didn't technically abandon me, she did die, and we knew it was happening, which felt like the same because I needed her. Which now feels so selfish.*

Me: *You weren't selfish. You were young. I think the two sometimes go hand in hand. It takes years to grow up.*

I realize that, in a way, I am excusing her behavior but then again, what are my options? What's done is done, and I've already decided to move forward—not look behind.

Penelope: *What I want is to move forward.*

Me: *You read my mind.*

Penelope: *How do we do that?*

Me: *I think we're off to a good start, don't you? It will take some work but we'll manage—I think it's a good idea to prioritize spending more time together—with Skipper of course.*

Penelope: *Of course. Yes, I agree that we should spend some more time together. And it means a lot that you're in town.*

Me: *Listen. I may be busy, but I know how to prioritize what's important—and that means SHOWING up—not just showing up.*

Penelope: *I agree.*

Yawning, I'm finally tired enough that I could drift to sleep with my phone in my hand, lying on the bed.

Me: *Thanks for the chat. I'm going to head to bed.*

Penelope: *Yeah, I've yawned about a dozen times already. Considering what a chill day we had, I'm beat.*

Me: *It was more emotionally draining than anything.*

Penelope: *It was, wasn't it...*

Me: *Good night, Penn.*

Penelope: *Night, Jack.*

Chapter 11

Penelope

My brother has decided it's a great day for a backyard barbecue, despite the colder temperatures late fall has brought.

His ex-teammates have been arriving, cars lining the street in our neighborhood and on my driveway and his. *How many people did he invite?*

And when did he decide this was a good idea?

It was last minute for sure. I heft a giant bowl of potato salad and carry it to the table. Most of the ladies agreed that the food should stay inside where it's warm. Men should stay outside near the grill, and everyone went in and out the big back patio door.

In a short amount of time, Davis and Juliet have managed to fill coolers with ice and beer, soda, and water, turning the potluck into a lunch of epic proportions.

Fruit platters, veggie trays, pasta salad, charcuteries—this spread has it all.

I make room for my bowl on the table, inching a few things that must be moved to accommodate one more item. Stealing a grape from the fruit platter, I pop it in my mouth.

This is one of the first times Davis has had a get-together where I wasn't the unofficial hostess. That's Juliet's role now.

It's a nice change, enabling me to mingle without worrying if the food needs to be replenished or the beer has run out or whether the cooler needs more ice. Or if the kids have enough to occupy them.

A few of them are in the pool, where the water temperature is guaranteed to be in the nineties. I'm sure Davis had to crank it up so it would be warm enough today.

I sit outside and spy Skipper on the swing set at the back with a few other smaller children while a few dads—all football players—sit in the loungers at the water's edge, watching the swimmers and laughing, while Davis flips meat on the grill. She waves at me, and I wave back, letting her know that I'm watching as she slides down the slide, showing off.

Goofball.

My stomach hits rock bottom when I turn around and almost bump into Jack Jennings as he comes through the back door, my little "Oh!" of surprise shocking us both.

"Hey there."

"You...you're here."

Miss Captain Obvious over here.

"I'm here." He looks around, and I can see when his eyes lock on Skipper at the back of the yard. He drags his gaze back to me. "Your brother invited me. Hope you don't mind."

My brother invited my ex-boyfriend slash father of my daughter to his "random, spontaneous, last-minute" backyard gathering? Gee, what a coincidence.

"No, yeah. It's fine. It's good." Stop talking. "We just got everything ready for lunch if you're hungry?"

"I can always eat."

He always could. Big guy, *big* appetite.

I stand stupidly next to the table as Jack begins making a plate for himself. It's as if he belongs here, comfortable in his own skin even surrounded by strangers. Sure, he knows most of the men here. My brother may not still play football, but the majority of his friends do. They are my brother's clients and best friends. His agent.

Jack clearly knows most of them.

He scoops a large heap of potato salad on his plate, followed by some watermelon, pasta, and three hot dogs, then he throws a hamburger onto the top. After he grabs a few napkins and a fork, he looks at me.

"Where do you wanna sit?"

Oh, he wants to sit together? I haven't put any food together for myself, nor have I put a plate together for Skipper, but she doesn't look nearly ready to come and sit for food. Best to just let her play, or she'll be a monster to deal with.

I take my time putting food on a plate because I'm in no rush to join him. I'm nervous at the prospect of being one-on-one with him. I trust him completely. I do. I'm not worried about him saying anything ruthless or insensitive. I'm worried about the feelings I've been having toward him since setting eyes on him on my brother's front porch.

I know that he wants to make this work. He hasn't said the words out loud, but I feel it in my bones.

I know Jack is a good man who wants to do right by his daughter.

Not once has he said anything about a paternity test. Not once has he thrown anything in my face. I guess the issue is that I feel guilty and don't know how to make things right.

The first step is the hardest. So I put one foot in front of the other and follow him, my heart thumping the entire way. It's cold, but we end up back on the patio, saved by the portable heaters my brother has set up every few feet. Most of the men have congregated out here while the women mingle inside.

I feel Davis's eyes on me when I have no choice but to plop down beside Jack on the pool lounger, resting the paper plate on my lap.

Davis raises his brows.

Is he serious? He's the one who invited Jack! What am I supposed to do, ignore the man for the first half of the party? Pretend I don't know him? Pretend I don't know he was invited because of some diabolical plan my brother apparently has that I'm just now finding out about?

What's his game?

"You look surprised to see me here," Jack begins, stabbing a hot dog with his fork and taking a bite off one end.

"I'll be honest. I wasn't expecting you, but that's not a bad thing."

"Good." He takes another bite. "I thought it was important to drop by one last time before I had to get home. Even though, you know—she doesn't know."

Right.

I shift uncomfortably, not sure how to respond to that. "The right time will come."

He nods, finishing off the hot dog.

Not three seconds later, Skipper is coming to a halt before us, hopping on one foot. "Jack! You made it!"

Hop, hop, hop.

"How did you know I was going to be here?" he replies with as much enthusiasm as she has.

"Because! I told Uncle Davis!" *Hop, hop.*

Get this kid a damn pogo stick. She's a ball of energy.

"You did? Thanks!" He holds out his fist so her little fist can bump it. "We have to stick together."

"Yeah!" She glances down at his plate. "You have two hot dogs!"

Jack holds up three fingers. "Nope, I had three. Just ate an entire one and gonna gobble up the rest."

"And a hamburger?" She looks shocked at the amount of meat on his plate and thrilled to discover there'd been more.

"Heck yes. Nom, nom, nom." They're grinning at each other, sending my heart into a tailspin with how much they look alike. "Hey now, where's your lunch?"

Skipper looks down at her empty hands. "I should eat."

"Why don't you go put a plate together?"

"By myself?" she asks dubiously.

I rack my brain, wondering if I've actually ever let her put together her own plate of food at a party before and come up empty-handed.

"Sure, why not?"

Clearly, Jack has never been around kids before, or he'd know plenty can go wrong at a food table with a child involved in serving themselves: overloading their plate. Only taking junk food. Only taking one of something. Not taking enough. Dropping their plate.

The list goes on and on...

"Mom, can I?"

Er. "Sure," I answer slowly. I mean, what's the worst thing that could happen? "If you need any help, give me a little wave. I'll keep an eye on you."

"I can?" she shouts, the hop evolving into a skip as she bolts to the house as fast as her purple My Little Pony sneakers can take her.

"She's easy to please." Jack is amused as we both watch her through the window. With a giant grin on her face and eyes as wide as saucers, she mulls over her choices on the food table. She looks each and every last thing over before grabbing a plate.

On her tippy-toes, it looks like she grabs some pasta first, then fruit—only strawberries from what I can tell—then a brownie and a hot dog.

Her small hand takes a fork and napkin, and with a nod, she carefully tightrope walks back toward where Jack and I are sitting, another adult helping her with the sliding glass door.

"She's so fucking adorable."

I glance over at him. "Yeah, isn't she?"

"Looks just like me, *obviously*."

Yes, she does.

It hurts my heart sometimes at how she looks like him so much. Every day is a reminder...

Once she reaches us, her little rear weasels itself between us, legs kicking back and forth since they don't touch the ground.

"Good job, buddy," Jack tells her.

"Thanks." She's already digging into the pasta salad, a colorful combination of red, green, and beige spiral noodles. "Mom, did you make this?"

"No, honey, I made the potato salad."

Skipper rolls her eyes. "You always make potato salad."

That has me laughing. "Well, it's one of the only decent picnic things I know how to make."

Cut me some slack, kid.

"I'm good at making cake," she tells Jack. "And also spaghetti."

He nods approvingly. "I love spaghetti. It's my all-time favorite."

"Mom, can I make Jack spaghetti?"

"Sure, sweetheart."

She stands.

"Not right now."

She sits, defeated. "When can I?"

Jack laughs. "Another time, squirt. I have to leave tonight and head back home. I live in Colorado. Do you know where that is?"

"Nope."

He holds his hand out sideways as if it were a map of the United States, pointing near the base of his thumb.

"We're here right now, and I live..."—he drags his finger toward the center of his hand—"right about here. See how far that is?"

"Yes, about two inches," Skipper declares matter-of-factly, happy to know this information.

"I have to take an airplane to get there."

Skipper nods. "I like plane rides, especially ones that take me to Disney."

"Have you ever been to Disney?"

"No, but I want to."

Jack seems to be making mental notes, nodding along as she prattles on.

"And I want to see the Statue of Liberty and be Rainbow Dash for Halloween... do you know who that is?" She eyes him skeptically.

"Er, no."

She points at the horse on her shoe with the flowing rainbow mane. "This is Rainbow Dash."

"Ah, I see."

"And I love jelly beans and don't really play with

Barbies, and I wish we had a pool and a dog." She gives him a pointed look. "A dog like Kevin."

"Ah yes, Kevin," Jack intones. "He's at a dog park right now playing fetch with his babysitter."

"It's so funny that he has a babysitter," she says, giggling.

"Well—I say babysitter, but it's actually a dog sitter, but they do the same basic thing."

"Because Kevin is your child."

Jack shoots me a look over her head. "Um, exactly."

"A dog can't be your child. Only a child can be a child."

He nods. "You're very wise."

"Thank you." She bites into the brownie from her plate and closes her brown eyes. "This is delicious. Not as good as cake, but delicious." Her eyes pop back open. "Did you see me on the slide before?"

"No, I only just got here."

Skipper hands me her plate. "I want to show you my tricks. Pay attention."

Off she goes to razzle and dazzle him with her theatrics, hanging upside down from the rings hanging off the swing set and climbing up the slide only to go down it again. Crosses the monkey bars, drops to the ground, then makes a show of crossing them again, skipping a bar this time.

Her eyes are trained on Jack to make sure he's watching.

"I wonder if she'll be an actress. She seems to love an audience."

I chuckle, biting down on my fruit. "She's not always like this. She's showing off for her new buddy."

"New buddy—ha."

The unspoken idea of introducing him as her father lingers above us like a heavy storm cloud, neither of us willing to say the words out loud but knowing they're not going away.

When are we going to tell her?

How are we going to tell her?

What will she say?

What will she say? I know she's going to be ecstatic, but that by no stretch of the imagination means we're going to simply blurt it out willy-nilly. There is a time and a place for everything, and this is the most delicate conversation I'll ever have had to make.

Had I had the conversation with Jack about being pregnant? That would have been it.

But I hadn't.

I had hid like a coward.

Skipper gallops around the yard, neighing like a horse, much to the amusement of everyone in the backyard.

My brother shouts, egging her on. "Giddyap, little horsey!"

"I'm a pony!" Duh.

Davis strolls over. I know he's been biding his time and giving us privacy and the time to...adjust to being in public together. Must have been driving him crazy to mind his own business.

I wouldn't say my brother is a busybody, but he certainly isn't one for holding back his opinion—not where his niece or I am involved.

His hand is already out, ready for a handshake. "Jennings, glad you could make it."

Jack stands, wiping his hands on the leg of his jeans. "Thanks for inviting me. I get to see what a little ham-bone Skipper is."

Davis looks over his shoulder at his niece, who's still prancing around the yard like a goofball.

"Yeah, she's not that shy." He grins. "Not sure where she gets it from since Penelope tends to be the quiet one around here."

Jack glances down at me. "She always was. Only spoke when she really had something to say."

That's true.

I don't talk to hear myself speak. I always believed my words had more power when they were used wisely—not that anyone gave a crap about anything I said.

"You in town much longer?" Davis asks Jack.

"No. I'm actually going to catch a flight tonight. I'm heading straight from here to the airport, but I'll be back before you know it."

Davis looks at me and raises his brows.

I wish he'd stop doing that! It's weird, and it's making me nervous, and all it does is draw attention to the situation. Ugh—freaking brothers, making everything awkward.

"If you two wanted to go somewhere and talk, I can keep an eye on PipSqueak."

Jack shakes his head. "Nah, I want to watch her race around and show off. She's living her best life right now."

I clear my throat, injecting myself into the conversation for the first time. "She wants to make him spaghetti."

Davis's eyes go wide. "Her world-famous sketti? Good for her. It's the best. You're going to love it."

Jack laughs. "Oh, I'm sure. I can't wait." He stuffs his hands in his pockets, looking bashful for the first time. "Thanks again for inviting me, bro—appreciate it."

"Don't mention it." My brother winks at me before saying, "Well, I'm going to keep mingling. Stay as long as you'd like."

And with that, he's gone.

And I'm not sure if he told any of his friends—or their

wives—to leave us be, but no one comes over. No one approaches us to make small talk or introduce themselves to Jack.

We sit on that pool lounger, watching our daughter in silence without speaking to each other. Skipper plays with the other kids. Skipper also goes down the slide again and again and again.

The sun begins to fade on the horizon, and in the background, guests begin saying their goodbyes. I hear a few of them mention Monday night football and needing plenty of rest. There is clatter in the kitchen as the dishes are piled up near the sink to be left for the cleaning women who come to Davis's home first thing Monday morning.

I had offered to do it at one point for extra cash, but he shot the idea down.

"Would you like to come over and read her a bedtime story?"

He looks at me, surprised. It's the least I can do, and she really, really likes him.

Any fool can see they already have a bond.

"Sure. Yeah, I'd like that."

Chapter 12

Jack

"**W**ould you like to come over and read her a bedtime story?"

Was she serious? Of course I want to go over and put Skipper to bed. Read the little shit a bedtime story.

I imagine that it'll be a production getting that kid to bed. Her high-energy theatrics haven't stopped since I arrived at the Halbrook's barbecue, her adorable little face seeking out mine all the while.

Is it weird to feel that she...knows?

Somehow, she knows.

Instinctually, Harper knows we're somehow cosmically connected, though she has no idea how.

It feels surreal being inside Penelope's house. Almost identical to her brother's, it's a spacious two-story with hardwood floors and gleaming wood I suspect she scrubs herself. Granite countertops, brick fireplace, winding staircase.

A punch in the gut.

The reality of seeing her house—a house provided for

her by her brother—is sobering. They should've been with me. That should've been me taking care of her like this.

I'm not going to say that I feel guilty, but I feel guilty. I feel misplaced guilt I know I shouldn't feel but feel nonetheless. All these years, I could've been providing for her. Correction—providing for us.

I know she wants to return to school to finish her degree, and that's something I could offer her. Something that would be easier if we lived closer. That's not a conversation I'm ready to have with her yet, but it's certainly something on my mind. How could it not be? I have a daughter now, so it stands to reason that I would want to make moves to involve myself in her life. To make up for the times I've lost out on. To start making memories with her.

With *them*.

Skipper practically drags me up to the second story, chattering the entire way about swing sets and a kid name Brian from the barbecue who tried to take her ice cream, showing me her bedroom and her toys and her crafts. It's a purple room with a cartoon horse mural painted on the wall and rainbows everywhere.

Cheerful.

Cute.

Exactly like her.

She has a bedtime routine and runs me through it, leading me into the bathroom and showing me how to start the bathwater. Penelope leans against the doorjamb with her arms crossed and a smile on her face.

I definitely don't feel comfortable giving her a bath, but it's adorable that she's showing me how it's done. As if I, a grown man, couldn't figure it out.

"You don't want the water to be too hot," she's telling me. "And you don't want it to be too cold. See?" She takes a

Sara Ney

bottle of bubble bath and hands it to me. "You add some of this to make the water bubbly. It's called Mr. Bubble."

Skipper watches as I twist the cap off and go to pour it. "Not too much."

I glance at Penelope over my shoulder. "Little hall monitor, hey?"

She scoffs. "Lord, you don't even know."

"Should I go pick a book out?" I ask her, not sure what to do with myself now that it's time to plop our daughter into the bath. I imagine that there isn't much that needs to be done. Skipper is seven and old enough to do most of the work herself. So the least I can do is busy myself by choosing a story to read.

"Good idea." She nods. "Her favorites are on the top shelf."

Nodding, I head back into Skipper's bedroom, her little voice following me out the door.

"Do you do voices, Jack?"

Voices? "What do you mean?"

"You know," she calls out. "When the mom talks to the baby, she uses a mom voice, and when the bear talks to Goldilocks, he uses a bear voice."

Oh, jeez. "Sure, I can do voices."

Not well, but I'll give it the old college try.

It takes forever for me to pick out a story, the stacks of books so high I'm not sure where to begin. I stare at the covers of each one, thumbing through the books that are actually filed on the shelves.

In the end, I choose three, and Skipper can have the final say.

The bath ends quickly, and before long, she's scampering back through her bedroom door, hopping on one foot with wet hair and purple pajamas and a giggly little grin that causes my heart to squeeze.

She gets right down to business, climbing onto her twin bed, with its pony blankets and pony pillowcase *and if I need to get her a gift, I'll know exactly what to buy for her.*

Her hands fold in her lap, and I get a whiff of her strawberry hair and pink bubblegum skin and want to hug her so tight.

Don't cry, dude.

Do. Not. Cry.

But it's hard. She's so damn adorable and so stinking cute.

Fuck.

Don't cry.

It's a story—just read the story, you got this.

"Did you pick one?" Her brows rise, and she looks so much like Penn and so much like me at this moment I wonder how I didn't see it that day in the green room at the stadium.

"I picked three. I was going to—"

"I get *three* books?" Her mouth forms an O of excitement. "Cool!"

"No." I laugh. "I chose three and was going to let you choose. It was a much tougher decision than I thought. You have great taste in books."

She nods solemnly. "I do."

I hand her the books, setting them on her pint-sized lap for her perusal, amused when she takes the task seriously, studying each one anew as if she's never seen these books before, which I seriously doubt is the case.

"Oh, this one is good. Have you read it before?" she asks me.

"*Gilly's Great Green Garden Patch*? Um, no."

"It's about a tadpole who lives in water but wants to have a garden. The pictures are so bright and cheerful, but it's kind of babyish."

Oh, shit. I picked a book that's too babyish?

Dad fail.

"Is this the book you might want to read?"

Skipper cocks her head to the side, debating. "I don't think so. Let me see *Ponies on Parade, Dash's Big Dream.*"

I hand her the purple pony book, and she immediately thumbs through it.

"I like this book because it's also a movie," she's telling me. "Dash has a dream, and this guy"—she points at a unicorn with a fire mane—"this guy tries to stop her."

"That sounds very interesting." I look up to gauge Penelope's thoughts, but she's no longer filling the doorway looking on. Nor do I hear her in the bathroom.

She's giving us our privacy, letting us bond.

It feels heavy. A weighty moment I'll remember for the rest of my life.

The first time I read my daughter a book.

It's then that I realize this is only one of many firsts. The first of hundreds of firsts in our lives—Skipper's, Penn's, and mine—this one shooting its way to the top of my list of memories.

I shake my head to stay focused. "I vote we read about Dash because you love ponies, and I want to know all about the things you love."

This seems to make Skipper happy, and she nods, setting the other two books on her bedside table and handing the keeper to me. She relaxes back on her pillow and folds her hands once again as she settles in for the story.

"Just so you know, I already brushed my teeth." She bares them to me as proof.

I laugh. "Great. We're off to a good start."

"Well, Mom always asks after she reads my story, so I'm just saying."

It makes sense.

I begin the tale, doing my best to use different voices but not coming remotely close to the original voices, too much timbre to mimic a girl pony, and not enough skill to do it without feeling like a major fraud.

"You're doing great, Jack," my seven-year-old praises, boosting my confidence. She laughs at all the silly parts and gasps at the dramatic parts even though she's heard it all before.

When I accidentally skip a page because of my fat fingers, she gently lets me know I missed a page.

When I mispronounce the evil pony's name, she gently informs me it's Prince Dancelot, *not* Prince *Lance*lot.

When I finish and get to the end, she looks up at me with those big, brown, puppy dog eyes and says the words parents dread to hear at night when they're done reading the bedtime story.

"Can you read it again? *Please?*"

"Um." I have no idea what to do. It took twenty minutes to get through that first reading, and now she wants me to read it again? How long does bedtime take? Does this go on forever?

"No, ma'am, he most certainly cannot read it again. What's the rule?"

Skipper purses her lips. "One story."

Penelope laughs. "Nice try, though. I admire the effort."

Our daughter has giggle fits, hunkering down beneath her blankets. "Oh, Mom!"

Penelope glances at me when I rise so she can kiss

Skipper good night. "Gee, wonder where she gets the willpower from?"

Another first.

Comparing her attributes to mine.

Willpower. Determination.

Nonstop energy.

Sure sounds like me.

I swear my chest puffs up from pride, that one sentence burning itself into my memory bank: *Gee, wonder where she gets the willpower from?*

"Night, sugar booger." Penelope is leaning down and smooching Skipper on the cheek, forehead, and nose. "Sleep tight."

"Don't let the bed bugs bite."

When she steps away, it's suddenly my turn, and I swear my palms get sweaty all over again. Something they don't even do while I'm at work, face-to-face with a three-hundred-pound defensive tackle.

Skipper yawns. "Thanks for the story. You have to work on your voices, but animals are hard."

"Yeah, they're hard, especially since it's a cartoon on television. I haven't seen that show yet."

"It's lots of shows and a movie," she tells me. "We can watch them tomorrow."

I won't be here tomorrow.

With a lump in my throat, I tell her, "We'll have to watch it sometime." Leaning in, I'm not quite sure what to do.

I can't kiss the child good night. I just met her.

Standing up, I straighten her blanket though it doesn't need to be straightened, and clear my throat, feeling my nose tingle.

You're not going to see her after tomorrow. This is it,

buddy—but this won't be the only time I get to tuck her into bed.

"I had fun today," I say. "You're one of the best...um..." I pause, unsure. "Hoppers I've ever seen."

"Thanks, that's what everyone tells me."

Thank goodness she's modest.

"Well, Skipper, I'm glad I got to tuck you in."

"Hold out your hand." Her little arm appears from beneath her purple bedding, palm shoved in my direction. "Show me your thumb."

She wiggles hers.

I hold out my hand and wiggle mine.

"That can be our secret handshake."

"Wiggling fingers isn't a secret handshake," I inform her, somewhat of an authority on handshakes, given that I'm a professional athlete who uses hand signals for a shit ton of things.

"Oh."

"Slap my hand, then go like this." Slap, wiggle, wiggle. "Now bump my elbow with your elbow." She bumps my elbow. "No giggling. This is serious business," I say. "Slap the palm, slap the palm, hook the pinkies."

Skipper's tiny pink tongue sticks out of her mouth from the sheer concentration and determination to get it right and memorize it.

"We can practice. Don't worry. Have you ever seen *The Parent Trap*?"

"No."

"Ask your mom to watch that movie and pay close attention to the scene where Martin the chauffeur drops off Hallie at summer camp. They do a secret handshake. It's not the same as our secret handshake, but you can see what one is."

"Can't I just google it?"

"How does a seven-year-old know what googling is?"

She shrugs. "I'm seven, Jack, not two. We know things."

Fair enough.

"But why do you sound like a thirty-year-old?"

"I'm not a grandma!"

She sounds horrified, still too young to know that thirty isn't old.

"Okay, okay, time for bed." Even to my own ears, I sound semi-parent-like and pat myself on the back for wrangling her back to the subject at hand. "Have a good day at school tomorrow."

"I will."

"Good night."

"Night." Skipper yawns. "I like pancakes for breakfast."

I chuckle as I flip her light switch off. "I'll give the message to your mom."

"Thanks."

I find Penelope in the kitchen wiping down her countertop—one that already appears clean and well-scrubbed. Her nervous energy vibrates when I enter the room.

She stands straighter. "Well. How did it go?"

"Good. We have a secret handshake."

"Oh, lord. Whose idea was that?"

"I'm not sure. She thought wiggling her thumb was a secret handshake, and I couldn't concede to that, so we made one up. I told her to watch *The Parent Trap* so she can see what one is, and she told me she could just google it."

"That sounds about right." Penelope pauses. "So what's the secret handshake?"

"Pfft. I can't tell you. It's a secret."

Penelope laughs and produces two glasses of wine from

the end of the counter, pre-poured, motioning toward the living room.

"Wanna go sit and talk? I know you mentioned the airport tonight, but I thought if you had a little bit of time...?"

I don't actually have time to sit around because my scheduled flight leaves in two hours, but a simple flight change in the app should get that fixed. After all, I'm seizing every opportunity here to learn about Harper and regain some footing, and yeah, reestablish a relationship with her mother.

"Sure. Yeah, I can do that."

We go to the living room and get comfortable on the couch, my eyes scanning the photos hanging on the far wall. They're framed pictures of Skipper, most of them school pictures and a few candids.

She sees me looking. "I can get you some pictures."

"Thanks."

I don't love white wine, but I sip from the glass, wanting to chug the entire thing in one swig to calm my nerves. I never get like this. What's my damn problem?

New territory.

Uncertainty.

It would make anyone insecure.

"I heard her telling you your voices suck."

"My voices don't suck. She did not say they sucked. She said I needed practice." Or she implied it anyway. Very strongly implied that I watch the show so I would know how the ponies sound. "I was set up for failure. I should have insisted on reading Greenies Green Garden."

Penn laughs. "*Gilly's Great Green Garden Patch*—god, I've had to read that book no fewer than sixty times. It's about a tadpole that sprouts legs and no longer wants to live in water even though he's a frog who has to live in the water."

"Sounds like classic literature."

"She loves anything with sparkly pictures and flowers."

I fiddle with the stem of the wineglass. "Well, I appreciate you inviting me over to put her to bed."

Did I tell her that already? I can't remember anything anymore, least of all what the hell I'm doing. I want to say fuck it all and do nothing but play with my daughter and take her places—to the park, the zoo, the grocery store. Anywhere, I don't care.

Penelope, too.

Goddamn, I've missed her.

I've always wondered about the woman she'd become, and now I know. She'd become a mother. A good one.

She worked hard.

She was funny yet shy, sweet and kind.

Her brother seemed to trust me. I'm assuming he now knows the entire situation. I wonder if he's always known or if he found out when I did. But why would she keep it from him, too?

"Can I ask you something?"

"Of course."

"How much did your brother know about...me?" *Being Skipper's dad.*

Her head dips for a few moments. "Honestly, Jack—nothing. He knew we dated, and he knew I was pregnant, but he didn't know for sure who the father was, and one day, he just gave up asking. I'm not even sure he had suspicions—like he didn't automatically assume it was you." Her shoulders rise and fall. "It was awful not only keeping it from you but also keeping it from him. I don't know how I did it or why. But you know—you dig that hole so deep, and at some point, you realize it's so deep you can't get out. Not even when someone throws you a ladder."

Holy shit! Davis Halbrook hadn't known?

Why does that make me feel some semblance of comfort?

It's so fucked up, but there it is.

My gut tells me that in another world, had Halbrook known...he might have contacted me and told me. He would have found a way. Not sure how I know this, but I feel it in my bones.

He would have told me.

Damn shame he got injured. He was one helluva player and a stand-up guy. A guy you're glad to call a friend.

He proved that by inviting me today when he didn't have to.

"That's heavy. Thanks for telling me that."

Penn nods. "So you know—I know it's asking a lot. It's asking the world of you, but...all I want to do is put the past behind us and move forward. Do you think you can do that?"

"Do I think I can do that?" I repeat. "Hell yes, I can do that. That's the reason I'm here."

Penelope smiles, hiding it in the brim of her glass. "Good."

Good.

Good.

We sit like this, making eyes at each other, filling our glasses for a second time, and downing those. Our evening unexpectedly turns from laughing and conversation to something else entirely.

I wouldn't say this is the Penelope I remember because it's been too many years. But I would say this feels as comfortable as what I remember—as intimate as the times we used to have.

Penn is beautiful, sitting there with her hair down. Wearing black leggings and an oversized sweatshirt, she has one leg tucked beneath her rear, her blue eyes so unlike mine and Skipper's.

And just as unexpectedly, we find ourselves sitting closer. Close enough that our legs are touching, and her hand gently taps my knee when I make her laugh.

"I've missed you, Penn." I find myself whispering words I've held inside, resenting the fact that I felt them. Why on earth would I purposely want to miss the woman who wronged me?

I should resent her, shouldn't I?

But that was then, and this is now—and we have a new understanding.

We have a new beginning, and I intend to take it. I have a family, and I want them in my life.

I want my family.

"I've missed you, too, Jack." Her nose is a bit red from emotion and the wine, and I lean forward, touching the tip of mine to the tip of hers, our wine-soaked breaths mingling.

Penelope inches her mouth forward by tilting her chin, lips touching mine. Again.

Soft.

Hesitant.

I take the wineglass from her hand and set both glasses on the coffee table, then pull her close, hands roaming her face so I can look in her eyes.

"I've missed you."

Don't fucking cry, Jack.

Her lips are the softest lips I've ever felt in my entire fucking life, and damn if I'm not underexaggerating. For a few minutes, we just sit here like this exploring each other's mouths tentatively—almost as if we were reliving the past and our former selves. Our former, younger selves. Those twentysomething kids who knew absolutely *nothing* about the life that they were heading toward when they thought they'd be together.

My fingers lightly caress her hair—those long silky strands I used to marvel at, especially when she curled them. I used to love when she would get all dressed up, pull her hair back and twist it so that later when we got home, I could take the clip out and let it fall down her back.

Our soft kisses become passionate. Tentatively, Penelope opens her mouth so I can explore it with my tongue. Our heads tilt. The kiss is wet and delicious and intoxicating. *An intoxication that has nothing to do with the wine.*

I swear I've been waiting for this moment for the past seven years. And now I not only have Penelope but we also have a daughter.

I have a family.

My parents are both gone, and I have no siblings, so I'm not about to let this opportunity slip through my fingers—to have a life I know we both deserve.

"God, I've missed you," she says, hands on my shoulders, kissing me senseless. Kissing me like this is the last time she'll see me.

Shit.

Maybe that's what she's thinking—that I'm going to leave and not come back again. Leave and not come back for days or weeks or even months.

I pull back. "How would you feel about coming to Colorado and catching a game?"

"Me and Skipper?"

"No, just you. Come to Colorado, come to a game, and let me show you where I live."

Maybe you'll want to live there, too.

"When?"

"Whenever you want. Next week." Tomorrow.

Tonight.

"My boss is going to kill me."

"Penn, I see no other way. At some point...you're going to have to make sacrifices to see where this goes."

"But...my job?"

I lean back on the couch, considering. "You're right. It's a big ask, asking you to miss work. Maybe just Monday. I have a Sunday night football game. We could spend Saturday together, and you could fly home Monday."

"I'd have to see. The only one I have right now to help me with Skipper is Davis, and it's hard. I can't keep relying on him."

"I get that." I pause. "Think about it. We can make something else work. I'll just fly back—it's no big deal."

"You can't..." She shakes her head. "I can't let you keep flying back and forth all the time. It's not fair." Another shake. "You're right. The time is now to make the hard decisions. I'll ask my brother and see what he has to say about watching Skipper for the weekend."

"Penn, I can hire you a nanny so you have more flexibility. I can—"

"Stop, Jack." She says it with a laugh, hand on my thigh. "I love that you're willing to do that, but ugh, this is all so overwhelming."

But she's going to think about Colorado.

She's going to think about flying to see me.

This...

...is what we call progress.

Chapter 13

Penelope

*I*f I hadn't only had two glasses of wine last night, one would assume I was hungover...

I'm surprised to see Davis and Juliet in my kitchen when I walk into it this morning, the sight of danishes, eggs, fruit, and drinks also greeting me.

Drinks?

"What on earth is going on in here?"

Juliet walks over with a champagne flute filled with bubbly orange liquid, handing it to me.

"Here, we thought you might need this after last night."

"Really, Davis, Bloody Marys and mimosas?" I hop up onto the barstool, pulling my hair into a ponytail and looping the rubber band around twice before leaning forward. "I'm changing the code on the garage door."

He points his spatula toward his girlfriend, Juliet, who shrugs. "Hey, don't blame me. It was her idea."

"Listen, there isn't much I wouldn't do for a breakfast spread like this."

"Okay, but it's Monday, and I have to leave for work in an hour."

My boss is not going to love the bags under my eyes.

"Lucky for you, I have nowhere to be, and *she* took a vacation day." He nods his head toward his girlfriend, who sits sipping her mimosa innocently while my brother drinks his Bloody Mary.

Ugh—I hate those things. Tomato juice has never been my thing. Once, when I was younger, I was on a plane to visit our father—the one and only time I ever went to see him after he left us—and decided a tomato juice was what I wanted to drink. I spilled it all over my lap, my new blue dress, and white tights.

Sad, sad day.

"So we noticed Jack's car was still here after everyone left last night."

If my brother is trying to be subtle, he is failing miserably. The raised eyebrows and the fact that he's trying not to look at me when he asks the question are dead giveaways that he's being nosy.

"How did you know which car was his?"

"Only one with a Texas plate. *Total* rental car."

Dang, he's good.

"You should become a private investigator," I sarcastically say, plucking a piece of bacon off the platter he's set on the counter. It's so good I close my eyes when my mouth closes around it.

Nom.

"That bacon is for the Bloodys," he complains.

I snort. "Three pounds of bacon for your breakfast cocktails?"

"Washes down better."

"Anyway. I might as well tell you that..." I hesitate, not sure how I'm going to word this. "Well. I'll just say it. Jack invited me to Colorado to spend a weekend with him. He wants..."

Davis and Juliet listen, hanging on my every word.

"He wants...to...um. Get to know me?"

"He wants to get to know you? I thought he knew you already. You have a kid."

"You know what I mean. He wants me to be a part of his family, and he wants"—I shrug—"to show me where he lives."

"Why does he want to show you where he lives?" Davis's brows are now firmly rooted into his hairline. Juliet smacks him in the arm so he'll stop talking and let me finish, but he cannot stop himself from interjecting. "He's not planning on moving you to Colorado, is he?"

I hadn't considered that. "No. Of course not."

I laugh it off, but a part of me isn't so sure. Jack seems hell-bent on reconnecting. He's already spent time with me twice in a matter of two weeks. It's clear he's sacrificing his time and his insanely busy schedule, and now it's my turn to return the favor.

"So what are you saying, Penelope?"

Davis isn't going to make this easy.

"I'm saying I should go. I don't want to take off work, but I feel it's important that I go. It's the olive branch I need to make things right."

"Because you lied to us and didn't tell him he was Skipper's father." My brother throws the gauntlet down as only big brothers can do. "When do you plan on telling her? When she's thirty?"

"Whoa, babe. That's not fair," Juliet says with a horrified look on her face.

Davis takes a few breaths.

Okay. Yes.

I know I hurt and pissed him off too, and I've only apologized to Jack, not my brother, for keeping it from him. None of it is fair.

All of it is true.

"He's not wrong." I take a deep, steadying breath. "You're right. I've done everything in the wrong order. But it's not too late to start over."

"Actually, yes, it is. Your daughter is seven. There's no turning back the hands of time."

"I get why you're upset, Davis, and it's a lot to ask for you to keep supporting me, but you're the only one I have right now." *Wait.* "Shit, that came out all wrong. I'm not trying to put a guilt trip on you. That's not at all what I meant. Shit."

No amount of alcohol first thing in the morning can cure this headache I have.

The more I speak, the worse I seem to make it, so I zip my lips and stay quiet, letting him process my words. Juliet's hands are on his shoulders, kneading them as she smiles at me. A kind, encouraging smile.

My brother runs a hand through his hair. "I know, Penn, I know. It's a lot to process, and I'm not even the one in the situation. But it kind of feels like a gut punch because I hadn't known who her dad was either, and I'm still processing all the information. That doesn't change anything, though. I'm here for you and whatever you need."

My body sags with relief. "It won't always be this way, Davis. I promise I'll get my shit together and become an adult someday. Unfortunately for me, Skipper is the more mature one of the two of us sometimes."

Juliet laughs. "Oh, come on. I'm sure that's not true."

"Certainly feels like it."

I take more bacon, then grab a plate and load it with

scrambled eggs and a slice of toast. I make a small plate for Skipper when she comes downstairs. She's sleeping late this morning but is due to come tearing down the stairs in a matter of minutes, making a fuss and a ton of noise.

"I love you guys." I push the food around my plate. "And I love this bacon. And I love these eggs."

"Hey now, you're not allowed to declare your love for bacon. Only people."

"Blah, let me eat in peace."

He leans against the counter, resting on his elbows. "So what did happen last night?"

Ugh, why are brothers so relentless?

"Well." I swallow the eggs I had in my mouth. "Jack did come over after the barbecue. I invited him over to help get Skipper ready for bedtime. I gave her a bath, and then he read her a story."

"Which story?" Davis wants to know.

"One of her Rainbow Dash stories."

"Ah," he says knowingly. *"Ponies on Parade, Dash's Big Dream."*

I'm stupefied. "How do you know this?"

"Because I've had to read it eight hundred times. I suck at the voices, or so I've been told."

We all suck at the pony voices. "It's hard to compete with a cartoon."

"Right." He pauses. "You're stalling. On with the story before Little Miss Nosy Rosey Skipper crashes our party."

I inhale a breath, letting it all out as I say, "So he puts Skipper to bed, and I can hear them talking. I obviously stood outside the bedroom door listening. And she compared their hands and corrected him a few times as he was reading. They came up with a secret handshake."

"Aw." Juliet sighs. "That's so adorable."

"I know. Melted my heart."

"Yeah, yeah." Davis isn't impressed. "A secret hand-shake, big whoop."

"Babe, don't be jealous. You're still her favorite uncle."

He gives me a pointed look. "Go on."

"After he tucked her in, he came downstairs, and I had glasses of wine for each of us, so I invited him to stay. We sat on the couch and talked a bit. Then he invited me to Colorado."

I leave out the kissing parts, but Juliet isn't letting me off the hook.

"That's it? You just *talked*?" She looks unconvinced and disappointed. As well she should. Juliet squints at me.

"No fooling around, just talking? Why don't I believe you?"

I set my fork down. "Fine. We kissed."

There, I said it.

"Who kissed who first?"

"I don't actually remember. I think we just…leaned into each other at the same time?" He was caressing my face, and I was touching his thigh, and one thing led to another, and we were kissing.

"And?!" She is so impatient for more details. "How was it?"

"Good? Fine? I don't know—great?" My toes curled inside my socks. That's all I know. But my brother is standing here drinking in every word, and I'm not about to say this to his face. He's annoyed with me as it is. He doesn't need to hear about me sucking face with a man he just found out is Skipper's father.

Dig that knife farther into his back? No thanks.

"And he wants to reconnect?" She uses air quotes

around the word reconnect, grinning. "This is great news. Very, very good news."

I thought so, too. "Next weekend, he has a game on Sunday. Sunday night football, and he was hoping I could fly in Saturday so we can spend the whole day bonding or whatever. Then Sunday I would go to his game, and Monday I'd fly home."

Davis is nodding. "Solid plan. Do you want me to take Skip? We can do the waterpark or something. Juliet, should we?"

"Yeah, that would be fun. Skipper and I haven't done any bonding lately."

She and my brother haven't been in a relationship long, so she's still getting used to the fact that Davis is Skipper's sole male role model, and he spends a lot of quality time with her. Juliet hasn't joined them on many of their outings, but she's a teacher and loves children. Skipper is becoming one of her favorite kids of all time.

I see a future favorite aunt in the making.

"Good, then it's settled." Davis nods. "I'll get Skipper from school and take her on Monday. Don't worry, we've got you covered."

Lord, I am so blessed. "Thank you."

I'm not sure if it's the mood or the alcohol in my glass, but I love them so damn much that I want to jump up and hug them and give them a million kisses.

Now if only my boss were this easy.

"Listen, Penelope, I want to share something with you." Davis gets serious. "You and I both know my history. I've had women date me when I was playing ball because I was playing ball. I want you to put it out of your head that you're like those women because you are not. You literally dumped the guy when you knew he was going to the draft and would probably get signed. You're the painful opposite of those women, so if you think for one second he's got that in his head, you're wrong."

He's saying all the things I've worried about, but this time, I know he's right.

"Today begins a new chapter for you, and for Skipper—and for him. Remember that. His life changed the second he showed up on my doorstep, hitting him like a Mack truck. Imagine how that all feels and go easy on him, yeah?"

"I have gone easy on him. I'm beating myself up about it."

"That's not going to do any of you any good. It's like being on the field, yeah? Looking back will only get you sacked. Run like hell toward the end zone."

Juliet and I both stare at him as if he's lost his mind. "Since when do you make football analogies?"

He shrugs. "It felt like a good time to start."

"That was so cheesy," his girlfriend tells him.

"Cheese!" he announces. "That's what these eggs are missing!"

～

I survived the day.

My boss didn't fire me for using a personal day.

My daughter is in bed.

I resist the urge to pour myself a glass of wine, instead deciding on a warm bath and a book. Hair wrapped in a towel, I submerge myself, carefully perching my phone on the edge of the tub, eyeballing it on the off chance it'll slip off the ledge and sink into the water.

It's happened before, trust me.

The bath bomb I added earlier fizzes and tickles the

backside of my legs—legs that could use a good shave, but I'm far too lazy to take on the task. Plus, I'm sure my razors are dull.

As soon as I crack open my paperback, the phone begins to buzz—the last thing I'm expecting it to do. Not only is it ringing, and not only is it Jack, but he's video chatting me.

Shit.

I'm in the bathtub!

Shit.

Shit, shit, shit.

My hands are dry, so I accept the call, holding the phone as high as I can so he can't see my boobs, though they're mostly submerged beneath some bubbles.

"This is a pleasant surprise."

That's the first thing he says.

The second? "You should move the phone so I can see your toes."

I laugh. "Nice try. This isn't a peep show."

He looks disappointed and is clearly sitting on his living room couch, kitchen behind him. Leather sofa (typical), probably a giant television on the opposite wall taking up the whole space.

"Well, what are you expecting me to say when you answer the phone completely naked?"

Is he flirting with me? It's such a foreign feeling! Makes me excited and nervous and pathetic at the same time. Pathetic because I have no idea when someone is flirting with me.

I'm so out of practice it's not even funny.

Come to think of it, when was the last time I went on a date?

Last year? Nine months?

Two years?

Shit, when was it?

The guy was decent enough but didn't make me laugh. He was way too serious and kept trying to impress me with all his "things." He talked too loud, and bossed around the servers, and okay—*so maybe he wasn't all that decent.*

"If I'd known you were calling, I wouldn't have gotten into the tub."

Ha!

"Touché." He pauses. "I assume by your soak that you've had a long day?"

I wiggle my toes. "Eh, it was decent. I wasn't in the mood for a shower and thought a bath would feel good. I have a book." I wave the book around in front of the camera before dropping it onto the floor.

"What book is that? I haven't read anything in a long time."

"A romance novel."

"What's it called?"

That makes me laugh. "It's nothing you've read."

"How do you know?"

"Because you just said you haven't read anything in a long time, and I'm going out on a limb to say it wasn't romance."

"Fine, you caught me. It was a sports autobiography."

"Shocking."

"But I have other interests, Miss Smarty Pants."

"Oh, yeah? Like what?" I move my free arm below the water, swishing it around to kick up the bath bomb fizz.

"Like Rainbow Dash and trampolines."

Cute.

Clever.

"Weird, those are some of my hobbies too."

I study him then, his face like a reflection staring back at me. He hasn't shaved and appears tired, hair smushed as if he's had a ball cap on all day.

Or a helmet?

Sweaty, like he needs a shower or just took one.

"What have you been up to tonight?"

Jack yawns. "Not much. Took the red-eye last night and slept all morning. Didn't have practice but had to work out, which sucked because I feel like I've been run over by a truck. Been looking at flights." He yawns again, and so do I. "And I thought I'd check in to see where you were at."

I giggle. "I'm home."

"No, I mean..." His voice trails off, leaving me to fill in the blanks.

"Ah, I see what you mean. Well, I talked to my brother and Juliet this morning—that's his girlfriend—and he volunteered to watch Skipper this weekend so I could go to Colorado. So it looks like we have a date."

"Saturday through Monday?"

"Yes, if that's still okay?"

"It's better than okay!" He genuinely looks excited, and I catch a brief glimpse of the youthful young man he used to be. He's older now, of course, with more laugh lines and a few wrinkles in his forehead. Not to mention more facial hair. "All my free time is yours, plus I may have a surprise or two up my sleeve."

I shake my head. "No. No, no, no—no surprises." I don't deserve one. "Please, let's just keep it chill."

"Sorry, request denied. And you should know I have no chill. That's where Skipper gets it from. Her old man, The Skip." Jack pauses. "When you brought her to the game a few weekends ago, did she see me play?"

"Um. Honestly, I'm not sure she was paying all that much attention. She's seven. She was more interested in the popcorn guy and the hot dog man who kept coming around." I sound apologetic because the man sounds like he really wanted his daughter to see him play. "She just doesn't understand sports."

Even though Uncle Davis watches them regularly and shouts at the TV while he does it.

Jack looks bummed by that news. "Well, there's still time to teach her."

"Always looking on the bright side, eh?"

"Eh."

We laugh. 'Eh' is something I used to always say, mimicking the accent of the Midwestern area where we grew up. Plus, I had a few Canadian friends in college who said it a lot too.

He leans his head against the back of his couch, suddenly joined by a copper-colored dog, jumping up and doing his best to lick him on the face.

"This is Kevin." He tries to make an introduction and fails miserably. "He's a pain in the ass. Kevin, stop."

Kevin does not stop.

"Dammit, Kevin." He laughs. "I'm trying to talk to my ex-girlfriend and the mother of your new best friend. Stop licking my face."

The mother of your new best friend.

Jack somehow manages to ward off the dog, wiping his face with the sleeve of his sweatshirt. "He was at doggy daycare today. I have no idea why he's so hyper. He had the zoomies before I called, so I thought he got it out of his system."

The zoomies. "Is that when they race around the house like they're on crack?"

"Yeah. Once, he broke a lamp. Yanked the cord right out

of the wall while he was trying to race under the table. Scared the shit out of us both."

I imagine having a Kevin is a lot like having a toddler.

Been there, done that.

Not that I wouldn't love to have more kids, just not a four-legged one that knocked things over and broke things.

"You probably won't get to meet the little scamp all weekend. We'll be busy, so keeping him home won't be fair." I can tell he's scratching the dog behind the ears. "And no, I'm not always gone this much, but when I am, I have a great sitter who either comes here, or he goes there. Everyone loves this nutty little dude."

It was on the tip of my tongue to ask, *"Why have a dog when you're never around?"* but now I don't have to.

"What are we going to do while I'm there this weekend?" Four entire days until I'm on the plane, which reminds me, I still haven't booked flights! I hope they're not through the roof expensive. It would kill me to have to dip into savings for a long weekend I hadn't been planning.

"Can't tell you, or it'll ruin the surprise."

"I hate surprises."

"I know."

"Once, when I was in middle school, my friends threw me a surprise party for my thirteenth birthday at my friend's house—it was a pool party. And when my mom dropped me off, I could hear everyone in the backyard and went running back to the car. I was so embarrassed."

"That doesn't mean you don't like surprises. Maybe it just means you didn't want a yard full of people."

I run a hand through the water to warm it back up. "Hmm. You could be right. I'd never considered it that way."

"I'm full of wisdom," Jack demurs. "So I'm going to

throw this out there and don't want you to feel weird about it, okay?"

Oh, crap.

I nod slowly. "Okay."

"I'm going to buy your plane ticket. I invited you out here, and I don't want you to worry about the expense."

Is he a freaking mind reader?

It's on the tip of my tongue to argue. Of course it is. The last thing I want to do is take help from him. On the other hand, I cannot afford an airline ticket right now. I have bills and groceries, and this wasn't in the budget.

"Will you let me do that for you?"

I find myself nodding again, this time more slowly. "Sure. Thank you, Jack. I appreciate it."

"Dang, that was easy. I was so confident you were going to give me a hard time about it." He laughs.

"I mean, I was going to give you a hard time, but for once, I stopped myself."

My skin is getting dewy, and the water is growing cold. I can't run the water without it drowning out the sound of my voice and ruining the conversation, but I also don't want to sit here in freezing water—no matter how badly I want to chat with him.

He's so handsome.

Looks so...happy.

At ease?

I shiver, shoulders above water getting goose bumps.

"Time to get out?"

"Probably. I think my toes have turned into prunes." I give them another wiggle, though he can't see them.

"Let me see."

Guess not.

I turn the camera in the other direction, pointing it at

my toes. They're hot pink, freshly painted during one of the girls' nights I have with Skipper.

Mani. Pedi. The whole shebang.

Her tootsies are always purple, and mine are always pink.

"You always did have pretty feet—even when they're wrinkled."

He always used to massage my feet any time we would be on the couch. He sat in the middle, and I was on the end. He'd always take my legs and pull them across his lap so he could rub my feet.

"I'm the one who should be rubbing your feet! You're the one who's been running around all day. All I did was go to class."

"Nonsense. Class is all the way across campus, and you had to walk. Give me these cute toes." He leans down and kisses my toes, biting the big toe before he begins pressing his thumbs into the heel of my foot.

"If the football thing doesn't work out, you can always go to work in a spa."

That makes him laugh. "And if the advertising thing doesn't work out, you can always be a foot model."

"Maybe I can be a foot model anyway as my side hustle."

Jack rubs and rubs and massages one foot, then the other, until they're good and relaxed, demurring when it's his turn.

"No, babe, I don't want you doing my feet."

"Why?"

"I like to spoil you."

"All you do is spoil me. You never let me spoil you!" It's really quite frustrating how much effort he puts in, bringing me small things that make me laugh and smile, like cookies and flowers—little things a student can afford but treats that cheer me up nonetheless.

He's way more creative than I am.

My contribution is picking out movies to watch and shows to binge or cooking him dinner after practice.

Lame.

"I'll have to rub your feet when you get here. You've been walking around in my mind all day."

I look back into the phone at him smiling through the screen, still petting his dog. "So cheesy, but I'll allow it."

"Can I tell you something?"

"Yes, of course."

"It's been a really long time since I've dated anyone seriously, so I'm nervous to bring you out here."

My mouth opens, then closes. I feel like a guppy searching for air.

"I'm nervous too." Actually, I've been a ball of nerves since he randomly showed up looking for me, nervous since he laid eyes on Skipper, nervous when we went for drinks, nervous...

You get the drift.

But I'm glad he admitted that because it makes me feel a shit ton better and gives me more to look forward to and less to be anxious about.

Chapter 14

Jack

To say Penelope is surprised to see me at the gate when she deplanes from her flight is an understatement. First, she looks around as if confused and unsure. Then she checks the signboard near the gate to verify she is indeed in Colorado.

"What are you doing here?"

"I said I was picking you up at the airport." Smugly, I walk forward and take her roller bag and tote, slinging it over my shoulder with mine.

"But you're not allowed through security without a boarding pass."

I give her a quick kiss on the lips. "I have a boarding pass."

"But..."

"I told you I had a surprise, didn't I? This is part of the surprise."

She follows beside me, reaching for my hand as we stroll past one gate after another, down the long stretch of corridor, garnering attention as passengers realize Jack Jennings is walking past. Though I'm in a ball cap and glasses, there's no mistaking my identity.

People whisper.

Point.

Stare as we walk past.

I double-check our gate, leading Penelope not to baggage claim where we would normally exit, but toward gate C19—one terminal over and toward our next destination.

"What's going on? Where are we going?" She sounds excited this time and less dubious as we walk past a Star-bucks with a line that's not to kingdom come.

I drag her over. "Do you want something? An afternoon pick-me-up?"

"Sure!" I swear, it looks as if she wants to twirl as we step into line, staring up at the menu, holding hands.

The kind of life I want.

I notice a man nearby watching us with his phone out and realize without a doubt he's taking photos of us.

Instead of frowning at him, I smile.

LOOK, EVERYONE! I'M HOLDING HANDS WITH A PRETTY GIRL, AND WE'RE GOING ON A DATE!

Print that on the internet for your headline, why don't you?

We place our order, stand off to the side for a full ten minutes, then it's off again to our gate. When we arrive, Penelope's eyes widen, and she looks at me.

"California? What are we going to do in California?"

"Well, I have a game against the Drifters, and I thought we could do some sightseeing."

"Ohhh, I thought your game was in Colorado. This is going to be fun. Wow! I'm...this is exciting!"

She bounces up and down, looking a lot like Skipper.

I pull Penelope in and give her a side hug, tucking her into my armpit as the gate agent begins the boarding process. We can board early if we'd like, or we can wait. It matters little to me as people stand to get in line, babies and grandmas and servicemen heading up the crowd.

Eventually, we board.

We buckle in and are served drinks, but it's difficult to chat over the jet engine noise, and both Penn and I have noise-canceling headphones, which rules out communication. But we continue to hold hands for the short flight, and that's even better.

Neither of us has checked luggage, so it's a quick jaunt from deplaning to the car rental when we land. I've rented a sporty convertible. The weather is beautiful, and the drive will be scenic, so it's perfect for the day trip I have planned.

After tossing the bags inside the trunk, I rub my hands together gleefully, feeling as giddy as a schoolgirl.

"Ready?"

Beside me in the passenger seat, Penelope grins. "Ready as I'll ever be."

Traffic cooperates, and the estimated twenty-five-minute drive from the airport to the Getty Museum is a breeze without bumper-to-bumper cars on our trip to Santa Monica.

We make our way slowly up the long, ascending drive, the view impressive once we arrive at the top. I've never been here before. Never had a reason to, but so far, I'm impressed and glad I made the decision to bring her here.

When I'd sent my agent a text, asking him to help me plan a day out, he'd shot me a list in return.

1. The Getty
2. A winery
3. Disneyland and California Adventure
4. Surfing

I'd had Disney on my shortlist but decided that was a better idea for three: Penn, Skipper, and I for a long week-end. Perhaps when the season was over, and I had more dedicated free time.

To be clear, I don't love museums.

They bore the shit out of me.

But there's more here than just statues and art, and with panoramic views overlooking the entire Los Angeles area, I didn't think the location could be beat. Shit, we can park ourselves on a bench and talk for hours if we want to, or walk the grounds—all seven hundred and fifty acres of it.

We're welcomed by a member of the Getty staff, who gives me her cell phone number in case either of us wants anything. Food, ensured privacy, a guided tour, and a golf cart if we have no desire to walk are just a few of the perks of being a celebrity and the five-star treatment I hadn't asked for.

We walk to nowhere in particular, into the large entrance hall, and toward the massive art gallery I have zero interest in actually looking at.

I'd rather study Penelope.

Is that weird?

There's an exit at the other end of the room, and we take it, stepping into the bright California sun and heading toward the garden. We find a bench and sit, gazing out toward the city below.

"Wow," Penn says, awestruck at the view.

"Wow is right." Except I'm not talking about the view,

I'm talking about her. Everything about her is right, especially at this moment. Her hair, her voice, her smile.

The way her eyes crinkle when she smiles at me.

It's a sight I've been waiting seven years to see, and now that it's in my grasp, I'm thirsty for it.

"They probably don't serve hot dogs here, hey?" Her voice drifts over in the airy silence, nothing but the wind and sun surrounding us.

"I imagine we could get a hot dog, but it would probably have a lobster on top with a French baguette as the bun."

"That actually sounds disgusting."

"This is why I'm a football player and not a chef," I quote one of her lines. I'm good at many things, but cooking, anything crafty, and singing are not included.

I give her a sidelong glance. "What two things do you love doing in your free time that have nothing to do with our daughter?"

Our daughter.

Rolled right off my tongue.

"Hmm, let me think." She ponders for a few seconds. "I love riding my bike. And this is going to sound super nerdy, but I really like needlepoint. It relaxes me."

"Needlepoint? What's that?"

"You know, cross-stitch? Your grandmother probably made patterns back in the day. Mine aren't flowers or anything. Mine are snarky quotes like 'maybe swearing will help.'" She puts her bag on her lap and riffles through it for her phone, pulling up her photo gallery. "Here, see."

I glance at the screen, at a photo of a little round cross-stitch that says, *"Hey Trainwreck, this isn't your station"* and another with a raccoon face on it that reads, *"To Me, You are Trash."*

My eyes get wide before the laughter comes.

"Penelope!" She seems so sweet and innocent, and here, she's crafting these sarcastic patterns? It kills me.

Her cell gets stuffed back in her purse with a laugh. "What? It calms me after a long day."

"I can see that. Guess I shouldn't piss you off, or I'll be on the receiving end of the snark."

"Ha. I don't do anything with them. Well"—she pauses —"that's not true. I love putting them on packages during the holidays as gift tags."

"What would you put on my needlepoint?"

"Good question. Hmm." Penn hums again. "Something like...Welcome to parenthood. I hope you like ibuprofen."

I stare at her, mouth agape. "Did you just pull that out of your ass? Because it's hilarious."

"No," she admits. "I've had that in the back of my mind for a while, but it's so accurate."

"You're cute. And funny." I sneak a kiss from her, then she kisses me back, and soon, we're making out at the freaking Getty, with who knows how many people spying on us.

Definitely Stephanie.

She's definitely spying on us.

I pull back. "We should probably discuss the tabloids."

She nods. "I've thought about that—obviously. And I don't love it, but I know it comes with the territory." Her shoulders move up and down in a shrug. "It is what it is."

"Well, don't believe everything you read. In fact, don't believe any of it. In fact, don't read anything at all." I laugh. "Stay off the internet and don't go looking for pictures or stories."

"Why on earth would I do that?"

"Trust me, you'll get curious and go look, and then...it's all downhill from there."

People will call her a gold digger. Say she got pregnant to trap me once the news gets out that we have a daughter. The press will print stories about our relationship without interviewing us, but they'll find people who knew us way back when and interview them. And those people will say anything for a payout.

And it sucks, and it hurts, but here we are.

"My job is to play sports, not to showboat around Hollywood or care what they say about me on television, but every once in a while, something gets back to me that really fucking grates at my nerves and hits me the wrong way, and those are bad days."

If I play great, I must be on performance-enhancing drugs. If I play terribly, I'm a curse to the team. Nothing is ever good enough for the press. The sports broadcasters—many of whom are my friends, but it's their job to entertain the masses for ratings—will drag me after games and then apologize later.

I've been called an old man. Washed-up.

Past my prime.

Ha—I am in my prime right now, motherfuckers!

"I just don't want you to get hurt by people who know nothing about you, or us, or Skipper."

It's inevitable, and it's going to cut deep.

"We'll get through it together."

Together but far apart.

We've only been reconnected a few weeks, but it feels like forever, and I already know what I want. It just hasn't been the right time to say it.

Penelope has proven that she scares easily. She proved that when she left me. But she's here now, which is something.

It's a start.

And little by little, I'm going to make her see that I'm dependable, reliable, and not going anywhere.

We make it to our hotel just two hours before our dinner reservations. It was another gorgeous ride into Santa Monica for dinner at the pier, arriving at the hotel as the sun in the distance fades into the ocean.

"Welcome to The Four Seasons, Mr. Jennings. We have two rooms set aside for you. Do two king-sized beds work for you? Otherwise, we have a two-bedroom, king suite, whichever you prefer?"

I turn to Penelope. "What's your preference? Two rooms with king-sized beds or one suite with two bedrooms?"

The decision is hers.

Penn wrinkles her brow, tilting her head. Then she moves closer and lowers her voice. "Why are we doing two separate bedrooms? I mean, it's totally up to you."

"You don't want your own room? I want you to be comfortable and to have your own space."

"Jack, I don't...*need* my own room."

"But do you *want* your own room?"

The front desk clerk averts her gaze, pretending to be examining some documents on the countertop and listening to anything but our exchange.

Ha!

"Do you want me to have my own room? I can't believe we're arguing about this."

I level her with a stare. "Okay. So what you're saying is...you want to do one room? The suite with two rooms or one room with one bed?"

"Oh my god, Jack, I'm going to strangle you."

Strangle me? I like this feisty side. "I'm just trying to make sure! Don't shoot the messenger."

The clerk looks on, no longer hiding the fact she's watching and listening to our fervent exchange.

Rude and unprofessional, but whatever.

"We'll take one room."

"A king, or would you like a suite?"

"A suite with a king. I don't need multiple bedrooms. It's just the two of us." I hand her my credit card, face on fire, ears probably red, too.

I feel like a teenager caught red-handed by my parents with my hand up her shirt. This woman knows we're probably going to be fooling around later. I might as well take an ad out in the *Wall Street Journal* to advertise it.

Jesus. She probably thinks this is a hookup.

"This is our first trip together," I tell the woman. "First trip without our daughter."

Her eyes grow wide as saucers.

Shit.

I just made this worse, reading her mind as her eyes go everywhere, including the hand where Penelope would wear a ring. "*Jack Jennings has a child with a woman he has never shared a hotel room with before? They stood arguing about it in the lobby...but they have a child? Is this his wife? Is this his fiancée? Can't be. There's no ring.*" The woman—Beth—does a poor job of schooling her expression, considering The Four Seasons is all about class and discretion and privacy. I can literally see what she's thinking. "*None of this makes sense.*"

Damn right it doesn't, Beth, but here we are!

Beth eventually hands me the key card to our room. A

beautiful penthouse room—despite not needing anything ostentatious, she upgraded us anyway.

"Oh my god." Penelope clutches my arm when we enter the suite, going straight for the bathroom. "I'm totally taking a bath in this." She twirls around. "This is incredible."

Like a kid would do, she oohs and aahs at the lotions set out on the counter, plucking up the shampoo and conditioner. "This is the good stuff." She sets it down. "Oh god, I sound so lame."

"You don't sound lame. You sound excited. And you should absolutely take a bath while we're here."

There's a hot tub, too, out on the deck, though that holds little interest to me. Too much time spent in them after games healing my body. Cold plunge baths and hot tubs in the training room ruin the appeal, but if she wanted to hop in, I'd do it.

"How do you think they got this fruit basket up here so fast?"

Good question. "They knew I was coming. I'm sure they already planned on me being in this room. They probably have a fruit basket in another room for you."

Penelope plucks a few grapes off the vine and pops one in her mouth. "Being pampered is so magical. It's been ages since I've done anything like this." She sweeps through the room to the window. "I haven't even had a girls' getaway in the past few years. This makes me want to plan one."

I want to go to her and see what she sees. Wrap my arms around her and kiss the back of her neck.

Instead, I drag the suitcases into the bathroom, setting them up on the luggage stands, unzipping hers and mine so we can start getting ready for dinner.

I need a distraction before I kiss her senseless and make us late, so I take what I need from my bag and give her privacy to change, do her hair, put on makeup—whatever women do to get gorgeous—while I get ready in the bedroom.

It's easy. All I have to do is change my clothes. Take off my jeans and throw on slacks and my button-down shirt. Throw on a tie and pick out some shoes.

I watch *Sports Vision* to kill time while I wait, nervously bouncing my leg.

Penn and I have been out before. This will be our second date, although that first date wasn't technically a date. It was...just catching up. Disguised as a date.

But that's before I knew she had a child—that we had a child.

Harper Halbrook changed everything for me. She changed the way I look at Penelope, she changed the way I view my job, she changed the priorities I never knew I had. Suddenly, being here with her mom is more important than anywhere else in the world.

Being there with Harper and Penn is where I want to be.

And it makes me nervous because I don't know if that's what Penelope wants.

So my leg shakes, and my palms get sweaty as I wait for that bathroom door to swing open, watching the shadow beneath the door as she passes by, blood coursing through my veins.

A few more passes by the door, and it opens.

I stand.

Game time, buddy.

Game time.

"You look...stunning."

She's in a satin green dress belted at the waist with large gold hoops in her ears. Her hair is wavy and loose—silky and smooth—and sways as she moves forward, blush already on her cheeks.

I wrap my arm around her waist and pull her in for a kiss. "You smell good too."

"Thanks, so do you. Smell good and look good." She's embarrassed to say the words, but she gets them out, almost shyly.

I don't blame her. We're not feeling ourselves these days, and every single moment we've spent in each other's presence feels vulnerable.

Arm in arm, we step through the hotel room door.

Chapter 15

Penelope

This entire day has been magical.

I feel like I'm sleeping, waking in my dream. I can't explain it, but something about being with Jack is intoxicating—not Jack Jennings, the football player, but Jack, the boy from my past and the man of my future.

Tonight felt like the first time he took me out on our very first fancy date. Neither of us had much money, but he'd made reservations at a fancy place along the river in our college town. A place where very few students ever went. That's how fancy and expensive it was.

But Jack took me there.

We'd been dating four weeks and had only done the usual: a few movies. A basketball game. Gone to a few Greek Week activities and a house party. Coffee. Target to walk around.

The usual.

Things kids do when they're broke.

There we were at the fanciest place in town, all dressed up in the fanciest clothes we had in our closets. I wore a black velvet dress that I'd worn when I'd gone through sorority recruitment (though I hadn't joined one), and Jack was in black dress pants and a baby-blue shirt with a matching necktie.

It was all nervous smiles and nervous giggles, accidentally touching because our knees kept knocking below the table.

"I'm way too tall for this table," he apologized for the second time. "Sorry."

"Gosh, stop apologizing. It's not as if you can help it. It's fine if you want to stretch your legs out."

He nods, readjusting the napkin the server had lain across his lap. "But then it'll look like I'm slouching, and I don't want to be rude. This is a fancy place."

I glance around, sitting up straight like the other women in the room, wanting to fit in though we clearly did not.

"Should we order an appetizer?" Jack was studying the menu again. "How about oysters on the half shell?"

I hated oysters. My roommate had gotten drunk one night on Saki bombs at a sushi restaurant and thrown up in our closet all over my shoes. Inside my shoes. Inside the file cabinet I kept in there.

I haven't been able to eat sushi or oysters since—not that I ever had the opportunity.

"If you want oysters, we can have oysters."

Not exactly a ringing endorsement, but I don't want to tell him I find them repulsive.

"Penelope, if you don't want something, just say so."

"Fine. I don't want oysters..."

That had been the beginning of me finding my voice with him. Knowing I could tell him what was on my mind, and he would accept it from me.

Still, some things weren't easy to admit.

Like the pregnancy.

"Oh look, they have oysters on the half shell," Jack is saying, grinning back at me, legs still too long for the table. "Remember when your roommate in college barfed in your closet after she got wasted?"

"Um, yes. But joke's on you because I can tolerate oysters now—especially if they're drenched in cocktail sauce and horseradish."

"Cocktail sauce and horseradish? That's cheating."

We tease each other all night. The staff at this restaurant leaves us alone, only coming over to bring food or remove plates.

Bring dessert.

The check at the end of the evening.

"Is the bathtub calling your name?" Jack is holding my hand across the table, stroking my palm with his thumb, the motion sending shivers down my spine.

I'm so easy. It's been forever since I've been touched, if I don't include this past weekend when he kissed me. But he hadn't put his hands anywhere else. He's kept them above board, not under my shirt, not over my shirt, not down my pants.

Chaste.

I've been restless since that night, my mind constantly wandering to sex—foreplay. Kissing. Touching.

Oral, even.

My entire body itches.

The ride back to the hotel takes forever. The concierge sent a car for us so we didn't have to drive ourselves. Jack's hand resting on my thigh practically burns a hole through the fabric of my dress.

It's the longest car ride of my life.

Tension fills the air when we arrive at the room. The sizzling, sexual kind. My satin dress caresses my legs with every step into the room I take, knowing it's going to come off and I'm going to slip inside the bathwater.

Invite Jack in with me.

Well, maybe not at first.

He makes himself busy while I run the water, setting a few towels on the edge, grabbing the soaps and shampoo and conditioner even though I pin my hair atop my head.

Leave the earrings in.

Finally, I step into the tub, getting comfortable, mostly submerged so my boobs aren't floating against the surface before inviting him into the bathroom so we can chat.

Jack sits on the edge, eyes scanning the surface of the bubbles the same way he'd done when we'd video chatted.

"I do love this habit of yours." His fingers flick at the bubbles. "I'll have to build you a bathroom with a giant tub."

"Does your place not have a tub?"

"No. Only a shower—a giant, marble shower with six showerheads."

"That sounds amazing, too. What's your house like?"

"I'm actually in a condo right now. I took the contract with Colorado, but we're never sure if we're staying to play, so I never went house shopping. Seven years and two championship rings later, it's a safe bet I'll be there a while."

"I like my house enough, but it's never felt like *my* house. I feel no sense in ownership because Davis owns it. Yes, he bought it so Skipper and I would be close, but it's not *mine*. It's this giant beautiful reminder of how indebted to him I am."

"You're not indebted to him. He did it because you're his sister, he can afford it, and he loves you."

I play with the bubbles, shifting them around, aware that Jack may catch a glimpse of my nipple.

His nostrils flare.

"Do you want to climb in?"

He inches forward. "I'm wearing clothes."

I roll my eyes. "I meant, do you want to get naked and climb in? I won't look."

He snorts. "I haven't got anything you've never seen before."

True, but the years have been better to his body than they've been to mine. I'm not the one who spends countless hours in the gym and on the field, honing and toning.

It stands to reason that I'm grateful for these bubbles floating around me, concealing my belly and whatever else I don't need floating about.

"Are you sure you want company?"

His hands are at his top button, hesitating, stuck between wanting to dive in yet maintaining some semblance of propriety.

"Like you said, you don't have anything I haven't seen before."

"A soak *would* feel good."

"Then you can get a good night's rest for your game tomorrow." Jack moans as if he hadn't wanted the reminder. "What, you don't want to play?"

"Not really, if I'm being honest. Or maybe I'm getting lazy now that I've taken some time for myself with you and Skipper. It's been ages since I've used my downtime for family stuff, you know. Usually, if I have free time, I use it to train. Which is work."

He laughs, standing, shedding his shoes and socks, then undoing his belt buckle.

I watch, transfixed, as his tan hands pull the hem of his dress shirt out of his pressed pants. Inch by inch, he removes it as if purposely going in slow motion to torture me—or put on a show.

A striptease.

Magic Mike has nothing on Jack. And yes, he has a farmer's tan when he finally removes his shirt, but the muscles and chest more than make up for it.

No complaints here.

I'm tempted to dunk my head under the water when his fingers go to the button of his pants, my warm face growing hotter by the second. I'm clammy and dewy and wet all over —and not from the water I've been soaking in the past few minutes.

Ugh.

No chickening out now.

When his fingers go to the zipper and pull it down, I almost squeeze my eyes shut, not wanting to stare at his dick when he pulls his pants down, or stare at it when he's completely naked and stepping over the side of the tub to settle in at the opposite side.

The water level rises by a good five inches as Jack sinks into the bubbles down to his chest, massive shoulders smooth and defined.

He has a body built like a god, but it's bruised and scarred, too.

A giant yellow and purple bruise on his collarbone draws my attention, and I ask about it.

"This? Who knows. It probably happened in the last game. Could have happened in practice." He rests his head on the back of the tub on the stack of towels there. "I was right. This does feel good. I usually hate the hot tub at the stadium, but this isn't anything like it. Plus, I'm usually in it with another hairy bastard."

I giggle.

Jack's toe comes up out of the water and sticks itself into my armpit, wiggling.

"Is this your way of flirting?" I tease, doing the same thing to him with my toe, but his armpit is way hairier than mine. *Aren't I glad I shaved my legs yesterday?*

His hand goes to my calf, and he begins a slow motion of caressing it up and down as we sit here, talking.

At one point, we have to add more hot water, thankful we're at a hotel with an unlimited supply of it, unlike my house where I run out all too often.

"What was your biggest fear in me finding out about Harper?" he says after a long lull. We're just sitting here enjoying the quiet time, the water around us, and the bubbles.

"My biggest fear." That's an easy one. "That you would think I was a terrible person. That I had bad intentions. I can't imagine what you were feeling when I told you."

He raises his head from the stack of towels. "Mostly shock. Call me crazy or call me naïve, or call me a fool, but... oddly, the biggest thing that pissed me off was the lost time. My mind didn't immediately go to anger, and I didn't run to my manager, publicist, or lawyer. They still don't know. I want to keep it private for now. Although after this weekend, I don't think that's possible."

No, it's definitely not possible with the fan photographing us at the airport and probably The Getty and probably the restaurant.

I haven't been online, but there's no doubt a story brewing there, false narrative or facts.

"I'm glad. Which sounds weird, but I was petrified and worried my whole world was going to come crashing down. It's all I can do these days to hold it together—which sounds terrible, but it's really difficult being a single mom."

"Especially knowing you didn't have to be."

I nod my head. He's so very right.

189

I didn't have to be.

I chose the path for myself and have regretted it since.

"What was your pregnancy like?"

"Good. Nothing out of the ordinary, thank god—no morning sickness, no nausea, no weird cravings. I cried a lot, though." I laugh. "Probably because I knew what I was doing was wrong, and I carried a lot of guilt with me, but I was too afraid at that point to say anything. It was stressful, and I'm lucky that everything went smoothly."

"I can't imagine the stress was good for the baby."

I shake my head.

No, it wasn't.

"Bet you were fucking adorable, though, with your cute belly."

I splash him with water. "No one is cute with a giant belly."

"Pfft, yes, you were. Don't lie."

Sighing, I laugh. "Fine. If you want to know the truth, yes, I did look great with a giant belly. I rocked it."

Jack grins. "See? That's what I'm talking about. You always look good, even in sweatpants and a ratty sweatshirt."

"When do I wear ratty sweatshirts?"

He pulls a face. "Uh... wasn't that sweatshirt you had on at your brother's house old as fuck?"

"Which time?" I laugh, splashing him again. "So I like to be comfortable! And so what if they're three sizes too big? I like what I like."

His head is back against his towel pillow, eyes sliding closed. "You were always a bit of a contradiction—not caring what anyone thought but also caring what people thought. Certain people. Like the girls on campus. I remember you worried they would judge you for dating me."

Is that what he thought it was? Hardly. "No, it was the opposite. I always thought they were judging you for dating me. I was so immature back then. It's embarrassing to talk about." All I needed was a few more years to grow up and form my own opinions and think for myself, and I would never have run away after finding out I was pregnant. I would have had a better head on my shoulders and wouldn't have been scared.

What's done is done, and I'm glad we can talk about it.

Jack nods, head still resting, eyes still closed. "Can you imagine how shocked I was when she told me her name was Skipper? If I'd have been sitting down, I would have fallen off my stool."

"Um, yeah. I could see it on your face."

"You know how I put two and two together? My buddy Robb Macenroy said 'Dude, that kid looked just like you. Put a wig on you and you'd be twins.' And I started thinking about it and thinking about it and was like—holy shit, he's right. She does look exactly like me! So I hopped on a flight and came right back."

"And here we are."

His toe drags itself down my rib cage, and his mouth curved into a delicious smile. "And here we are."

Jack looks relaxed and half asleep, the same way I feel.

His eyes come open eventually, and he sits up, pulling back from against the tub side and sitting up straight.

"I have an idea. Do you want me to wash your back?"

Wash my back? *That sounds more like an invitation to put his hands all over my body.*

Do I want his giant, strong hands all over my back? Um, yes. Still, I demur, a bit shy. "You're the one who's constantly getting your body beat up. I should be the one rubbing your back."

His head lolls from side to side as if he's working out a kink. "Probably, but when's the last time you had someone give you a back massage?"

It's been ages, actually. Getting a professional massage is a luxury I can't afford and would be the last thing I spent extra cash on.

Still.

"How about I wash your back first, then you can wash mine?"

There. That's a sound, reasonable compromise.

"Alright, if you insist."

"I insist."

Jack is massive. His back is broad and muscular. One of those backs you see in a fitness magazine where the person is flexing, the tendons and cords visible. He is a work of art. He is firm *but soft too* as he sits with his back facing me, my hands beginning at the base of his neck.

My hands are not nearly as strong as his are as they massage, my eyes scanning the tub for the bar of soap I'd set out so I can use it when the time is right.

I knead. Push.

Work his muscles best I know how, unsure if he's getting any actual benefit from it or if it's too light of a touch.

Smooth, sexy skin...

My palms graze his flesh, exploring over his shoulders and down his arms, then back up again. Down his spine. Up his spine.

This body has covered mine in the most intimate way.

I'm just playing, really—sadly, there is less massage to

this massage and more greedy wandering, my fingers itching to tease.

He is so freaking gorgeous...I would lick him.

Eventually, I grab a washcloth and rub the soap bar around the material, lathering it up, placing it in the center of Jack's back and caressing his skin with it.

He isn't dirty at all, but my thoughts about him are...

"What's going on back there?" His voice interrupts, and I realize I'm just sitting here, letting my mind roam, unable to stop the fantasies and daydreams. "You stopped."

"Sorry."

I can see his mouth grinning from behind and bite down on my bottom lip to stop the nervous giggle bubbling up inside my belly.

"I'm not very good at this." *The concentrating part, not the cleaning part.*

It's as if he knows exactly where my mind is at as he glances at me from over his shoulder.

"Your turn."

I nod, still holding the washcloth and turning my body into position, back in the middle of the bathtub facing him, water sluicing, flirting with the edge and in danger of spilling over the side when he slides his long legs around my body and pulls my back against his chest.

Well okay then, do it your way.

How we even fit in this tub is a mystery, but we do, comfortably.

Everyone is wet, making it easy for his palms to glide over my flesh, fingers kneading at my shoulders, digging but not too deep. They glide to the center, down my spine as if calculating each vertebra, massaging at the base of my back, just above my ass.

My head dips forward, eyes closing so my sense of touch is heightened, and I can feel every movement.

His hands go slow. *Deliberate.*

They're calloused but gentle. Firm but skilled.

"I feel like you've done this before." Now, why did I go and say a thing like that? I sound as if I'm digging for information on other women.

Ugh, Penelope.

"What I meant is, it feels like you know what you're doing."

I can feel him nodding. "I have a physical therapist and a massage therapist who work on me a few times a week. I've picked up on a few things. If this football thing doesn't work out, I can work as a PT."

"Someone would definitely hire you."

"You think?" His voice sounds close to my ear, and I shiver.

"Yeah."

Jack's fingers push a few stray hairs to the side so they're out of his way, then his lips softly trail against my back, his warm breath heating my insides.

I shiver again.

"Cold?"

I roll my eyes. He knows I'm not cold. "Knock it off."

"You want me to stop kissing you?"

No. "I meant, you know I'm not cold."

I don't know how it happens, but his hands are around my waist, pulling me even closer. I'm suddenly hyperaware —as if I hadn't already been—of the cock pressing into my ass though Jack does nothing more than hug me tight while breathing into my neck.

Lips pressing my skin.

Tenderly.

It's an embrace filled with emotion, considering we're in the bathtub, but emotional nonetheless.

And tension.

Plenty of that, too.

I let my head tip back against him and just breathe. I tilt my neck when he continues to kiss it, water up to my chest, skin dewy and moist, beads of water dripping from my arms.

We fit perfectly together and always have.

His lips move from the nape of my neck, to the side of my neck. Just below my ear, nibbling at the lobe.

My jawline.

I turn my face, and our mouths meet, his hands unclasp from in front of me and spread over my belly, thumbs stroking the underside of my breasts.

Every nerve in my body tingles.

His hands are huge. They feel amazing, and it's been so long. *I'm not desperate for any touch. I'm desperate for his.*

We kiss, open-mouthed and wet, his hands sliding to cup my breasts until I want to drag one down and put it between my legs. It feels so good I want to weep.

I want to turn my body and straddle him. Feel the length of his cock against my pussy. I'm so turned on I can't kiss him enough.

Apparently, he's had enough too.

Abruptly breaking the kiss, Jack pushes to stand, water cascading off his hot, firm body. Reaching for my hand, he pulls me up, too.

"Come here." He hauls me up out of the water, and I'm convinced we're both going to slip and fall and crack our skulls open on the tile floor. But he scoops me up before I can protest and carries me in his arms across the bathroom to the bedroom, setting me in the center of the bed.

Sara Ney

He crawls onto the bed after me, pushing my legs apart, palms holding my knees.

"Oh my god," I moan when his tongue licks between them. "*Oh my god.*"

"God, I haven't been able to stop thinking about going down on you." His fingers play with my folds, spreading them apart.

"Really?" I prop myself up so I can look at his face.

"Yes. I thought about it all day today. Now stop talking and lie back."

I want to die.

I want to die like this.

It's heaven.

It hardly takes anything for my body to react. It's been so long since a man has gone down on me that I'm basically a sure thing. I swear I would come a dozen times if he stayed down there like this, licking and sucking my way into heaven.

Turns out, he doesn't have to because it barely takes much.

I'm moaning and groaning, head thrashing back and forth against the comforter when my orgasm hits, my entire body shaking. Jack absolutely has to keep my legs apart when I come because it hits me so hard.

Breathlessly, I lie there, spread out, his face still between my legs, leisurely stroking my inner thigh as if it were a marvel, clearly enjoying his view.

I enjoy it too. Jack's tight ass propped up behind him, squatters glutes and hips.

Wide shoulders and sinewy biceps.

The top of his head. His thick hair between my fingers.

We're damp and naked, getting the comforter wet.

I wonder how he can lie like that and if his dick hurts

pressed into the mattress. If I should blow him to alleviate the problem. But Jack is making no move to continue the foreplay—no moves to have sex or climb on top of me.

It seems he only wants to cuddle. "Let's get under the covers."

~

JACK

I can do nothing but stare at Penelope, reaching for the clip in her hair and removing it so her hair falls down around her shoulders.

I want to run my fingers through it.

The sun has long gone down, and the room is dark. We've been in the bathroom since we got back from dinner, my clothes and her dress in a heap on the cold tile floor. We can get to that later after we've slept. Our wake-up call will come early enough given the football game I have to play at noon but leave for much earlier.

We're drier now but still naked. I am one lucky SOB that I didn't slip on the water and kill us both when I carried her in here, but it was well worth the risk.

Having her in my arms again?

Better than I could have imagined—and trust me, I've imagined it often.

Every waking hour and every second of my sleep, I can't get her out of my mind.

My hand caresses her cheek, and she scoots closer to kiss me on the lips, her hand going to my hip.

I'm still hard, dick still throbbing—but tonight isn't about me or having sex. It wasn't even my intention to go down on Penelope, but she's so sexy I couldn't stop myself once my hands were on her wet tits in the tub. I had no control over myself, climbing out like that and taking her with me.

Now we're lying here staring into each other's eyes, covered by the thick blankets, my fingers running through her hair. She smiles into my hand when I cup her cheek.

So beautiful, just like when we were younger, only more mature. It's clear she's had her fair share of worries, judging by the lines around her eyes.

Natural.

Smooth skin and pouty lips, I see the face of our daughter when I look at her, which only makes me love her more.

I part my lips to speak but close them.

"Tired?"

She nods. "It's been a day."

A long, busy day.

"Ready for sleep?" I ask.

"Are you?"

No, not really. I want to lie like this and talk, but I can also feel my eyes getting heavy. Whether from the warm bath or from the emotional heaviness I've felt the past two weeks, I'm not sure.

"Yes, we should try to sleep."

Penelope yawns, snuggling down further.

It's not long before we're both fast asleep.

Chapter 16

Penelope

I've only felt out of place a few times in my life.

"Who are you?"

"My name is Penelope."

"That's nice, but what are you doing *here?"*

What was I doing there?

Honestly, I didn't know.

I was at the football house off-campus after the first game I watched Jack play. He'd picked me up from my dorm and brought me here, thinking it would be a fun way for me to meet a few of his best friends—and teammates.

The trouble was, I was shy and didn't love parties, or drinking for that matter—and this house was full of loud, rambunctious people. Wall-to-wall people. Girls who didn't look anything like I did, girls who wanted to be noticed, girls who looked at me as if I were invading their territory.

Jack had left me standing here to use the bathroom, holding a beer cup I wasn't drinking from and doing my best to smile at anyone walking by.

"I'm with someone," I told the girl who seemed more keen to ask questions than answer any herself—and what did

she care who I was and what I was doing there. Who was she, the gatekeeper?

"Who?" Her eyes scan the crowd of students. It's a sea of people, all of them here to celebrate the team since they had won their game this afternoon.

"Jack Jennings."

Her chin tilts up. "You're here with Jack?" I can't hear her scoff, but it's implied.

And so very rude.

But I was in no position to defend myself when I wasn't even sure what I was defending myself from. All I knew was that she was making me feel shitty, and I didn't like it.

"Who are you here with?" I volley the ball at her, irritated with the set of her eyebrows. She's taller than me and staring down her nose with a critical eye.

They all did. This was nothing new, but that didn't mean I had to like it.

"Friends."

Friends? "Oh. I thought maybe you were dating someone on the team, too."

That was as close as I got to insulting someone.

"I'm here to see Stan Millbauer."

"Good luck with that then. Say hello to his girlfriend for me."

I didn't know who Stan Millbauer was, but the look on the girl's face was satisfaction enough for me, although guilt set in as soon as Jack returned from the bathroom and to my side, arm sliding around my waist and kissing my temple.

"Who was that?" he asks as the girl sidles away, weaving through the crowd, back on the prowl.

"I didn't catch her name." I sip from the beer in my hand that had grown warm, barely tasting it. "She's here to try to hook Millbauer."

I use the kid's last name the same way I hear Jack refer-ring to his friends, and it makes him laugh.

"Millbauer? She can try to hook him, but I'm pretty sure he has a long-term boyfriend back home. Good luck to her."

He kisses my cheek, pulling me along with him.

I spent the rest of the evening listening to him and his buddies joke around, giggling nervously and making small talk with the girlfriends—or girls hanging on them, anyway. It's hard to tell who is who or what to the guys...

"Hey there. I was wondering if I would see your face again!" A familiar face comes toward me down the row I'm sitting in, reaching over to tap me at the crook of my arm. "You were with Jack Jennings at the Sprinters game a few weekends ago."

She plops down beside me, setting her purse in her lap.

I can't remember her name, but boy am I glad to see her face.

"Lana Macenroy," she provides, blonde hair in the perfect coif. She looks so elegant. "We met in Chicago."

"Yes!" I thrust my hand out. "Penelope Halbrook."

"I remember who you are." She winks and begins rifling through her purse. "I don't know how long I'll stay. My mom is with the kids back at the hotel. We were going to take them to Disneyland this afternoon. Little one needed a nap first, or she's a monster."

Lana pulls out a pack of gum. "Want a piece?"

"I'm good, thanks."

She unwraps a stick and pops it onto her tongue, eyes out on the football field. "I'm at this game because I needed some alone time. Isn't that hilarious?" She nudges me. "My mom lives in Santa Ana, so it's the best of both worlds. She gets to see the kids, the kids get to see Disneyland, and I get to see Robb play and have a second to think."

The crowd goes wild to punctuate her words, the noise level deafening.

Lana laughs.

"Jack surprised me with a date. I thought we would be hanging out in Colorado. I didn't realize the game was here."

Despite my brother having played professional football, I should mention I know nothing about football. All I see is grown men running back and forth around a big field with lines and numbers on it, screaming people, and big dudes gathered on the sideline who may never get playing time.

They're already playing the second quarter, Colorado up by two.

"Oh, Robb used to do that when we were dating, randomly fly us places. You know, they get so bored sitting at home. At least Robb does. He has to be busy. I haven't noticed that about Jack, but we haven't spent much time with him socially. It's more difficult with the players who don't have kids."

Now is not the time to break the news to Lana that Jack is indeed a father. It's not my news to tell, and I have no way of knowing she won't go to the press, or their managers, or the coach.

I don't know her at all.

She seems friendly, and I'm grateful for her company since the other women look at us but don't approach.

Lana notices me noticing the other women and begins pointing a few of them out. "That's Sissy Whitnall—her husband is a linebacker. They have three kids, and she almost never comes to games. That here is Portia Stubbins. She's engaged to Travis Blake, number nineteen." Lana leans in. "Good luck with that one, Travis." She sits back. "Not that I don't like her, and I'm not trying to gossip, but he hasn't known her long, and he's young, so it's...you know." Her shoulders shrug. "She likes the lifestyle, and if he's not careful, he'll be broke when he retires."

And in this game, that could come sooner than you were planning. Just ask my brother.

I nod. I see where Lana is going with this monologue, and while I prefer forming my own opinions, Portia stands out like a diamond in a coal mine with her sparkle and designer bag and stiletto shoes she has propped up on the seat in front of her.

Red bottoms.

Giant rock on her finger.

Actually, Portia has several rocks on several fingers— bling, bling.

"Anyway, I've talked your ear off, and you've only been here three minutes." Her hand taps my knee. "How's it been going otherwise?"

Gee, where do I even start.

I open my mouth to speak, but Lana interrupts before I can pull a sentence out.

"How old is your daughter again?"

"Seven."

She nods. "Oh yeah, that's right. She's the same age as Presley, my older daughter. Peaches is three."

They have a daughter named Peaches?

I don't ask because I don't want to be rude, and for all I know, Peaches is a nickname the same way Skipper is Harper's nickname.

"She's at home with my brother and his girlfriend. They're having a weekend of fun, which they haven't had in a while, so...it'll be good for them." At least that's what I tell myself to appease the guilt of leaving for the weekend.

"Oh, sure. When Robb played for Detroit, my sister

moved in with us for a while to help out, but when he signed with Colorado, she wanted to move back to California and went back to her day job." Lana sighs. "Damn, I miss having her around."

"Yeah, when my brother got his first big paycheck, he bought two houses side by side, which I thought was obnoxious at the time, but I've come to see it as a blessing."

Not to mention when he'd bought the two houses, Mom was alive, and she lived with Skipper and me, and well, those are years I'm grateful for and wouldn't give back for all the money in the world.

"The man sounds like a genius."

"It's worked more in my favor than in his. He has no kids, so mine is always at his place, getting in his business." I laugh. "Can you imagine being a single man and having your seven-year-old niece policing the place while you're trying to bring dates home? Worst cockblocker ever."

"I can imagine. Presley never stops talking, and it's worse when we're in the car. That kid couldn't care less about watching TV in the back when we're driving somewhere. She wants to talk. About everything. Literally makes up stories just to hear the sound of her own voice."

Sounds about right.

"Skipper has the garage code to Davis's place, and the first night his girlfriend stopped over, guess who was patrolling the yard? His niece. Sequesters the poor woman outside, gives her the third degree, wants to know what her name is, where she's from, and does she like brownies."

"Oh, so the important stuff!"

"That child loves baking, but damn, it's such a mess."

"I have put the kibosh on baking and slime."

Oh my god, slime. "Slime isn't allowed in my house anymore or glitter. I had so much glitter on me once I looked like I'd taken a bath at the strip club. Couldn't get it out of my scalp or off my skin, just terrible."

Lana and I are laughing and sharing stories as the game plays on in front of us. Her declaration of leaving early fizzles with every move executed. Every point scored. Every penalty.

"How long have you and Jack been together?" She finally gets around to asking, politely refraining from asking anything too personal until we've laid some groundwork.

"Actually"—I clear my throat—"we dated in college for two years."

"College!" She twists her body to face me. "Robb and I met in college." She moves closer. "Okay, confession time. I never wanted to go to college. I just wanted to get married and have a family and be a mom. The same way my mom was, you know? So I basically used college as a way to meet my future husband. How terrible is that?"

The Mrs. Degree.

"Not terrible at all. I knew plenty of girls who just wanted to get married and have kids."

"I know, but people judge, especially when it turns out you end up dating football players. I didn't plan that part, I swear." She holds up three fingers in Scout's Honor.

Oh, yeah? Bet I can one-up that one.

Confession Time: *I managed to get pregnant while I was dating a football player, dropped out, didn't tell him, then had to watch him on national television for seven years until one night he showed up at my doorstep and shocked the hell out of me.*

I wonder what Lana would say to that little factoid.

She'd probably spit out the beer she just ordered.

"So you met in college...?" she hedges, urging me to go on, watching intently.

"We met in college and dated for two years. I didn't stay and didn't finish. That's one of my biggest regrets."

"Not staying with Jack or not finishing school?"

"Both."

Lana is quiet for a few seconds, doing the mental math in her head. I can see it in her eyes, the calculating ticking of the time continuum, subtracting what she guesses my age to be, back seven years.

She and I both know there's more to the story than I'm letting on.

"Why didn't you finish?"

The moment of truth.

I can either lie to her face and wind up looking like a fool when Jack announces to the public that he has a child—a first grader—or I can tell her now the reason I didn't finish my degree and graduate.

"I got pregnant." I pause. "I wasn't in a space at the time when I was tough enough to stick it out and see it through. I wasn't strong enough to stay on campus while I was pregnant and go to my classes with a baby bump. So I dropped out."

Lana nods, speaking slowly. "I remember what girls were like back then, especially if you were dating an athlete. Cruel from jealousy. You must have known then that he was going to the pros."

"Yes, we knew. Or we'd definitely been talking about it. He had gotten himself an agent, and it all went so fast." My hands make a globe over my belly, pantomiming pregnant. "And then..."

She makes a humming sound. "I probably would have done the same thing."

"Anyway, to answer the rest of your question, Jack and I

reconnected almost three weeks ago, so our reunion wasn't that long ago. We're still getting to know each other again."

"But you still had the spark?"

I smile. "We still had the spark."

Lana shifts in her seat, edging closer, encroaching on my space as if we've been friends for years, and she wants to share a confidence. "Can I ask you something personal?"

"Sure." I don't sound sure. I sound scared. *Ha!*

"Does Jack know?"

"That I got pregnant?"

She nods. "Yes."

"Yes, he knows."

"Is he...?" Lana sits back upright. "I mean, I saw your daughter, and there was no mistaking the resemblance. Robb wouldn't shut up about it once he got home that night. He said, 'Lana,'" Lana deepens her voice. "*Lana, did you see that kid? Jack's got himself a fuckin' daughter.*"

"Oh god." I facepalm myself, feeling my face get flush. "Yeah, he has himself a daughter."

"Holy shit. Does anyone know?" She scoffs. "I mean, of course no one knows, or it would be all over the news. Damn girl, buckle up because the ride is about to get real bumpy." She covers her mouth with her hand. "I'm sorry, I shouldn't have said that. Yes, it's going to suck, probably for a solid week, but then some other news will come along, and the worst will be over, along with the prying eyes and the requests for interviews." She pauses. "And they'll follow you, of course. Probably show up at your daughter's school to try to get photos. It'll be a real circus. I fucking hate the press."

She pats me on the hand. "Jack and Elias will take care of it. Once Jack is ready to share the news, there will be a whole media plan. I wouldn't worry, but I would try to prepare."

"Have you ever had to deal with anything like that?"

Lana laughs so loud that a few people around us turn to stare. "Are you kidding me? Oh, god. Three years ago, right after Peaches was born, there were rumors that Robb stepped out on me."

"Stepped out on you?"

"Cheated." She plucks at some pilling on her Colorado sweater. "It wasn't true, but that didn't stop the media frenzy. Those bastards camped out outside the house, called my phone, showed up at the grocery store—so thirsty for a story it almost destroyed us. That sometimes happens, especially when they travel and we're not with them. Groupies try to sink their claws into our men. It's disgusting, but if a man wants to stray—" She points at the football field. "There's the door. I hope she gives better oral than I do, fucker."

Whoa, the mouth on Lana.

"All I'm saying is, she better be worth it, and most of the time, they're not. And trust me, we've seen it all." She motions to the group of women sitting around us. "Some of these women have gone through some really hard times. That's why we have to stick together, and why we're so leery of new women entering the circle. We're a family."

It makes sense.

And fills me with hope.

"Jack is older and wiser. He's no rookie, so his head won't be turned by giant boobs and silicone lips." Lana purses hers. "If he even went through that phase, it was probably years ago."

The thought of him going through a phase where he slept around with random women suddenly fills me with jealousy. It had never crossed my mind; I've always been consumed with my own issues and my own problems to have considered he had a life after I left.

Maybe he drowned his misery in alcohol. Maybe he slept with half the female population at school.

Maybe he, maybe he, *maybe he*...

All the possibilities swirl through my head. Lana sips on her beer, oblivious to everything weighing on my mind. She has no way of knowing that Jack only found out three weeks ago he was a father. No way of knowing I lied to him for seven years. No way of knowing how remarkable he has been or how forgiving when I undoubtably do not deserve it.

Back at the hotel, I tell Jack about the conversation when he sits at the foot of the bed, removing his shoes and pulling me over to sit on his lap.

I wrap my arms around his neck, wanting him to see that I'm at ease with him. I want to find that flirty, youthful side of myself again that I might have lost while busying myself with becoming a mother.

I did myself no favors by not dating when Skipper was growing up. But I suppose the universe had a plan for me, and that plan was to wait for Jack Jennings to reappear.

And he did.

"Lana Macenroy, hey?" Jack rubs my back. "I like her. She's funny."

I play with his hair. It's damp from the shower he obviously took at the stadium before returning to the hotel. "She doesn't seem too worried about the media. She thinks it'll be a solid week of being stalked, but at that point, the excitement will fizzle out, and the press will move on to something more exciting."

"Something more exciting than us?" He gasps. "What could possibly be more exciting than us?"

"I don't know. What's more exciting than ponies and brownies made by a seven-year-old that sometimes contain glitter—and not the edible kind?"

Jack laughs at that. "Sounds pretty damn good to me. The perfect life, actually."

"There is no such thing as the perfect life." I find myself stating the obvious, despite not wanting to be a downer.

"There may not be a perfect textbook life, but I have an ideal life in mind—a goal for myself and my future family that I would say I'm damn near close to getting." He's still rubbing my back, running a large palm up and down my spine; it's soothing and reassuring and feels amazing. "Did you talk to anyone else today?"

He changes the subject away from us, and I let him.

"There were a few people who introduced themselves once the game was over. A fiancée named Portia—she was nice but was totally checking me out. I don't think I was fancy enough for her, but she was pleasant enough. And a Beth Cartwright? She had her son along. A few of them were going to Disney tomorrow or visiting friends and family."

"Yeah, they do that sometimes, depending on where we're at. It's a good way to multitask. We spend more time together in the off-season, though because it's easier. And we're all so fucking tired, so no one wants to play host unless it's summer and we can shoot the shit and lay around." He pauses. "But I have a condo and no one fits in it."

"No one fits in it?"

"Just me and Kevin. I'll need a house now if I'm going to have Skipper running around."

A house.

A yard.

Jack lets his body fall to the bed, pulling me along with him, rolling so I'm beneath him, our legs still hanging over the side of the mattress.

He shifts us so we're in the middle of the mattress, adjusting himself to hover above me. "I'm glad you're here this weekend. I always feel like I'm...missing something."

Missing something.

He sounds so serious as he continues. "I was excited to get back, knowing you would be here waiting for me."

I swallow the lump in my throat. "Lana had invited us to Disney with them today, but I told her we'd be busy."

"Busy? Doing what?" He's cupping my cheek, fingers straying down my neck, causing me to shiver as they fiddle with the string on my team logo'd hoodie. I bought it at the game during halftime because I'd gone wearing a button-down plaid shirt and felt conspicuous and boring—especially compared to Lana and Portia and Beth and all the other wives and girlfriends who were decked out in team apparel.

It cost me sixty freaking dollars.

"Busy doing...*this,* I guess."

Jack lowers his head to kiss me, warm lips pressed against my mouth, working their magic and wreaking havoc on my body. I trail my hand over his back up to the nape of his neck, threading my fingers through his hair.

It feels amazing with him on top of me, kissing me.

His hand lowers, down over the thick fabric of my hooded sweatshirt, down to the hem—then beneath it, his fingers skimming their way up my stomach. His thumb caresses the swell of my breast over my bra.

"What did you think of my playing today?"

His playing?

Um.

Is it bad to admit that I hadn't paid much attention because Lana talked my ear off, filling me with information and gossip? Will he be offended if I say it out loud?

He leans in and kisses my neck. "Hmm? Did you see me knock that pass down on the line of scrimmage during the second quarter?"

Er, no. "Is that what that was? I'm still learning."

Judging by the coy grin on his face, he knows I didn't watch the game.

"Did you see anything at all during the game?"

"Of course I did! Pfft, it was very exciting."

His palms skim my rib cage. "What was the score?"

Dammit! Is he being serious? "Why are you asking me such hard questions?"

"That's the easiest question I could have possibly asked you."

"Ask me another one."

Jack considers it, then says, "What color is my uniform?"

I laugh. "Bright green and white."

"What's on the side of the helmet?"

I have to think about that one for a few seconds. "Silver...horns?"

His fingers trail along the cup of my bra. "How confident are you?"

"Pretty confident."

"Confident enough to place a bet?"

I nod enthusiastically. "Yes."

"Okay. If you're wrong, you have to take this hoodie off."

Oh—so he wants me to strip, does he? "And if I'm right, you have to take everything off."

His face falls. "Damn. Now I wish I was going to lose."

Jack pulls his phone out of his back pocket and googles, speaking out loud as he types. "What is on the helmet of the Colorado Mountaineers." He holds the screen toward me.

Silver mountains grace the side of the green helmets.

"Dammit!" I laugh, giving him a push so I have the room to remove my hoodie, pulling it up and over my head and tossing it to the ground, lying there in just my bra. "Happy now?"

"Very." He lowers his head again, kissing the globes of my breasts, finger hooking the bra and tugging it to the side so he can kiss my nipple and suck on it.

I squirm on the bed, plunging my fingers into his hair. "Don't start anything you're not going to finish."

He lifts his head. "Who says I'm not going to finish it? This is our last night, and I probably won't see you for a week, so we're going to make it count."

A whole week.

I've gotten used to his presence by now—him popping up on a semi-regular basis, taking me out or spending time with Skipper and me—that the thought of not seeing him for an entire week makes me...sad.

Sad. Is that right?

How can I be sad when he has his mouth on my tits and hand slowly creeping into my pants, fiddling with the button on my jeans?

"If you want me to get naked, you have to get naked—or at least take something off first so it's even."

"Done."

Jack doesn't even sit up to remove his shirt, peeling it up and over his broad shoulders as if his life depended on it.

Our lives.

I'm grateful that it's not pitch black in here and that it

hasn't gotten dark outside because I want to see his body. And I want him to see mine. I feel sexy not just because he's attracted to me but because I've had a baby—his baby—and he's excited about it, and he wants to make things work. Jack wants to try again, and that is incredibly sexy.

Effort is incredibly sexy to begin with.

We are both still wearing bottoms, the jeans I had on for the game are unbuttoned yet remaining, and Jack is wearing athletic pants. My fingers go to the drawstring waistband, and I untie them, sliding my hand inside and over the thin cotton fabric of his boxer briefs. They feel like compression shorts, hugging his ass and thighs—I wouldn't hate it if he got up and stretched it around the room to give me a better view.

I want to get him out of these pants.

I push them down at the waist, hoping he'll assist me in getting them down around his hips. Undressing someone while lying down isn't the easiest task, and help is always appreciated. Together, we work them down over his legs until he's kicking them off and onto the floor.

"Well, well, well," I say. "Isn't this a pleasant turn of events?" Seems that it's always the woman who gets naked first, and I appreciate the fact that I can admire him before taking my own pants off and getting naked. I feel like I deserve it for waiting seven years.

I give him a nudge so he's lying on his back the same way I had just been and hover over him. When I lean forward, my hair dusts his chest before I close in and kiss the valley between his pec muscles. I give his nipples a lick —those are my favorite part of a man's chest, odd enough.

I don't actually have a plan but I find myself moving down his body, kissing my way down his sternum, belly, to his belly button. He has the most glorious happy trail that disappears into the waistband of his boxer briefs, and I want to discover where it leads.

I see his intake of breath when he clenches his stomach; it's a move that fills me with boldness. It's one that tells me I'm in control now.

I feel powerful and sexy, propelled to pull at the elastic band and stretch it, pull it down, down, his hard dick finally peeking out. I swear it's bigger than I remember it, or maybe I'm just so horny and filled with lust that I'm not thinking clearly.

Dicks aren't pretty, but I'm convinced this one is.

My mouth waters. I swear it does.

What is your problem, Penelope? Dicks are not cute, so stop staring at this one.

But it is.

It's hard and perfect, and when I touch my lips to the tip, Jack and I both groan out loud, his louder than mine, but still.

We groan, his hands finding my long hair and burying themselves inside, fingers gathering up piles into a ponytail.

I literally haven't given a man a blow job since Jack; in fact, he is the first and last man who's dick I've ever sucked, the few people I've dated in the interim either weren't into it or did not care about receiving oral.

I would be lying if I said I wasn't worried I'm doing it wrong or that I feel rusty because I've been out of practice for so long. Still, I feel like it's somewhat instinctual, and enthusiasm counts, so I lower my head until he's inside my throat. Sucking, I decide to have fun with it.

Fun?

Not something I normally associate with a blow job, but here we are.

I visualize the pornos I've watched in the past; the technique the women used, the way they bobbed their heads, the spot they put their hands. I remember reading something in a magazine once about paying attention to the balls and not neglecting them, so I move a hand from his shaft and place it beneath him.

Jack groans again. One arm was now thrown over his eyes, the other still in my hair holding it back.

I suck. Move my hands up and down.

Honestly, it's wet and messy, and I gag a few times—not that he's bothered by the fact. It seems to make it hotter. Sexier. *Watch me gag later when I brush my teeth, ugh, like that wouldn't be embarrassing.*

Jack is not fazed by any of this. In fact, he seems to like it.

"I don't want to come in your mouth," he finally groans, giving my shoulders a tug the same way I had when he'd been going down on me.

"Why? I want you to."

"I don't want to come in your mouth, or on your face, or in my own hand. I want to come inside you."

Oh.

Oh...

"Get on top, Penelope."

Should I?

Can I?

It's been so long. What if I forget what I'm doing, and instead of moaning or shouting his name, I start...*barking?*

Ha!

Still on the bed with my jeans on, I have those to remove before we can think about getting busy, our excitement and urgency making the whole thing that much more fervent.

I lift my head, wiping the drool from my mouth,

glancing down one last time at Jack's gorgeous, thick cock, and go to work unbuttoning my pants so we can get them onto the floor along with all the other discarded clothes.

Not in the mood for any more foreplay, I climb on top of Jack, our bodies pressed together, my boobs squished against his chest. I love the way it feels, him under me. Me looking down into his face, kissing his lips whenever I want, however I want.

His hands go up and down my back while his cock is nuzzled comfortably between my thighs.

I bring my face down, laying soft kisses on the corner of his mouth.

Once.

Again.

Open-mouthed. A little tongue.

Gentle, flirting. Exploring.

Not a frenzied make-out session but romantic, quiet kisses.

It's gotten darker in the time I was blowing him, dimmer in the room than it was earlier, and I can see less of his face.

We're becoming shadows in the dark.

"God, I want to be inside you so bad," Jack was saying, his voice cracking a bit. It was the first time we were having sex after dating for a few weeks. He had wanted to wait—I had not. I wanted to feel close to him and didn't feel the need to put off what our bodies wanted, but he had way more self-control than I did.

"Just wait a second," I told him, liking the feel of the tip at my entrance, wanting to prolong him burying deep inside me. I knew that once he entered me, I would be done for. I knew we wouldn't be able to control the temp once we started.

"Jesus, I'm going to explode."

"You'll live."

"I feel like I've been waiting forever," he says, and I remind him that he's the one who wanted to wait. That I was the one who wanted to have sex after our third date. He's the one who wanted it to be special.

I shift above him, lining him up, dry fucking him until he moans.

"Do you like that? Does it feel good?"

He nods, lips parting.

Good.

Something is powerful about making a man like this lose a little bit of control. Always has, but it's this man and this man only whose face I want to see like this; eyes glassing over, nostrils flaring, hands and fingers digging into my hips.

This big, strong, strapping professional footballer is under me, waiting for me to slide on top of him and sink him deep inside. *For the love of god, Penelope, fuck me already.*

He hasn't said it yet, but I can see it in his eyes and feel the tension in his shoulders when I kiss his collarbone.

The tip of his hard dick rests right between the folds of my pussy, and it's making me just as wild as it's making him, probably even more so. But if there's one thing I've learned, it's to savor the moment, and I want to remember this one for a long time.

I kiss him again.

And again.

Move my body up then back, up and back, easing it in, centimeter by centimeter, excruciatingly slow.

I'm so wet.

He is so hard.

I'm so hot for him I can barely stand it myself.

Self-control can kiss my ass.

I swear on the heavens above I see stars when Jack is inside me, all the way in. I sit up, wanting his hands on my breasts, leading them there before leaning back a bit, savoring the sight of myself riding him.

I'm no longer *just a mom*. I'm a sexy, bad-ass woman.

"God, you're sexy," Jack mutters, playing with my boobs, thumbs stroking my nipples. His hands roam everywhere—my rib cage, boobs, waist, everywhere.

I lower myself, kissing his neck, inhaling how incredible he smells, settling my mouth there as I rock back and forth. The pressure is intense, the feeling...

Intoxicating.

Jack's arms hug me, his moaning getting loud. He was already worked up from the blowie, so there's no doubt he's at the brink of coming. I'm almost there, too.

So close...

So, so close...

I come first, and after I do, Jack lifts me off, tosses me onto the mattress, and comes on my stomach, breathing hard and sweating, beads of perspiration from our five-minute screwing session on his forehead.

He collapses beside me. "Sorry about that, but we didn't use protection." He breathes in and breathes out. "I'll get you a rag."

"Wait. Stay for a second." I don't want the heat of his body leaving me just yet. I felt it when he pulled out and hadn't wanted to lose the contact.

I kiss his shoulder, then he kisses mine.

Jack eventually rolls off the bed and pads to the bathroom, returning with a wet rag to wash my stomach, and we both change into our pajamas after that and get ready to sleep.

Tomorrow morning will come soon enough, and so will the reality of our real lives.

When we drift off to sleep, my head is on Jack's chest, and all is right with the world except for two things:

1. Skipper isn't with us, and
2. She still doesn't know Jack is her dad.

Chapter 17

Jack

I've gone over and over and over with Elias about something romantic I can do for Penelope after our date this weekend as a token of my appreciation that she flew out to spend time with me.

Took a day off.

Had to find a sitter for Skipper, albeit her brother.

Elias, who is not much of a romantic and is more of a playboy, had a few useful things but nothing I wanted to actually do. First, he suggested I send her flowers and a balloon bouquet—too basic. He then suggested I send those flowers to her job, which I didn't think her boss would appreciate barring she wasn't thrilled Penn took a personal day.

"What does she like, dude? Send her a gift card."

"I'm not sending her a gift card. That defeats the purpose of sending her a gift."

"How? A gift card is literally a gift. It's called a *gift* card."

I massage my temples with my thumb and forefinger. "Please stop saying the word gift. You're not being helpful."

I don't just want to show my appreciation. I want it to be romantic. And thoughtful. And brighten her entire freaking day.

"Sexy lingerie is out of the question?"

"This is why you don't have a girlfriend. Your ideas suck."

"That idea does not suck; maybe this is the reason you don't have a girlfriend, did you ever think of that? You've spent the past seven years pining for this woman, and now you're going to send her a sweater."

"I never said anything about a sweater, asshole. All I said was I wasn't going to send her lingerie." There's a time and a place for everything, dude; time and a place.

Elias sighs loudly over the phone. "Okay, well. Jerome Dupre just gave his wife a massive diamond band as a push present. You could do something like that."

"What the hell is a push present?"

"It's to thank her for having their baby, but I secretly think she picked them out herself and made him buy them for her so she could show them off to her friends." Elias blows his nose. "She's posted more about the ring than the actual baby."

"A diamond ring?"

"Yeah, it would blind you. I don't think it actually fits on her ring finger with her other ring. Have you seen the size of the middle stone?"

"Dude, what the fuck? No, I haven't seen the size of the middle stone. I barely know who she is." Why would I even care to look?

I can practically hear Elias shrugging. "Listen, as my clients, I'm obligated to follow all of y'all on social media on the off chance someone goes off the rails and posts something stupid, and I have to save you from yourselves." He blows his nose again. "Charlene is one of those people who may need to dial it down or their house is going to get robbed."

"Are you getting a cold?"

He sniffles. "Gee, what gave it away?"

"This is why women say men are pussies when they're sick. You're being so dramatic."

Elias grumbles. "Leave me alone."

"Is that any way to talk to your favorite client?"

He laughs. "Ha. I don't play favorites. You should know that."

"Yet another reason you don't have a girlfriend..."

"Bye, asshole. I'll talk to you later."

I laugh when he cuts the call loose, staring at my cell, googling gifts and going back to a jewelry website. Maybe Jerome Dupre is on to something. Maybe I should try to find something here.

There is a store not too far from her house; it's more than likely I'd be able to have it delivered today and not have to wait.

The famous aqua blue banner of the online store, with its shiny gold and silver objects, has me wondering if I would be able to choose something that wasn't over the top yet simple enough not to overwhelm Penelope.

I look through the necklaces, then the bracelets.

I waste a solid hour of time I'm supposed to have been at the gym scrolling and scrolling until I'm damn near cross-eyed.

Satisfied with what I come up with, I write the item number and description on a piece of paper before turning my attention to a gift for Skipper.

This gift will be easy.

Horses.

Specifically, rainbow horses and ponies, my only conundrum is choosing between the hundreds of items that pop up online and getting it there today.

I hate waiting.

When I make up my mind about something, I want it, and I want it now, and I want those gifts hand-delivered before dinner time today.

I shoot Elias a text.

Me: *Can you get in touch with Maggie? I need her to find a concierge in the area who can shop and deliver. Today.*

Elias: *Sure thing, boss.*

Seven years ago, when I was a rookie and just starting out, I wouldn't dream of contacting my agent about running my errands or buying gifts, but I've come a long way since then.

Maggie is Elias's assistant, and every so often, I lean on her for things like this because I don't have an assistant of my own like a lot of my teammates do. Or their wives.

Their assistants have assistants. Their nannies have assistants.

I wouldn't be surprised if some of these dudes hired someone to wipe their asses for them in the off-season.

I am not that guy. But I do occasionally need a hand executing the impossible, and today? It's jewelry and ponies.

Sweat beads down my spine, soaking my tee shirt as I walk into my condo, flipping the light on and tossing my keys onto the kitchen countertop.

It's dark outside, and both Kevin and my stomach let me know I've been gone far too long, both of them rumbling.

Food goes into Kevin's steel bowl; food comes out of the fridge for me to eat.

There isn't much; I've been traveling way too much, but I manage to scrounge up leftover pizza, leftover poke bowl, and a salmon filet I had Friday night before flying to California.

It should still be good, yeah?

I don't bother sniffing it. My plan is to throw it all onto one plate, nuke it until it's lava hot, then eat it as fast as I can and avoid having it touch my taste buds.

Kevin and I both eat our dinner and I fiddle around with my phone, staring at the last few text messages from Penelope. Her gifts were delivered earlier; I got confirmation from Maggie that they were dropped off at the house around four thirty and Penelope was indeed there to accept the packages.

Everything was gift wrapped.

According to Maggie, Penelope was as sweet as pie, both of my little ladies at home when the delivery woman stopped by, Skipper having done a happy jig on the front stoop when the delivery person had handed her a bag with her name on it. It wasn't her birthday, why was she getting a present?!

I shovel a forkful of rice into my mouth as my phone rings—that weird ring that lets you know it's not a regular phone call but a video call, and when I look down at it vibrating on my counter, I see Penelope's face lighting up the screen.

Quickly I wipe my hands before hitting accept.

"Hey there!"

Her face fills the screen, smile beaming back at me. She holds up a bag; it's not large but it's that famous blue color with a large silky bow tying it closed.

"Jack Jennings, what is the meaning of this?"

"It's a present. Nothing big." I shrug it off, embarrassed. Shit, was the gift too much? Wait. "Have you even opened it yet? How can you yell at me when you don't even know what's inside?"

"I—"

"Are you talking to Jack, Mom? I want to see! Mom, I wanna talk to him!" I can hear her hopping up and down next to her mother, and the next thing I see is her cute little face, hair and head covered by a Rainbow Pony mane, hands stuffed into plush hooves.

"Wow, look at you!"

Skipper neighs like a horse. "This is the best costume I've ever had! Thank you, Jack, thank you!"

"Yeah—thank you," Penelope deadpans. "You only have yourself to blame when she wears it in public and sounds like a horse instead of a little girl."

I'll live for that moment. "Can't wait. I hope I get to see it in person soon. She looks amazing."

Our daughter seems to have lost interest in our phone call already, galloping into the living room, going around in circles on the carpet, hooves poised in the air, round and around she goes.

Neighing, obviously.

"She was so excited to get a present she couldn't wait to open it."

"But you could?"

"I wanted to prolong the anticipation and draw it out." She smiles shyly. "Not to make it weird, but I don't get presents very often, so I wanted to make it last. And I wanted you to watch me open it, of course."

"Alright. I'm waiting on pins and needles. Open it up."

Penelope nods. She's seated in the kitchen at the

counter, bag resting in front of her still tied up neatly. The white bow is glossy under the overhead lights, and she takes each end between her fingers and gently tugs, loosening it. In an excruciatingly slow manner, she pulls it apart, letting it fall to the counter, then setting it off to the side.

Could she *be* going any slower?

This is torture.

Penelope pulls the bag open and peers inside before reaching in and taking hold of the small blue box nestled within. Her expression is one of excitement when she removes it, her mouth forming an O of surprise.

And delight.

It's a square box, tied with another pretty ribbon, the entire process repeating itself until the box top is ready to be removed, Penelope's hands shaking a bit from her eagerness.

Anyone else wouldn't notice, but I do.

I wish I were there with my arms wrapped around her, kissing her neck as she unwrapped it. Whispering in her ear as Skipper danced around the house dressed like a goofy little lavender pony.

Those two—they're my family.

A lump forms in my throat when I watch Penn lift the top of the box and set it off to the side. Then she plucks at the white satin filler and removes that.

She peers inside at the gold chain bracelet there.

On that bracelet is a charm; a baby shoe with a one karat diamond—Skipper's birthstone—dangling along with a gold football. One charm to represent me, one to represent our daughter, both representing the fact that I wasn't there when she gave birth and even if I had, I wouldn't have had the money to buy her a fat diamond band as a push present.

I had the money to buy her one now, but chances are, she wouldn't have wanted one. That is not Penelope's style.

Sure, this may be too sentimental of a gift, but I want her to have something that reminds her of me, but also lets her know I would have been supportive seven years ago, and I would have been happy, and I would have held her hand through the entire thing.

Shit.

I don't have a tear in my eye. I don't.

Kevin stares up at me from the floor as Penelope holds the bracelet up in front of the camera, inspecting it, turning it this way and that so it catches the light.

The stones sparkle and shine—simple but flashy, if that's even a way to describe it.

"Jack, I don't know what to say." She certainly looks as emotional as I feel.

It's just a bracelet, and it wasn't that expensive. At least, not to me, based on what I earn.

In my mind, it's all relative.

"I wish I was there so I could put it on you."

Her head gives a little shake as she sets about undoing the clasp and putting it on. "Funny enough, I've learned some tricks to putting on my own jewelry over the past few years—not that I *have* a lot of jewelry, but you know what I mean."

I catch another glimpse of Skipper in the background, dancing around the living room in front of the television, still duded up in her new costume.

She's so stinking cute.

My heart squeezes watching her hop around, so excited and...loud, and I feel like an asshole that I'm not there with them both.

Yeah, yeah—it's not my fault, I get that.

But that doesn't make it feel any better.

"What do you have going on this week?"

It's Tuesday, and the only thing I have going on is practice now that the Sunday football game is out of the way and I'm days away from the next one. Just conditioning and practice and a few meetings—same shit, different day.

Penelope sets the phone back on the counter and leans in, bracelet already shining on her wrist. "Well, let's see. This Thursday Skipper has a Fall Concert at school."

Say what now? "A Fall Concert? What's that?"

She shrugs. "You know—it's singing, mostly. They do one in spring, one in fall, and one at the holidays. It's a total racket and lasts way too long, but I'll tell you—that child really gets into it. If she doesn't beg me to wear that horse to sing in, I will be shocked."

"Are you going to let her?"

Penelope laughs. "No! Absolutely not. It would be so disruptive. Besides, she picked out a dress when we were at Costco a few weeks ago, so she can wear that."

"It's Thursday?"

She nods.

"I could do Thursday." I'm nodding too, already planning in my head, buying an airline ticket, renting a car, getting to the school on time.

Yeah—I can swing it. Make it work.

"You do not have to come on Thursday for an hour-long concert." She pauses. "Okay, it's more like two hours. The point is, you do not have to fly here to watch a kid's concert."

"My kid's concert," I correct her. "And I know I don't have to but also, yes, I do. Besides, I want to, so—this isn't actually a discussion because I've already made up my mind."

Penelope seems to weigh her arguments; whatever reason she was about to come back with gets swallowed.

"Just to be clear, this is a rinky-dink children's concert; half of the kids are too embarrassed to sing, the other half stand there giggling and laughing. The rest stare off into the crowd of parents and wave."

"Sounds like my kind of concert."

"I just don't want you coming here and being disappointed or annoyed. I want you to manage your expectations."

"Penelope, I'm well aware that this is a children's concert where there will be children singing. I've sung in a few of them myself back in the day. I'm not expecting Billie Eilish or The Weeknd to come busting out on stage. I know this isn't a halftime show at the Super Bowl."

Her shoulders rise and fall. "Okay, I'm just letting you know..."

"Penn." I take a deep breath. "Don't feel guilty that I'm willing to fly in to watch a two-hour concert. This is what airplanes are for."

She laughs. "Spoken like someone who can jet-set around without overthinking it."

Ha. "I bust my ass and have ruined my body, and they pay me a shit ton of money for it. I had nothing to spend it on; no wife, no family, no house. And now I do—Skipper. And you. So if you're worried I'm wasting money, don't. It is a non-issue."

Her mouth is in a straight line. "Alright, I won't worry about it then."

Briefly, I wonder about the stir it's going to cause when I show up at school. How many parents will hound me for autographs or whisper during the concert? Then again, her brother is a retired professional baller, and I assume he's been present for most of the performances, knowing what I know about him.

Davis Halbrook is a stand-up dude.

"Hey, Skipper, come here for a second," Penelope calls over her shoulder to our daughter, who I can see running over, carrying a stuffed pony while dressed like one. Her little, sparkly purple and rainbow mane flaps as she runs.

"What?" She can't stand still, curious to look at the man in the phone and know what the conversation is about.

"Jack is coming to your concert on Thursday. What do you think of that?"

"I knew he was!" she shouts with a laugh.

"How did you know? I just told him about it."

"'Cause I knew he would come. Jack is my friend. We have a secret handshake." She winks at me through the phone. "Can you come over so we can practice?"

"I can't, buddy. I'm in Colorado. It's too far."

Her face falls. "But you'll be here on Thursday, and we can practice then."

"Yup."

"Cool!" She skips off again, Penelope calling after her. "Don't get too comfortable. We have to get you in the bathtub soon—then it's bedtime."

Bedtime.

Sounds good to me, too.

"Check in with me later, okay? Send me the school's address and the time the concert starts."

"I will," Penn says, fiddling with the charms on her wrist. "And thank you for the bracelet. It's beautiful."

Her praise embarrasses me, but I have no idea why. "You're welcome."

"Talk to you soon."

She makes a goofy kissy face at me before ending the call, and my heart tugs again, knowing I'm missing out on bath time, story time, and bedtime.

231

Chapter 18

Penelope

T wring my hands nervously, watching cars drive into the parking lot, wondering which one is Jack. Since he has a rental, it's hard to tell which one is him as car after car passes by despite it being the middle of the day.

Skipper is already inside with her class, while Davis and Juliet are saving Jack and me seats inside. I hadn't wanted him to walk in and not know where to go, so here I am, waiting by the curb for his car to arrive.

A black sedan pulls up, and the window rolls down. "Going my way, sweetheart?"

It's Jack, and he's grinning ear to ear, sunglasses perched on his nose, looking as handsome and sexy as ever, especially behind the wheel of a slick, black sedan.

"I'll wait here while you park."

"Or you can hop in, and we can make out before we go inside."

I hesitate, wanting to. *Live a little, Penelope, stop over-thinking it. Get in the car and let him flirt with you a few seconds before we're inside surrounded by people.*

I pop open the passenger door and climb inside, and

when I do, Jack immediately leans over to my side and kisses me on the lips, lingering a bit too long, considering cars are waiting behind him to pull into the parking lot.

I blush down to my toes, fixing my hair in the overhead mirror as he slowly creeps around the lot, looking for a space to park. He finds one at the back of the lot, near the playground and overlooking the little concession stand they have by the adjacent soccer field.

He puts the car into park and looks over, hand already on the back of my seat. "Come here."

I lean in so he has easy access to my lips, opening my mouth, missing him bad.

It's been a few days, but it felt like an eternity, and I wonder how I made it through those early days when I broke up with him and was still in love with him and pregnant with his child.

How had I done it? Where had I found the willpower because these last few days? Torture.

I hate it. Hate leaving him now and hate when he goes. There is so much to catch up on and make up for.

"You taste so good."

"I had a cookie." I say it dumbly, because I had eaten a cookie. One from the little bake sale they have set up inside, a fundraiser for the school's extracurricular program.

"Yummy." He leans in again, but this time, I laugh and reach for the door handle. "We don't have time to sit in this car making out like teenagers. Davis will take one good look at me and know we were up to no good!"

"We have a daughter. He already knows we were up to no good."

"Seven years ago." I move for the door again, but he pulls me back. Again.

"Which means we have a lot of catching up to do. And I

have a plane to catch at the ass crack of dawn, so this is the only time we're going to have alone."

"You're leaving tonight?"

"Yeah—I have a meeting in the morning with my agent about some endorsement deals. It was at ten, but I pushed it back to noon so I wouldn't look like I had a hangover."

"You're only here...what. Five hours?" I'm horrible at math and don't try to figure out the numbers, but five hours sounds about right.

"Landed an hour ago, fucked around at the rental car place, concert, fly out at..." He checks the watch on his wrist. I'm almost positive it's a Rolex, one of those watches that cost thousands of dollars and not an Apple Watch like so many people wear these days.

I have neither.

"Four thirty." We both pull faces.

Kiss again. "There's something I want to talk to you about. And I wanted to do it when we had more time and weren't rushed, but I can't wait anymore, Penn. It's driving me nuts."

"Oh god, this doesn't sound good."

He has one of my hands in his and kisses the knuckles. "It is or it isn't, depending on how you look at it."

The phone in my back pocket pings, and it can only be one person: my brother, checking to see where I'm at, probably wondering if I've been abducted or stolen.

I try to pull away, nervous, not wanting to hear whatever it is he has to say because it scares me.

"Penn. Wait. I'm serious."

I relax back into the seat. "Jack, just say it."

Tell me it's over.

Tell me you're taking me to court.

Tell me you want fifty fifty custody.

Tell me...

"I want you to consider moving in with me." He inhales a deep breath. "I know it's a huge ask and something you obviously have to put some serious thought into, but I want to be with you. At least for the season, I have so many months left, and it's only going to get worse as we get closer to the playoffs and the Super Bowl."

He wants me to move in with him. "Me?"

Jack laughs. "You and Skipper, silly." He boops me on the tip of the nose but I can see that he's as nervous now as I am.

"You want me to move?"

He nods solemnly. "Well, for at least half the year. I don't know how you feel going back and forth, but Skipper is still young she might see it as more of an adventure than we do."

Move. He wants me—us—to move in with him. To Colorado.

That's hundreds of miles away!

"Can you tell me you haven't thought about it?"

Have I? I'm not sure it's crossed my mind, too busy was I considering the other logistics; him flying back and forth, only seeing him a few times a month, how it might be impossible to continue this way.

Move in with him.

I mean—what will Davis say?

Does it even matter what my brother thinks?

Of course it does, I include him in all my decisions and this certainly affects him..

But who is most important here? You, Jack, and Skipper? Or your brother and his opinion of the situation?

"Shut your brain off for a second," Jack tells me, staring hard. "Relax."

I can't relax. The words are out there and they're going to be on my mind until I make a decision.

How long have we been sitting in this car talking? Five minutes? Fifteen?

Twenty?

Shit!

"Let's go!" I urge, desperate to get out of the car and into the fresh air. "The concert starts in fifteen minutes."

As we're walking across the parking lot, Jack takes my hand; holds the door open for me when we reach it, puts his hand on the small of my back as we walk into the auditorium and find our seats.

My brother is taller than most men; Jack is too, so he's easy to locate toward the middle row, even easier because his hawk eyes seek me out. His hand goes in the air to wave when we make eye contact.

His fingers do the 'over here' motion.

Once we're seated and Jack make pleasantries with Davis and Juliet, telling them hello, asking how they've been, we settle into our seats to the quiet voices of the people around us. The hushed whispers, the speculation.

"Is that Jack Jennings?"

"No, it can't be." Pause. "Sure looks like him though."

I stare straight ahead, dying to look behind me to see who's talking—maybe they'll stop.

It's worse than the movies and these are grown-ups!

He wants me to move in with him. Move!

To Colorado.

"Babe, here they come." Jack takes my hand again and squeezes my fingers as the risers on stage begin filling with students, the little ones, starting with kindergarten.

They really truly are so damn adorable.

They sing three songs, pantomiming along to the lyrics

—quite horribly, I might add—waving to their parents, guardians, family from their place on the state. One little boy has his hands up his shirt and appears to be itching his belly; another is waving to someone in the crowd.

There's a little girl with her face buried in her hands, making me wonder why we put everyone through these programs.

Kindergarten out. First grade in.

Jack sits up straighter in his seat, neck craning for a visual on Skipper as she marches proudly onto the stage, lavender dress swinging to and fro, her dark hair in two French braids that hang down her back. White socks up to her knees. White dress shoes.

It's an outfit better suited for an Easter brunch or a summer wedding, but this is the outfit she chose and nothing was going to change her mind. She knew Jack was coming today and dressed to impress.

Her little beady eyes do nothing but scan the crowd for a peek at him.

Skipper shields her eyes as she looks for us, blocking the spotlight glare.

Jack stands and waves, not caring one iota that he is blocking the view of everyone behind us, apologizing as he sits down, "Sorry." He waves at a few people in the back rows. "Sorry, that's my daughter up there."

More whispers, this time more fervent.

The couple in front of us turn in their seats at the man who had the audacity to stand up to get his daughter's attention, the man putting his hand on his wife's arm just as she's about to say something nasty to Jack.

I catch his eye and give him an apologetic smile, but I think it's cute that Jack is so excited and enthusiastic; he's not been to one of these events before. He's never had a daughter before, this is all new and he deserves to hop out of his chair to wave.

Dammit!

Let the man live his best life!

Skipper sees her dad, waving back enthusiastically, bouncing on the heels, ready for action. She's being silly, showing up and singing loud, has the four of us cracking up at one point.

Jack continues to hold my hand. He also continues to wave, surreptitiously sneaking them in now and again, no shame. *Dang he's enjoying this.*

The little stinker up on stage does the same. She thinks she's being sneaky, but she's up in front of an audience where anyone and everyone can see her.

When it's over, there won't be an opportunity for Jack to say hello, goodbye, or to hug her—she'll go back to class, and I'll go back to work, and he'll head to the airport, and this will be a blip on our radar of memories that pass in the blink of an eye.

The lobby is a crush, some people noticing Jack's presence and ignoring it, others pointing, others saying hello and shaking his hand—mostly men, of course.

The principal comes over and greets us and for the first time, Jack introduces himself as Harper Halbrook's dad.

Harper Halbrook's dad.

He sounds so proud, the words leaving his mouth with zero hesitation.

We haven't told her yet, and my mind shifts to Mom Mode, worried that the principal will tell her he met her dad. Or one of her classmates will ask if Jack Jennings is her dad and confuse her.

She's smart; I wouldn't put it past her to put two and

two together and confront me about it—after all, she's asked me several times before and she has Jack on the brain.

Considering Jack flew all this way to be here for two hours, we only have time for a hour or so before he has to get to the airport and return his rental, so he follows me home.

Parks in the driveway, hands at my hips when I punch in the keypad on the laundry room door, lips already at my neck. He lifts me then, picks me up and carries me upstairs to the bedroom, kicking off his shoes along the way.

Shirt comes off; mine and his.

I wouldn't call it frantic, but it's close—two people who know they're going to be parted but only just found one another after too many years. *It's sad and blissful both at the same time.*

I'd worn a cute dress today knowing I was going to see him; it's long sleeve and roughed with two sides down my hips. Probably too sexy for a school function but I have few opportunities to flirt with him and I'm taking each one I can get.

Jack doesn't fuss with the particulars; he pulls the darn things straight off me, lobbing it to the ground. Kneels at my feet to unbuckle my cute wedges.

When he stands I unbutton his polo shirt. Belt buckle.

Jeans.

Remove his sunglasses with a laugh. "Do these actually work as a disguise for you?"

"No. Nothing works as a disguise for me. I could wear a wig and people would still recognize me."

That sucks.

I would hate it.

Will hate it, I'm sure, once we go out into public together more often, which I know is inevitable. I have a lifetime ahead of me of being seen in public with him, as Skippers father.

It will be second nature to her once she gets used to it but I doubt I ever will.

"That dress was so fucking sexy." He's saying as he pulls his own shirt over his head.

"Then why'd you take it off so fast?"

"Because you're sexier without it, you goof."

I run my hands over his bare chest, loving the way his warm skin feels beneath my fingers, loving the smatter of hair there. It makes him look masculine and strong. Strapping.

The vee that disappears into his waistline draws my eye the same way his pleasure trail does, and I work his jeans down his hips so I can run my hands over that, too.

"I wish we had more time."

"I know, babe."

That's the second time he's called me babe today and it feels so...definite. Permanent.

Couple-y.

Our tongues entwine even as we fall to the bed, laughing the entire way down. I still have my bra and underwear on, Jack still in his pants which are mostly down around his knees. He kicks and until they're off as he lays on his back, then pulls me on top of him, hands immediately straying to my ass.

His boxers. My briefs.

Thin material doing nothing to prevent the sensation of his dick from making my lower half tingle when he nestles it between my legs.

I tingle harder when he moves the cotton fabric so his thumb can brush up and down my pussy, round and around in circles so I get wet.

News flash: I've been wet for him since the kiss in the car. Since he picked me up and carried me up here.

I'm a walking, talking, teenage hormone and Jack is a teenage dream.

God he's sexy.

I can barely stand it, having his hands on me, I want to self-combust.

Wanting to be under him, I roll off the top to the mattress and he follows, settling between my legs, arms braced on either side of my head.

Our tongues are wet.

Our patience is short.

Our underwear? *Off.*

"You're so fucking wet," he moans into my mouth as his cock slides back and forth over my slit, getting me wetter still.

I moan too, wanting him inside. Insatiable for him.

"I'm wet for you." *Just you.*

"Fuck babe, I love you underneath me."

"I want you inside me," I tell him, unabashed, wiggling, and somewhat desperate. The clock is ticking as we lay here. Every second we're not having sex is a second closer to him having to roll out of bed, get dressed, and leave.

"Then have me." My voice is brimming with emotion as Jack slides in slowly, adjusting himself until he's all the way in. I grab his hips, knees on either side of his hips as he thrusts and thrusts and thrusts, our lovemaking fast.

I wouldn't call it a quickie, but there is no slow burn to how fast his orgasm comes.

Mine? Not so much.

Jack pulls out, spilling himself on my stomach with an apology, breathing heavy as he lays his head on my chest.

My mind whirls. My lower lip juts out into a pout.

Rude! Only one of us gets to orgasm?

I don't think so, buddy....

As if he were reading my mind, Jack finally lifts his head. "Let me get a rag and clean you off."

He hops out of bed and brings a terry cloth towel from the sink, wiping the liquid off my lower belly before discarding it on the tile bathroom floor.

His eyebrow is raised when he looks at me. "Do you have a vibrator?"

Oh thank god he's asking.

I don't mean to be a brat, but I would have been pissed if he hadn't planned to make me come.

"I sure do." I point at the bedside table. "Second drawer down."

Jack climbs onto the bed and hangs over the other side, his gorgeous body stretching to open the drawer, all smooth muscles and firm curves. While he's rooting around in my sex toy drawer, I run a palm along his backside, stroking his ass and admiring it at the same time.

I'm still wet and still turned on.

So close was I to climaxing before he beat me to it and pulled out, the retrieval of the vibrator the only saving grace for him right now.

He fumbles with the power button until it comes to life.

I roll to my back, spreading my legs, bending my knees —my plan is to allow him to worship me and do all the work while I reap the benefits of the vibrator.

It's blue and one of my favorites; tried and true, it's a basic wand that has never let me down.

Well. Only when the battery dies mid-masturbation.

Hate that. We call that a fail.

But today I'm in luck because not only is the vibrator fully charged, Jack seems to know how to use it on me, finding the sweet spot between my legs and holding it there.

Lowering his head, he sucks on my nipple at the same time, and the sensations melt my entire body from the inside out.

God, it feels better than his dick did—and that's saying a lot because his dick feels incredible. Still, vibrators and other kinds of foreplay have their moments, and this is one of them.

I watch as he plays with me, the fire between my legs only intensifying, wanting to come but also: not wanting it to be over so soon since our initial screwing lasted, oh—about three minutes.

Jack licks.

Jack sucks.

Jack applies more pressure with the blue wand, moving it slightly to the left. Up. Down. More toward the middle of my clit, it's so incredibly sensitive and feels so incredibly amazing that I moan out loud.

I don't care how loud it is. I am going to have an orgasm, dammit! And if Jack Jennings moves that vibrator or stops using it, he is a dead man.

Everything is so sensitive.

So good.

So...so, "Ohhh..!"

Jack's mouth leaves my breasts so he can kiss me, the intoxicating way our tongues mingle sends me over the deep end, waves of pleasure shooting through my body as the orgasm hits me hard.

So, so sensitive.

So, so good.

I lie there afterward as he flops down next to me, lips on my shoulder.

I can feel him smile and I?
Smile too.

In the morning, I wake up alone, and my smile has faded into a frown.

Jack is so busy—this dashing back and forth between states and cities isn't sustainable—not in the long run. He's having fun now, and he loves seeing Skipper and spending time with us, but it's so much work.

And so much money.

A pit forms in my stomach as I roll over to grab my phone off the nightstand. I check the time and breathe out, staring up at the ceiling.

He's right. We can't keep doing this.

All the back and forth, there and back?

He can do it, but I cannot.

I have a job, would like to finish my degree so I can get ahead, and a daughter in school...I can't date someone that far away, no matter how flexible he's pretending to be, whenever he chooses.

He'll have the off-season, though. There's that...

Right, but the off-season is only four weeks.

Four.

Big whoop.

See, this. *This* right here is the reason I didn't want to be in a relationship with Jack when I knew he was going to be drafted into the NFL. The travel and the go-go-go and him moving from our home state to...wherever the team is that he signed with.

If you'd been in a relationship with him and stayed, you'd be with him in Colorado and not here, my rational self argues. *You wouldn't have to decide if you were going to move—you would already be living together. Maybe we'd even have more kids.*

Always rational.

Always worried.

I always play it safe.

I can't help it, that's part of who I am, and I won't apologize for it. But I'd be lying if I didn't say it hasn't bitten me in the ass more than a few times.

1. My pregnancy obviously being the big, glaring one.
2. A job offer I turned down because I didn't have a degree and therefore didn't think I had the qualifications - even though they offered it to me.
3. Dating a few nice, stable men because in the back of my mind, I was always hoping somehow, someday, Jack would return to my life.

Okay so that last one has nothing to do with playing it safe and everything to do with me being scared and being used to being alone.

Single, not ready to mingle.

A single mother who went to bed dreaming of a boy she left behind, wondering what he was like as a grown man.

And now I know.

And now I have to decide—again—what to do.

Chapter 19

Jack

My flight home is pensive; I can do nothing but think about the distance between Penelope, Skipper, and I, nor can I be the one to pack up and move across the country and resettle myself to spend more time with them.

I mean—I *could*. Plenty of guys do it who play football, baseball, or any other professional sport. In the off-season, so many of my buddies live in different states.

I wonder how Penelope would feel about that as an option?

I wonder how she would feel about being closer, *period*.

I want them to move in with me.

I want to have my family together.

Glancing over at the clock, I turn my head and my muscles throb. Today's meeting went longer than I'd hoped, a pitch for a sport drink company that wants to give me three million dollars per year to drink that shit in public for four years.

When my parents were still alive, my father always told me to 'Make hay while the sun still shines,' and that's what I intend to do. If I have to drink blue piss to ensure my future financial stability with a career that could end tomorrow, I'll drink blue piss.

Three million dollars.

I let out a whistle and grab my phone, settling on to the couch with Kevin, who's constantly irritated with all my traveling. Seriously, the dog has an attitude with me now, and I don't blame him for giving me the cold shoulder.

"Don't worry, pal, I'll find you a friend. I'm working on it."

A little girl friend who happens to be seven years old, if I have my way—but first, there's something I have to do.

Me: *Hey, pretty lady, what are you up to tonight?*

Penelope: *Just got done folding clothes. It was a long day. You?*

Me: *Do you have time for a video chat...?*

Penelope: *Mmm, my hands are full—can we just text so I can keep working? I have to start a bath soon and it might be easier.*

Huh.

She can't video chat while she's folding laundry?

A nervous knot forms in my stomach at her lame excuse; she clearly doesn't want to talk to me right now.

I mean, I get it—I dropped a bomb on her yesterday, she has a lot on her mind.

Me: *No worries, just thinking I'd love to see your pretty face. And Skipper's. What's she up to right now?*

Penelope: *She's actually with Davis and Juliet, they ran grocery shopping because Davis wanted chicken tonight and didn't have any—promised Skipper ice cream as a bribe for going along.*

Me: *She's not a fan of the grocery store?*

Penelope: *Not really, she thinks it's boring unless I let her ride inside the cart, which I hardly do because she's getting way too big and I have no room for food.*

Me: *Ha. I bet.*

I rack my brain, wanting to say more but not wanting to do it in a text.

Me: *Is everything good?*

Penelope: *Sure, everything is good. Why do you ask?*

Me: *I don't know...something feels "off."*

Penelope: LOL. *You can tell something feels off from a text?*

Me: *Sure. You're usually way more bubbly. And you usually want to video chat if I ask...*

Penelope: *Ah.*

Ah? What kind of an answer is that?

Me: *So what's going on? Are you thinking about what I said yesterday, is that it?*

Penelope: *Obviously I'm thinking about it. It's the only thing I CAN think about.*

Me: *What are your thoughts about it? If this is going to work, you have to open up to me, Penn.*

Penelope: *I know. That's the thing—I wish you were here so we could discuss it more in person.*

Me: *Does that mean you miss me?!*

Ha. I can get my flirt on during a serious conversation.

Penelope: *Of course I miss you. I miss you every day you're not here, which isn't very often.*

Me: *I know distance bothers you because it bothers me too. Which is why I think we should live together.*

Me: *Is the issue that you think...it's too SOON to live together?*

Penelope: *No, no—that's not it. I feel like even though*

I haven't seen you in seven years, we haven't missed a day. It feels as if we were never apart. Is that weird? And now I'm just lonely for you and...

I can almost see and hear her shrug from here.

Me: *Lonely?*

Penelope: *Yes. I'm lonely. Are you?*

Me: *Yes, Penn, I'm lonely too. Do you know how rough it is meeting your daughter and then having to say goodbye, and not get to see her again for days? She's with you, but it's not the same, it's like...she's ripped from me over and over and over.*

Penelope: *I hadn't considered it like that.*

Me: *Every time I see you two and connect with you two —then leave—I have to reconcile it from the beginning each time. Not really sure when I'll see you again, then the past comes rearing its ugly head. How I felt finding out I had a daughter.*

Me: *It's rough. All my brain does is work in overdrive. I can't shut it off. If you thought I had dreams about you before —I go through my days sleepwalking, thinking of only you. You and Skipper.*

Penelope: *I'm sorry, Jack.*

Me: *I wasn't saying it to make you feel bad. I said it to put things into perspective for you. I know you hate the distance, but I do too, and I'm trying to figure some shit out.*

Me: *You just have to be patient. This is never going to be perfect, but this relationship is OURS, and we are the only two who can figure it out.*

Penelope: *I don't NEED perfection.*

Me: *Then what is it you think you need?*

Penelope: *Just... I just want... you to be present. Or me to be present. I don't know, LOL.*

Me: *Which brings us to our current predicament.*

Penelope: *And here we are.*

I know it's been seven years, but she's right. When we're together, it's as if we were never apart. Some of the best days and nights I've ever had with another breathing human have been with Penelope Halbrook.

In college, we rarely fought. I picked up my shoes and kept the lid to the toilet seat down because that's how she liked it. I always pitched in around her place, and even went as far as helping her roommates. She tidied up my place, and I tidied up hers. We were a well-oiled—albeit young —machine.

Me: *You know, I didn't mean we had to move in together tomorrow, Penn. I know it's freaking you out...*

Penelope: *I'm not trying to hurt your feelings. I don't want you to think I'm freaking out. It was just unexpected and caught me off guard. I mean, we were walking into our daughter's concert. What were you expecting me to say?*

Me: *That you'll consider it.*

Penelope: *I'm considering it.*

I wish I could see her face.

Hear her voice.

I wish she would video chat with me. No good comes from straight-up texting, especially not when it's a serious topic of conversation. She could have been typing that sentence with a smile on her face, but I most certainly didn't interpret it that way.

I resolve not to bring it up again. Instead, I switch gears because I need to see her again.

Five hours in one day was total bullshit, and we both know it. Still, I was there for Skipper, and that's all that matters in the long run.

I am not going to miss any more milestones, big or small.

Penelope: *I'm trying to open up to you, Jack. I promise I am. I'm open-minded about the whole thing, and I'm thinking about it. I owe you that much.*

My body relaxes as if on a sigh.

Me: *That's all I'm asking. You to be open-minded and to see my side of things until we figure our shit out. Until we figure out what we're going to do.*

We have options. PLENTY OF THEM.

1. I move to her during the off-season—in an apartment or in a condo or in a house. I don't give a shit where; I'll stay where she tells me to stay, even if it's with her.
2. Penn and Skipper move here, permanently, but I'm sensing now that may not happen. Not with how cautious she always is.
3. I continue flying back and forth for the time being (which is what I'm already doing), and we revisit the situation in a few more weeks. Which I *do not* have the patience for.
4. Um.

See? We have options. She's just too stubborn to see them.

Penelope: *I just worry you're too busy, Jack. I woke up this morning thinking about how you're doing all this chasing back and forth and—*

Me: *All this chasing? It's only been a handful of times.*

Penelope: *Alright, fine. If you want to be literal. But I woke up thinking about how none of this is sustainable long term.*

Me: *News flash, Penelope Halbrook: PLENTY of people have successful long-distance relationships. And PLENTY of parents co-parent long distance, too. They make it work, and we will too if you don't want to live together. Or near each other.*

Penelope: *You're right, you're right. I just don't want YOU to do all the heavy lifting because I can't afford to be hopping on an airplane and flying Skipper to Colorado, and vice versa.*

Penelope: *And don't say "Lucky for you, Penelope Halbrook, I can afford to fly you back and forth," because that's not what I want.*

Me: *Okay, but that's the reality of it, Penn. The hard TRUTH is that you can't afford it, and I can. I can, and I will. Not because I have to, but because I WANT to. Pay and fly. I'm not trying to be a dick about this, but you have to just LET me, okay?*

Penelope: *I know, but...*

Me: *Penn, I was in a meeting this morning for Sport Aide. They want to pay me THREE MILLION DOLLARS per year for FIVE years to drink their sport crap. That's FIFTEEN MILLION DOLLARS to smile for a camera, chug, and say cheese. I can afford the plane tickets. I can afford the hotels. I can afford to move you here. I can afford to buy you a house. I can afford the child support.*

Oh shit. Child support.

I had to bring that up, didn't I?

Fuck.

Back up, rewind.

Lucky for me, she doesn't latch on to that one little last sentence.

Penelope: *You're right. It's just hard letting go. I've* *been alone for a while, you know? It's a pride thing, and it's going to take time to get used to having your help.*

Me: It's not my help, Penelope. We're partners now. Whether you like it or not, LOL.

Me: And not to brag, but I have at least four other endorsement deals that pay me a shit ton of money for products I already use, on top of my salary and bonuses for championship wins. So we're good. Can we not ever argue about money again?

Penelope: *Asking me not to argue is like asking Skipper not to wear her pony costume to the grocery store.*

Me: SHE DID NOT.

Penelope: *She did. You should have seen the look on my brother's face when your daughter went galloping out of the house and climbed into his car.*

Me: My daughter. Do you have any idea how much I love the sound of those two words? I swear, I'll never get used to them.

Penelope: *LOL. It's the little things in life.*

And I won't take it for granted.

Penelope: *So what next?*

Me: You keep thinking over what we discussed, and when you're ready, we can discuss it again.

Me: And I hate to have to say this, but we're going to have to see each other soon. I KNOW, I know—shitty of me to bring it up given that you just told me you feel guilty about it, but yesterday made me feel a certain kind of way.

Penelope: *What did you have in mind?*

Me: I don't know—something we can do as a family?

Penelope: *Hmm. Well. Actually, I do have something in mind if you're willing to come back to town next week...*

~

And *that's* how I found myself on the Tilt-A-Whirl one week later, spinning around and around, wearing sunglasses and a baseball cap so fewer people recognize me—but there are a shit ton of people at this Family Fun Fest, and most of them are staring.

I'm going to barf.

Why the hell am I on this ride?

I hate the Tilt-A-Whirl.

The last time I was on it, I was probably twelve and threw up on Becky Albright's new white sneakers.

"We're going to have to go on something slow after this one. I need to settle my stomach."

Skipper pulls at my shirt sleeve. "You need a Sprite. Mom always gives me clear soda when my tummy hurts." Her hair whips in the air, the pony mane atop her head is topped off by a crown, glittering and sparkling for the occasion as it catches the sun.

"I'm fine, kiddo." I just need everyone to stop talking to me until we're off this godforsaken ride. Not sure if I'll be able to walk straight or if I'll be a tippy canoe, cockeyed as if I were hungover.

It's happened to me before.

I cannot do twirly, swirly rides.

Desperate to make eye contact with the young guy operating this ride, hoping that I can telepathically make him stop the ride before it's over, I inhale deeply in and out. In and out.

In and... "Oh shit."

"Jack, are you going to puke?"

"Don't say puke," I moan, clutching the side of the ride.

"Wasn't this supposed to be tame? This is worse than the wheel of torture."

"What's the wheel of torture?"

I manage to wave a hand precariously through the air. "That Ferris wheel thing in California with Mickey's giant face on it."

Skipper giggles, clutching the metal bar keeping us from flying off the ride and into the spinning core.

Stop, I pray silently. *Please don't.*

My own child is out to get me even though she doesn't know she's my child.

"Whose idea was this?" I groan.

"Yours." Penelope laughs, looking all kinds of adorable in her bright yellow skirt and sneakers, boobs looking incredible in a white ribbed tee shirt. "You said you wanted something we could do as a family."

Sunshine.

She smells good, too. I know because I took a whiff.

I flew in yesterday for the carnival in town, a fundraiser for a new youth student center the city is hoping to raise money for, an entire city block blocked off for rides, food, and fun.

This ride?

Not fun.

"You need bubbles, Jack," Skipper says again, eyeballing me suspiciously, hair whipping around.

Soda. Bubbles.

A quiet bench in the shade where I can breathe into a paper bag...

"Jack, you don't look so good. We can have them stop the ride?"

I nod. Pathetic, I know, but here we are.

"We can't just make them stop the ride, Skip, but I appreciate you."

Skipper pats me on the arm sympathetically. "Mom, we need to get Jack a soda."

I glance up miserably. "How come neither of you are sick?" I can't be the only one who wants to throw up over the side of the teacup.

Penelope shrugs. Or at least that's what I think she's doing. It's hard to tell when there are four of her spinning in front of me. "I don't know, babe. We just don't."

Is she yelling, or is it just me?

Finally, the speed of the ride decelerates.

Slows.

Cups stop turning, the attendant operating the ride making eye contact and walking over and THANK GOD it's to release us first, and why are there suddenly four of him?

I wobble, trying to stand.

Skipper takes my elbow to guide me as if I were drunk at a frat house and need to be led to the door. "Here, Jack, this way."

Breathe in.

Breathe out.

"Here, take my hand and follow me. We'll grab you something quick to ease your stomach." There's a popcorn and hot dog stand not fifty feet away, and she hands over five bucks in exchange for a big gulp.

I chug it, wincing at the onslaught of carbonation hitting my throat, but the ice and the pop and *the cold just makes my brain feel so much better.*

"Yeah, it does, doesn't it?"

"Shit, did I say that out loud?" Because I sound like a tool.

"You did." Penn laughs. "I drink a diet soda when I have a migraine. It usually works to take the edge off." She gathers our things, backpack with the water bottles, and makes sure everyone has all their things before looking around for our next destination.

Something more chill, I pray.

The carnival is crowded but not packed with people, mostly due to the fact that it's cold outside. The jean jacket in Penn's arms gets thrown on as soon as we begin strolling toward the Fun House.

The Mega Slide.

The dizziness and queasiness wouldn't have happened if we'd gone on the Bumper Cars or the Bumble Bees like I'd wanted, but my daughter declared the bees were too babyish, and she wasn't a little kid anymore.

She leads me by the hand, playing tour guide, walking the three of us to the Super Cyclone, a mini roller coaster that looks harmless enough despite the screaming from a few kids currently riding it.

Okay, tiny roller coaster, I can handle you.

Finally, something that won't make me ill.

When it's our turn to board, we hand the dude four tickets each and choose our cars, Skipper in the first car with her mother and I in the second.

I barely fit.

Who designed this damn roller coaster car?

It's a tame ride compared to some coasters I've been on, but still faster than the caterpillar kiddie one at the entrance of the carnival. Penelope grins, looking back at me, most likely to see if I'm going to barf or not.

I stifle a laugh.

Actually, this little ride isn't half bad...and it's over in the blink of an eye, and we're deboarding for something new to see.

This whole day has been an adventure, and we haven't even had lunch, if you don't count churros, ice cream, and cheese curds as lunch.

Or popcorn?

And a giant cone cup filled with slushy?

Yeah, *I didn't think so either.*

As if it were the most natural thing in the world to do, I take hold of Penelope's hand while Skipper once again takes hold of mine. The three of us hold hands, dodging people, and every so often, I have to reach up to adjust the brim of my hat so it covers my eyes and disguises my face, but overall, we're left alone.

I'm pretty sure it has a lot to do with the fact that the carnival itself is charming and quaint, with a decent size pumpkin patch at the exit, surrounded by a white picket fence and hay bales.

Full of families and noise, zero people expect to see a professional football player walking amongst them, so of course they don't see one even when they're looking straight at me as I waltz around the joint.

"Mom, look—pumpkins!" Skipper announces when we reach the patch. "Can we look at them, Mom?"

All I see when I look at this patch is all the hard work it took hauling all those orange things from a farm in the country to this carnival in the middle of the city.

My back hurts thinking about it...

"I guess so," Penelope says. "It *is* almost Halloween."

It's almost the month of October, so I guess that counts. Cold enough to be, that's for sure.

"Pumpkin carving?" I squeeze Penelope's hand with a

mock whisper. "That might be a fun thing to do when we get home."

She nibbles on her bottom lip. "Yeah, actually, that would be fun. I didn't have anything else planned. This was our big event."

"And!" I enthuse. "I'll order food, so neither of us has to cook."

She offers me a fake swoon. "My hero."

I pull them along. "Let's grab a few pumpkins then—or maybe just one big one we can all work on together."

"Teamwork makes the dream work," Skipper chimes in, making us both laugh.

Because of all the action nearby, the pumpkin patch isn't crazy crowded, and we're able to take our time selecting one. It's a decent variety, big and small and everything between. Skipper sits on a few and wants her photo taken, and Penelope obliges, gesturing so I hop in the frame, too.

Smiling big, I put my arm around my daughter's tiny shoulders, and we grin wide.

"Should we take this one?" She pats the one under her rump. It's large and oval and probably weighs twenty pounds.

"Sure. Just this one?"

Skipper glances around, hands on her little hips. "Maybe that one too, if it's okay? Oh!" She gasps. "Should we get three? One is you, one is Mom, and the small one is me."

"A trio."

"A family," Skipper corrects, bounding off to find a third to represent herself, and I catch Penelope's *'did she just say what I think she said'* expression.

"I thought we were only going to do one!" Penelope groans.

"We're outnumbered."

"But there's only one of her and two of us."

"She's the one with the puppy dog eyes."

Penelope pouts, jutting out her bottom lip. "Does this count?"

I laugh. "Not even a little, sorry."

The pumpkins cost an arm and a leg, not that I'm complaining, but holy shit. Who can afford this?

I mean—I can, but still.

We're able to easily get everything back to Penelope's car, each of us carrying the pumpkins Skipper chose for us, placing them in the back cargo space before we're on our way.

We don't bother with showers once we arrive back at her place, but we do change out of the clothes we wore to the carnival and in to more comfortable attire; leggings and sweatshirts for the girls, and mesh track pants and a hoodie for me.

While I order delivery to feed us, Penelope roots through the kitchen cabinets for cookie sheets, then through the drawers for spatulas, knives for carving, and spoons for digging out the seeds and the guts of the pumpkins, while I spread newspaper on the kitchen table.

"Am I missing anything?" She taps her chin. "Oh! Paint!"

She finds markers, glitter, glue, and rhinestones in Skipper's craft cabinet so we can bling out rather than *carve* the pumpkins—which seems way easier in my opinion. But Skipper wants a Rainbow Pony pumpkin and has an idea.

"What if we use the pieces you carve and make a mane for the pony?" She's running a hand down the back of her head to demonstrate. "Like this. Down its back like a real horse."

It's brilliant but probably going to be a painstaking pain in the ass, considering how small her pumpkin is. The pony design would work better on the large pumpkin, but she has declared the big one is *mine* and would most likely take all night.

I use the smallest knife, my daughter breathing next to me, giving me instruction, oohing and aahing at my skill.

It's a real ego boost having this little kid tell me how amazing it looks.

I feel like a goddamn master at this, and it's really truly the only pumpkin I've ever carved in my entire life. I don't remember my parents being all that interested in holidays except for Christmas. Both of them worked too hard and were busy, and often forgot about more commercialized holidays like Halloween and Valentine's Day.

They'd be so proud to see me now, carving with my cute family and doing cool dad shit.

I brush the thoughts of my parents aside; now isn't the time to get emotional—not when I have a pony to perfect. One wrong move, one slice too thin, could ruin the entire aesthetic and put me in hot water with a certain seven-year-old.

While I'm chiseling away at Skipper's pumpkin, Penelope is painting hers with a bright floral pattern, a large letter P in the center surrounded by bold colors. Her concentration game is so strong that the tip of her tongue is sticking out of her mouth.

The hours tick away, Skipper hovering nearby but eventually abandons us for the living room and one of her pony shows.

It takes me forever to get this project done; so much time that I have none left over for my big, orange beast, and we collectively decide to put it out on the porch intact, as is

—without carving it tonight—arranging the trio where passersby can see.

I put my arm around Penelope's waist as we stand on the sidewalk admiring our work, Skipper running up to fiddle with the candle stuck inside her pumpkin, the pony eyes and mane an impressive display of skill on my part.

"Is there anything I can't do?" I sigh in the most unhumble way.

Penelope laughs. "One thing you can't do is...beat me inside the house."

She makes a run for it, racing to the porch as fast as she can—but I'm quicker. Quicker and stronger, scooping her up as Skipper giggles hysterically, swooping us all inside to begin cleaning up and getting the bedtime routine going.

Get us to bed.

"I think we should tell her in the morning."

"Tell who?"

I'm running my fingers through her hair as she lays facing me, naked as the day she was born, bedhead from thrashing it against the pillowcase while I thrust into her.

The more time I spend with Penelope, the deeper and deeper I fall. Our connection grows stronger by the day. I guess that's to be expected, considering how in love we were back in college, how abruptly it ended, and how we're going to be in each other's lives forever now that we have Skipper.

"Tell who what?" I repeat obtusely.

When she trails a finger down my sternum, I shiver. "Harper. I think we should tell her you're her dad."

I swear my heart stops beating with those words.

You're her dad.

I think we should tell her.

They're the words I've wanted for over a month, but the same ones I've feared, both at the same time.

"You do?"

She nods enthusiastically, still running her fingers over my chest, tracing the muscles there. The valley between my pecs. My clavicle and shoulder blades.

"Yes, Jack. If you're ready, I think we should tell her." Penn lets out a content sigh. "She's spent quite a bit of time with you, so even though it's only been a few weeks, I don't think we should let it go much longer. She's comfortable with you, and she asks about you when you're not here." Another sigh. "I don't want her to think you're just my boyfriend. She's going to ask pretty soon, and when she does, I don't want to lie and say yes when that's not the case."

"You don't consider me your boyfriend?"

Penelope laughs. "Of course I consider you my boyfriend. My point was that's what you are to her and that's not the reason you're back in my life." She pauses. "Did that come out wrong?"

"I know what you meant."

"Good." She nods, resuming her exploration of my front side. "She needs to know. I'm starting to feel like we're keeping this big secret, and it feels like we're lying, and I hate it."

Same. "No, you're absolutely right." I'm still digesting the words. "How?"

She rolls away from me and stares up at the ceiling. "At breakfast tomorrow? We'll make it a feast, and I'll explain to her how you and I met and go from there."

"You think it will be that easy?"

Her mouth contorts. "I don't think it will be easy for us,

263

no. But I think she'll be excited and that's what's important. But..." Penelope clears her throat. "Once we tell her, she'll want to be with you all the time."

I go still.

Penelope keeps going. "I love being with you, Jack. I think the universe put you back in my life for a reason, and the last thing I want is to lose you again."

"You're not. You won't."

She shakes her head as if she knew she hadn't chosen the right words to explain herself and starts over.

"I love being with you, and I think you're right. We need to look forward and spend more time together, and I think our daughter deserves both of us as often as we can be there for her. And..."

I hold my breath.

"...and..." She gulps. "I want to try. I'm willing to move to Colorado for the season so we can be with you there."

What is she saying? "What are you saying?"

"That we'll move in with you."

"Not in a condo? 'Cause I can get you a condo—maybe even in the same building or an apartment. A nice one, not a shithole. Whatever you want, Penn," I ramble on. "Or a house. You don't have to live with me. I don't want you to feel uncomfortable. I—"

"Babe. *Jack.*" She puts a finger over my lips to shush me. "No. I don't want a condo or an apartment or a house of my own. We've been alone long enough. Skipper has lived without you long enough. Davis is great, but he's not her dad—you are. I want her to know what it's like growing up with you. Me. Us. Together."

All this information is a hell of a lot to take in.

First, she tells me she wants us to tell Skipper in the

morning that I'm her dad, and now she's giving me the green light on moving in together.

Holy shit.

Am I dreaming? Because if my heart hasn't just stopped beating from shock, my name isn't Jack Jennings.

I reach for her but am almost too afraid to touch her. "Seriously?"

She nods her head, biting down on her bottom lip. "Yes."

Yes.

No prettier word has there ever been in the human language than Y-E-S.

"Are you sure, because—"

Penelope laughs, rolling toward me again. "Oh, so now you're going to try to talk me out of it? It was your idea to begin with."

I laugh, too, the giddy, nervous kind you belt out when you're high on adrenaline. It sounds almost manic, even to my own ears.

"Jesus, why do I feel so insecure all of a sudden?" I muse out loud, taking her hand and kissing her fingers. Her nails are light pink, the same color she used to paint them in college.

"I feel to blame for that. It's partly my fault. I've been wishy-washy and scared of my own shadow when it comes to you, but I don't want to be that person anymore. I'm a grown woman, and this is my choice. You are my choice."

You are my choice.

"You are mine. You and Skipper." Short of declaring my love for her, this feels a lot like that. The feeling, the butterflies in my stomach of certainty. It feels very heavy but also as if a weight were lifted off my shoulders.

I no longer have to wonder.

Thank god.

"How am I supposed to sleep?" I grumble with a smile, pulling her close so I can wrap my arms around her. "I feel like it's Christmas Eve, and we're going to wake up and run down to see what Santa brought us."

"Do you still believe in Santa?" she teases me.

"Are you being serious? Of course I believe in Santa. If you don't believe, he doesn't bring any presents." I kiss her on the lips. "And you have to be a good girl, too."

"I am a good girl." Penelope swings a leg over my thigh, draping herself over me, kissing me back.

We share an open-mouth kiss, my dick beginning to twitch, ready for a second round. She reaches between us and begins stroking me. "I think my dick likes this news."

"Feels like it."

"Seriously. I swear it's hard from the adrenaline pumping through my body, not from being turned on."

"Should I be offended?" she says between kisses, her tongue entwining with mine.

"Probably. I could probably fuck all night right now. I have so much blood coursing through my veins." This is better than any rush I've ever had on the playing field. Not even that first game as a rookie beats this feeling right here.

I'm the luckiest son of a bitch in the world.

Chapter 20

Penelope

The smell of bacon wakes me up, followed by the sound of clinging pans in the kitchen, the television—laughter between two people.

Jack and Skipper are apparently hard at work making breakfast and probably a giant mess in the process.

I throw back the bed covers, then put on my robe before heading downstairs, greeted by the sight of Skipper kneeling on a barstool at the counter watching Jack flip pancakes next to a pan of sizzling bacon.

I can see the grease splattering from here but zip my lip.

It's Sunday, and it's early, and I don't want to begin the day off by nagging.

"Mom, we're making breakfast." Skipper's wide eyeballs are on the frying goodness, and she licks her lips to punctuate her sentence. "Look at these pancakes. They're hearts."

"Awww, how cute!" I pat Jack on the butt as I slide into the duo. "Look how creative you are."

"I'm a man of many talents."

Talents that make my toes curl. Talents that have my stomach fluttering. Talents that make me go Mmm.

"Get your mind out of the gutter," he mutters, nudging my boob with his elbow in a covert attempt to flirt, and I skirt on past, grabbing plates out of the cabinets.

"I have a feeling my mind is perma-gutter when you're around."

"Well, brace yourself 'cause soon I'll be perma-around."

Shit, that's right.

I agreed to move in with him and move to Colorado, at least for the next few months.

Am I crazy?

Honestly.

Or just crazy for him?

I pour myself a cup of coffee and make myself comfortable at the kitchen table, one leg crossed beneath me, snuggling up in my robe as I watch the two of them. They're having a good time making a mess; as well they should—breakfast looks yummy and delicious, and I don't often make pancakes.

Definitely don't make them into fun shapes like hearts.

Lately, we've been more of a cereal and yogurt—or a bagel and cream cheese—on the fly kind of family. So I know this little spread is going to be quite a delight for Skipper.

Jack seems to be enjoying himself, acting like a modern-day Julia Child and whatnot, casually flipping the pancakes in the air as if being a chef was his part-time job. *He could seriously be a line chef at a breakfast buffet, and I would sit at that buffet bar and watch him work his magic. Preferably, he'd be wearing an apron with an open back...*

Ha!

Jack brings over a platter piled with pancakes, sausage,

bacon, and eggs and sets the large oval plate in the center of the table. Skipper is hot on his heels with the butter and maple syrup.

"How many people are we feeding? This is obscene!" I'm eyeballing the stack even as I stab two flat cakes with my fork, plopping them on my plate.

"I used way too much pancake mix, and at that point, it was too late to put it back."

I shrug. "Guess we'll be having breakfast for dinner tonight. Maybe I can roll these sausages inside and make yummy breakfast burritos." Yum.

Skipper nods, filling her own plate like a big girl and grinning from ear to ear as she takes her first bite.

I have a few myself before resting my fork on the side of my plate and making eyes at Jack.

Ready? I silently ask him.

He stares back blankly, clearly not understanding where I'm about to lead the discussion, so I proceed.

"Hey, sweetie?" I say.

"Yeah?" Both Jack and Skipper answer, each of them assumes I'm talking to them and calling them sweetie.

Um. "Skipper, sweetie."

She giggles and pokes Jack with her little index finger— one I'm confident is sticky and has syrup on it.

"Hey, sweetie," I start again. "Remember how you always want to know what it was like when you were a baby and love hearing stories?"

She nods, chewing.

"I told you that story once about my college boyfriend. You know what a boyfriend is?" I explain it just so she has a tiny bit of an understanding. "Jack and I used to go on dates like to the movies and football games, and sometimes we would dance."

"And kiss." She says it nonchalantly without a care in the world.

"Yes, and kiss." Am I blushing? Ugh. "Well." I wipe my sweaty palms on the napkin I've placed on my lap, anxious.

"I was your mom's boyfriend, and she was my best friend." Jack chimes in.

Best friend. The words make my heart melt a little, and my lady parts tingle. I mean, I knew this, but nonetheless it feels good to hear the words spoken out loud.

They fill my love bucket, and it's already almost spilling over the brim.

"So Jack was my boyfriend, and he was also one of my best friends and...well. As you know, seven years ago, I had a baby. You."

Jack goes still even as Skipper eats between us, blissfully unaware. With bated breath, he waits to hear what I say next. Honestly, he could cut in at any time.

I feel like I'm dying here.

Why is this so hard? Skipper is seven!

"Is Jack your boyfriend now?" She lifts her gaze to look at the two of us, glancing back and forth, still eating.

"Yes." He takes my hand across the table and gives it a squeeze of encouragement. "Your mom is my girlfriend."

"I wish I had a boyfriend," our daughter answers, surprising us both. "He could bring me flowers."

I laugh. "Maybe when you're older, you can have a boyfriend."

"Much, much older. Like, thirty," Jack intones with a fatherly tone.

"Anyway, sweetheart, as I was saying. Back when I was in college, Jack was my boyfriend at the time I got pregnant with you. And I got really scared."

She squints as if she were doing a difficult math problem. Her wrinkly little nose is adorable just the same. I want to poke the tip of it with my finger and kiss it. Smush her, she's so sweet.

"You got scared? Of what?"

"Well, I was young and didn't know anything about babies. And Grandma was still here at the time, and she told me if I moved home, she would help me take care of you. So I left college and didn't tell my boyfriend that I was having a baby."

Skipper pauses, squinting again. "Jack was your boyfriend."

"That's my girl," Jack proudly says, beaming. He knows she's clicking in the puzzle pieces on her own, using the small clues we're giving her because:

1. She's too young to give the hard truth to—that I was foolish and scared and worried my boyfriend was going to do something stupid, like leave school, too.
2. I can't just blurt it out. We have to ease into it so we don't shock her or scare her. Let her get used to the idea as the small clues come.

"That's right, Jack was my boyfriend. And I know you're seven years old, and you've asked me a few times about your dad, but the truth is..." I swallow the lump in my throat. "The truth was that I didn't know how to tell him we were having a baby because sometimes it's scary being honest with people."

She nods knowingly. "Like when I wrote on the couch with Sharpie marker and didn't want to tell you because I was scared."

"Wait. What? You wrote on the couch with Sharpie marker?"

"Penelope, focus." Jack laughs so I stay on task.

"Right. Sorry—yes. That's exactly it. Sometimes, it's scary being honest because you don't know what they are going to say or if they're going to be mad or disappointed—but I was too young to know that, so I left school and came home." I pause. "And I did not tell Jack that we were having a baby."

I repeat the fact so it resonates with her, stating it again, waiting for the lines to fall into place.

"Sweetie, do you know what I'm trying to tell you?"

"I think so?" She nibbles on a piece of sausage, making the sounds people make when something tastes delicious. "This is so good."

Jack laughs, ruffling her hair. "You're adorable."

She side-eyes him. "Are you my dad?"

"Yes, I'm your dad."

She puts down her fork and wipes her hands, holding her hand up and wiggling her thumb. "I knew it. Because we have the same finger."

Jack's rumbling laugh is loud and full of humor, nervous but happy. "You are really something, kid, do you know that?"

She resumes eating, stabbing more eggs with her fork as if we haven't just dropped a life-changing bomb in her lap. "Can I call you Dad instead of Jack?"

"I would love it if you called me Dad instead of Jack."

"Thanks, Dad."

My heart melts, and I have to wipe my eyes with a napkin. They're tearing up, and I can barely take it. I'm so happy right now. All this time I'd been worried I ruined both their lives and having to tell her would be traumatizing, but instead, she's taking it like a champ.

Which makes sense because her father literally is one.

A champ, that is.

He's got his arm around her chair and kisses the top of her head, the way dads do, already stepping into the role as if he were born for it.

"Wait a minute." Her fork gets set down again. "Does this mean... I have a *dog*?"

"A dog?" I furrow my brow, confused. We don't have a dog.

"Kevin. Is he my dog now?"

"Kevin is absolutely your dog!" Jack announces. "And I've been telling him all about you!"

Skipper sits up straighter in her chair, eager for more facts. "Like what? What did you tell him?"

"I told him you were excited to take him for walks and give him treats and that you were going to play with him and be his friend. I told him you were in first grade and you love horses and that your stuffed animals are not toys."

She soaks this in. "I might let him play with one, though."

"That would be very nice of you."

"I like sharing." Skipper takes a sip of water, and while she's doing that, Jack catches my eyes over the top of her head.

"I love you," he whispers to me, his eyes glassy from emotion—the same way mine are.

"I love you, too, Dad," Skipper cheerily replies, not a care in the world, happy as a clam.

I don't think now is a good time to drop more news into her little lap, so we let her keep eating. She goes to play shortly after, taking her plate to the sink before going to the backyard to her swing set.

"I think that went rather well."

We're side by side doing dishes when there's a knock on the door, followed by the sound of my brother announcing himself as he rounds the corner into the kitchen. As if he were going to catch Jack and me doing something scandalous—or catch us naked.

"Knock, knock!"

I roll my eyes, putting a pan back into the lower cabinet now that it's clean. "We're decent."

"I saw Jack's rental in the driveway and thought I'd stop in to say hey." He holds his hand up. "Hey."

"Hey." Jack laughs, putting his hand out for a shake.

"When did you get here? If I'd have known, we could have gone to dinner or something."

"He got here Friday, but we did bonding things. You know that street carnival in town, the fundraiser for the youth center?"

He nods.

"We did that last night, then carved pumpkins."

"Saw those on the porch. Yours is obviously the pony pumpkin," he says to Jack with a grin, stealing a sausage that's been put on a plate. "How long are you staying?"

"Heading out in a few hours. I have a game tomorrow and a team meeting tonight I won't be able to miss."

My brother knows what that's like; jet-setting around before his games, visiting girlfriends but needing to be back. It wore on him the same way it would surely wear on Jack if we hadn't committed to moving in together, something I have to tell my brother.

I open my mouth to speak, but we're interrupted when Skipper comes busting through the back door, hair wild, galloping like a pony, decked out in head to toe purple—as usual.

She immediately goes to Davis, hugging his waist and squeezing.

"Uncle Davis, that's my dad!"

My brother's eyes go wide with shock. It was news he already knew but wasn't expecting to fly out of his niece's mouth.

"He is! How wonderful!"

"Yeah, he looks just like me," she tells him, bragging about their similarities. "We have the same hair and eyes, and when we smile, he has the same dimple." She demonstrates, tilting her head. "Dad, smile."

Jack smiles and tilts his head.

"Oh yeah, would you look at that." My brother remains visibly shaken, while I am internally shaken. I hadn't realized my daughter was aware of the resemblances she and Jack had, down to the dimples in their cheeks. Or their dark hair or the same color eyes.

It just goes to show how observant kids actually are and that they're not to be underestimated.

I won't be making that mistake again. Ha!

And like that, she's gone again, only coming inside to grab her pony animal and returning outside with it.

"So you ripped off the Band-Aid, eh?"

"It was harder than we thought it was going to be, but she took it really well."

That's an understatement if I've ever heard one.

"Obviously," Davis remarks, his eyes on his niece in the backyard, in the sandbox with Rainbow, her horse. "She's been asking about her dad for a while, and no offense, but at one point, she thought it was me."

I cringe.

But it's true, she did.

"You know she's going to be asking about him nonstop now. What do you plan on doing? Like what's the next step?" He watches us intently, always keeping it real, pushing the envelope, and wanting to be honest.

It's now or never.

I have to tell him the plan, tentative or not. "Well." I clear my throat, uncomfortable.

Jack puts his hand on my lower back. "We've been talking about moving in together. Or at least, for this football season or after it. Sooner than later, though we don't have firm details."

Davis stills, then nods slowly. "Makes sense."

I wish I could read his mind.

"It's only been days since the subject was brought up," I say hastily, wanting to ease the hurt he's probably feeling. "It just feels like the right thing to do, especially now that she knows. She's growing attached, and I want their bond to be strong. I..."

Owe it to him.

Of course, I don't say those four words out loud. To my brother, they might sound self-deprecating. To my brother, he might say I don't owe Jack shit.

"No, man, it makes sense. Penelope, I get it. I would do the same thing. If I found out Juliet and I had a child, I would want to be there for her, and I understand that Jack's life is in Colorado—not that his is any more important than yours, but it's not as if he can pack up and move at the start of an NFL football season. And I understand how you wouldn't want to wait five months."

Five months isn't that long when I think about it.

"We have a few options." Jack scratches his chin. "I can buy this house from you so this can be home in the off-season—or we can go house hunting and get something different, although I realize you might take an aversion to that."

Davis looks at me, and I feel a blush creeping onto my cheeks. This isn't at all how I'd planned to discuss this with him. I'd planned to sit him down quietly, maybe over dinner, just the two of us, and break the news.

No time like the present, they say.

And Jack dives right in.

The thing with my brother? He's always been supportive even when my decisions have been stupid and foolish and irresponsible, and I can see him thinking through Jack's words.

"I think keeping the house is a great option for now. It will buy you time to figure out what you really want to do and where you want to be. It's big enough for the three of you, plus another one—ha-ha." He laughs. "We'll just operate business as usual until you have a plan, yeah?"

We all nod, but I feel sick to my stomach.

Why is being an adult so hard?

Why do I feel like I'm disappointing my brother in the process of making my partner and daughter happy?

This sucks.

"Penn," Davis says. "Look at me."

I look at him.

"This is what I want for you. Stop feeling guilty. This isn't about me, do you hear me? It's time you did what's right for you. The only thing you've done for seven years is do what's right for Skipper, and the right thing for her now is her dad." He nods toward Jack, who has his hand on my shoulder. "I'm not going to be pissed if the house is empty for a few months. I can come to see you in Colorado. It's not the end of the world."

I break away from Jack and go to my brother, hugging him as if our lives depended on it.

"You've always been here for me. When am I going to be there for you?"

He squeezes me hard. "What are you talking about? When Mom died, you were all I had. When I broke up with Willa, who was there for me? You were. I love you, sis. It's time to be a little selfish and do something for you for once."

The tears stream down my face and onto his polo shirt. "I love you."

Another pair of arms go around me as Jack makes the hug a sandwich, squishing my brother and me.

"I want a hug."

"Dude," my brother eeks out. "You're making this weird."

"Dude, get used to it."

Epilogue

Jack

Four months later...ish

I t's been years since I've been to an actual Super Bowl Party at the stadium, typically choosing to stay in the comfort of my own home if my team isn't playing.

But this year is different. This year, I have Penelope and Skipper. And this year? I want to show her off to my friends.

So we flew to Detroit for the occasion, which is where the game is being played, and I'm so glad we did. The party has been a blast; food, booze, swag. Elias hasn't missed a beat, throwing together a table for the women of donated cosmetics, apparel, and jewelry in lacquered black gift bags Penelope was giddy over.

Women love free shit.

Elias loves women.

Can't sustain a relationship to save his soul, but he's a good dude with a big heart and plenty of romantic ideas—good and bad.

He's the one who'd coached me through some of the rough patches with Penelope. He's the one who helped me

pick out gifts for her and Skipper. He's the one that found a
real estate agent who found the house we moved into back
in December.

Yeah—in the middle of fucking December.

It was great having Christmas there, though. The view
of the mountains is spectacular through the panoramic
windows at the back of the house, and you can't put a price
tag on that.

I mean, you can. That view cost seven point four
million dollars but is worth every last cent.

Especially the last few times Penelope has taken a bath
in that gigantic tub, filled it with bubbles, her perky tits
were visible above the water. I'm convinced she does that
shit on purpose to torture me, and you won't convince me
otherwise.

As soon as she saw that tub during our house hunting
search, the house was as good as ours.

Elias offers her a glass of champagne.

He's the one hosting this modest shindig in one of the
stadium suites, surrounded by my teammates who are his
clients—plenty of players who play for other teams—
managers, assistants, wives, and significant others.

The place is packed, and the liquor is flowing.

"All settled in to the new house?" Elias is asking Penelope, who'd been chatting with Lana Macenroy, who has
become one of her closest friends and confidants. Lana has
been showing her the ropes and introducing her around—
not to mention, the kids all get along, which has been great.

They've been over at our new house a lot, and us to
theirs.

"So far, so good. We didn't have a ton of stuff to unpack
since Jack was coming from a condo, and all my things are
back in the Midwest and technically don't belong to me."

They belong to her brother, who offered up the contents if we needed them—which we didn't. But it was gracious of him anyway.

Good dude.

We've gotten close in the past few months, and it's almost as if he were my brother now, too. But not in a weird way.

Ha!

My agent looks me up and down with a laugh. Of course, he's been drinking so everything is funny to him right now.

"What's so damn funny?"

"You. You're so domestic now."

"I wasn't before?"

"No, before you were a hermit. I wouldn't call that domestic."

"There's nothing wrong with being home all the time. I find nothing interesting about going out and partying and meeting random women."

He puts his hands in the air in a surrender motion. "I get it. I get it. All I'm saying is, you'll never see me tied down."

"You know what we call boasting like that? *Famous. Last. Words.*"

"Ha," he says, drinking from the amber bottle in his hands and stealing a shrimp kabob from the server passing by. "Can you see me with a dog, a white picket fence, and a kid?"

Not really, if I'm being honest.

"Do you know what they call men like you in romance novels?" Penelope pipes in.

"What?"

"A rake. You'll make the best boyfriend when you're

reformed." She takes a dainty nibble of the cake pop she's holding. "Reformed rake."

"You can't compare me to anyone in your romance novels. It's not the right time for me to be dating."

"It's never the right time," Penn says wisely. "If everyone waited for the right time, we'd be waiting around forever."

"So wise." I kiss her on the temple, pulling her close. "But he's right, babe. Elias, here, would make a shitty boyfriend."

"Hey!" he sputters. "I never said I would make a shitty boyfriend. I said I couldn't be tied down."

I glance around the room. "Who's trying to tie you down? I don't see a line forming."

"Screw you." He laughs, looking down at Penelope. "How do you put up with him?"

"Easy. He's my best friend." She twists the giant emerald ring on her finger. It's the one I got her for Christmas, an exact replica of the cheap plastic one I won for her eight years ago at the fair doing the High Striker.

Except this one is real.

It glitters and sparkles like nothing I've ever seen, especially beneath the overhead lights in this room.

My agent feigns a gag. "Don't say he's your best friend so loud. You'll make everyone jealous."

"But not you?"

"No. Never me."

Penelope isn't convinced. "The perfect girl will sweep you off your feet, Elias, and you won't even know what hit you."

"Sweep *me* off *my* feet? That's not how that works." He sounds so disgusted it makes me laugh. "If I was going to meet someone, I would have met her already."

It's true; he's surrounded by women everywhere. Every game, every party, every city he's visits to sign new players. He gets hit on constantly by mothers, sisters, and team owners' daughters. Publicists and reporters.

The list goes on and on.

Not once has a single one of those women caught his eye.

Penelope tilts her head, nonplussed. "Want to bet?"

Elias stares down at the hand she has extended. "You're trying to bet me that I'll meet someone?"

My girlfriend nods. "Yes. You'll meet someone, and it's going to hit you like a Mack truck. Then you'll come crawling to Jack and me for advice."

Elias laughs. "You sound way too confident for someone who has no idea what she's talking about."

He's not wrong.

Penelope has no idea what his track record is and how many women he's dated that he had no actual interest in. But it's fun to watch them spar; go back and forth arguing.

"You sound scared you'll *lose*," she taunts, the champagne giving her a bravado I rarely see in her.

"Fine." He holds out his hand and clasps it in hers. "You have yourself a deal."

The End

The Make Out Artist
Releasing July 19

I've known plenty of men like Elias Cohen before; smug, arrogant—*too flirtatious and cocky for their own good.*

He won't charm *me* with that crooked smile and dimple in his chin. I won't let him.

When he knocks on my bedroom door during a house party after I spent the night playing wingman for my friend, I'm tempted to slam the door in his face.

But I don't.

Because if there's one thing I am, it's curious.

And that never ends well for me, *does it?*

Available for Pre-Order Here!

About Sara Ney

Sara Ney is the USA Today Bestselling Author of the How to Date a Douchebag series, best known for her sexy, laugh-out-loud sports and contemporary romances. Among her favorite vices, she includes: traveling, historical architecture and nerding out on all things Victorian. She's a "cool mom" living in the Midwest who loves antique malls, resale clothing shops, and once carried a vintage copper sink through the airport as her carry-on because it didn't fit in her suitcase.

For more information about Sara Ney and her books, visit: https://authorsaraney.com

Also by Sara Ney

Printed in Great Britain
by Amazon